# REVENGE

## A Claire O'Shaunessy Mystery

## Sue Myers

Badcat Literary Creations

# Badcat Literary Creations

Copyright © 2017 by Sue Myers

Cover Art by Julie Kukreja, Pen and Mouse Design

Cover Photography by Alexis Lindell

Edited by Diane Piron-Gelman, Word Nerd, Inc.

Printed in the United States of America

10 9 8 7 6 5 4 3 2

# DEDICATION

To my husband, Gene,
for his incredible love and support.

To the LHS Class of 1964.
Thank you for the memories.

# OTHER NOVELS BY SUE MYERS

A Claire O'Shaunessy Mystery Series:

Deception

# ACKNOWLEDGMENTS

Once again, I would like to thank my husband, Gene. I couldn't have written *Revenge* without his continued unwavering support; and, my cousin, Bonnie Gardner, who unknowingly provided me with the idea for this story.

I want to thank the team that actually put *Revenge* together: my editor, Diane Piron-Gelman, Word Nerd Inc., for giving my book the final touch, Julie Kukreja, Pen and Mouse Designs, for another great cover, and Alexis Lindell, for her fabulous photography skills on the cover.

A major thanks goes to Michele May, author of the Circle City Mystery series, for her constant support and guidance, and computer skills. Again, my sister-in-law, Patty Schreck, who graciously stepped up to the plate with her red pen to save me from my grammatical errors, and, Pat Camalliere, author of the Cora Tozzi Historical Mystery series for her kind review.

Many thanks go to two great past co-workers, Joan Schumacher and Debbie Miroslaw. Also, Dustin Ver Steeg and Kelly Miroslaw were very generous with their time and expertise for my research. I need to thank two dear friends for their constant support, Arlene Erlbach and Patty Cletcher Tennerman.

A quick reminder, *Revenge* is a work of fiction. This means, I made it up! I've enjoyed including local history, sites and a ghost. Any errors are mine. Hope you enjoy reading *Revenge*!

# Chapter 1

The squad's flashing red and blue lights added an odd festive effect to the late fall evening sky. The vehicle blocked the back entrance to the Cook County Morgue pending the arrival of Chicago Mayor Michael Keeley's sister. The air crackled with excitement.

Derek Ruger's pulse quickened. The evening chill cooled his perspiring neck. His hands gripped the Nikon camera as he scanned the crowd. Through the lens, he checked the entrance of the morgue's parking lot and waited. A small crowd gathered from nearby apartments.

Most of the television news crews had set up their equipment at the main entrance, on the east side of the building. Only one local station remained staked out at a spot along the back fence near the north corner entrance. Using the bushes along the west side of the parking lot as cover in the dark, Derek watched Jillian Garcia talking with her cameraman. He didn't approve of how the station treated her. She rarely caught assignments on warm sunny days. More often her live reports on car crashes and house fires from bridges and street corners occurred as rain or snow pelted her. He bet her boss had told her she had to pay her dues.

He knew what that was like. He had paid dues his entire life for the sins of the mayor's father, Timothy Keeley. Now Derek would collect his just reward. He could almost taste the flavor of payback and bittersweet revenge. Nothing could turn back the clock and make his life right. However, this would make up for some of the pain inflicted on his family. Today he took his revenge to the next level. One more step after this and he would accomplish his lifelong goal. Timothy Keeley had caused the destruction of his family life. Now, he would destroy Keeley's favorite son, Michael. The shrill sound of approaching sirens interrupted his thoughts. A squad car entered the parking lot followed by a transport van and

1

another squad car. He could see Mayor Keeley in the front seat of the first car. *Michael, how does it feel to have someone you care about taken away?*

With a click, his camera preserved the pain on Michael's face. The car disappeared around the privacy wall in front of the morgue's bay doors. Everything happened too fast. He snapped a final picture of the van carrying the body of Elizabeth Keeley O'Connor, before it vanished behind the wall. Derek wanted to see the results of all his actions. He'd earned it. He hadn't worked for that lousy undertaker on his days off from his regular job to miss this moment. He strained his neck to see more, but his hopes were dashed by the long privacy wall blocking his view. He felt robbed.

To his surprise, a car entered the parking lot and stopped directly from across his position on the sidewalk outside the morgue parking lot. Quickly raising his camera above the bushes, he recorded a striking slender redhead emerging from the car dressed in jeans and a black leather jacket. A man accompanied her. He shot several more pictures as they raced toward the bay door. *Who was she?* He couldn't place her. He'd never seen her before. He thought he knew everyone in the Keeley family. She must be from Michael's wife's side. They all had red hair.

*Stop!* he said to himself. He must concentrate on Michael. But that woman's red hair ignited his attention. Her presence refueled him. The sight of her blew life into him. He had to have her. *No*, he thought, *remember why you are here.* A slight smile crept up the edges of his mouth. Why couldn't he have both, Michael and the redhead? He drew in a breath laced with the scents of fall. Even though only a week remained before completing his master plan, he'd make time for her. She'd be the icing on the cake, or even better, the red cherry on top of the sundae!

He hadn't decided what he would do with her, yet, but that didn't matter. He knew he had to have her. He must have patience, one of his greatest strengths.

An hour passed. To his disappointment, nothing else happened. He spent the time pretending to adjust his camera and shoot the sunset. He watched Jillian tape her final on-the-scene report for the late-night news. Afterwards, her crew packed up their equipment and left. Even the flashing lights no longer glowed, though the squad cars still blocked the parking lot entrance and exit. He knew he had to move on or risk being questioned about his presence. He couldn't have that happen. He had too much to do.

Again, his thoughts strayed to the redhead. Who was she? The question whirled in his mind. He wanted to see her again, and he would. He squeezed his camera case with anticipation. She was waiting for him right inside his camera. Perhaps she deserved a place on his wall.

# Chapter 2

Dr. Claire Marie O'Shaunessy rushed down the hallway and dropped her leather jacket on the chair in her office. Convinced the leather would absorb the morgue odors, she never left her good clothing in the locker room. While the smells didn't bother her at work, she didn't want them following her home.

Ian's voice echoed from behind her. "Hey, Dr. O'Shaunessy."

Claire turned to see her favorite tech. "So, they called you in, too?"

"Yes, Dr. Johnson called in everyone. They didn't tell us what's going on. We never do autopsies after five. Who is this, the Queen of England?"

"No, it's Mayor Keeley's sister."

"You're kidding me." Ian stopped, then ran to catch up with her. "What happened?"

"That's what you and I are going to find out. All I know is, she had a hysterectomy a couple of days ago and then her temperature spiked. Let me change and I'll meet you downstairs in the autopsy room."

"Okay. By the way, how's your brother doing after his heart attack?"

"Patrick is pissing and moaning just like a homicide detective, which means he's getting better. He should be home from the hospital tomorrow."

"How long before he goes back to work?"

"Soon, but he'll be on desk duty for a month."

"Ouch. He'll hate that."

"I know. He's not one for sitting still."

Claire changed into the County's blue scrubs and tied her hair back before entering the autopsy room. She gowned, gloved, adjusted her face mask, and took in a deep breath. She'd known Elizabeth Keeley O'Connor a long time. This would be one of those cases when, no matter how tight she closed her eyes at night, the memory would never fade.

Homicide Detective Jack Miller, her brother's partner, stood gowned just inside the autopsy suite. Jack's superior, Captain Ramos, had ordered him to accompany Claire to the morgue and attend the autopsy. When it came to the mayor's sister, Captain Ramos wouldn't leave anything to chance.

They were visiting Patrick at the hospital when she and Jack received the calls regarding Elizabeth's death. Claire didn't comment as she watched Jack smear a healthy dose of Vicks Vapo Rub over his upper lip and up his nostrils to kill the strong morgue odor. After all, Jack had signed up to serve and protect the people of Chicago, not watch her perform autopsies.

The door to the x-ray room opened and Thomas, the x-ray tech, pushed the metal cart with Elizabeth O'Connor's draped body into Claire's bay. In spite of the type of work they did, Thomas always had a big smile for everyone, but not tonight. It seemed the mayor's loss weighed heavy on everyone's hearts. Chicago might be a big city, but it was made up of tight-knit communities. During her high school years, Claire babysat Elizabeth's children. Thomas's mother worked for the mayor's parents. She could think of another half a dozen ways their families were all connected.

Claire looked down at Elizabeth's body. She hated autopsying kids and friends. Of course, this case she would never think to refuse. Michael had personally requested her services. Their families had grown up on the same block. Until Elizabeth entered Chicago General Hospital for a scheduled, routine abdominal hysterectomy, she had been a healthy fifty-three-year-old mother of six children. Three days later she was dead. These were the bare-bone facts.

"Ready, Dr. O'Shaunessy?" Ian asked as he uncovered Elizabeth.

She swallowed the lump in her throat. "Yes," she replied.

Claire collected cultures from the surgical and IV sites. Afterwards, Ian washed the body. Next she made the classical 'Y' incision across the collar bone and down the center of the trunk to the surgical site. Usually, Claire and the staff would make a comment about the case during the autopsy or chit chat about prior cases, but tonight, no one spoke unless absolutely necessary. Even though she was the only one in the room who knew the deceased personally, she could see the sadness in her co-workers' eyes as occasional tears wet their cheeks. Elizabeth had been well known in Chicago for all the programs she'd created to help children and the less fortunate. She would be missed.

Gently, Claire folded back the outer tissue, exposing the body's abdominal organs and rib cage. She'd be Elizabeth's last chance to speak. That's the way it was for everyone who passed under Claire's scalpel. If she missed something, the deceased's final words went unspoken. They came to her as they would be forever. They no longer could change who they were. They couldn't go back and lose ten pounds or learn Spanish. After their bodies told Claire the last tale of their lives, they lay naked and dead on the cold, metal shelves waiting for their final resting place. Some would have the luxury of a satin-lined casket, while others would have only the scent of a fresh pine box to comfort them.

Before Claire completed the autopsy, each organ would be weighed and tissue specimens sent to the morgue's histology lab with a blood sample to toxicology. At the moment, a sweet, foul smell coming from the surgical site drew her attention. Prior to the incision, Claire had noticed inflamed and firm tissue surrounding the hysterectomy incision, but no drainage. Once she opened the surgical site, the story changed.

"Quick, Ian, grab a specimen jar," Claire requested.

"What is it?" Ian held the jar open for her.

Claire used the sterile hemostat to drop what appeared to be large flakes covered with a yellow bubbly fluid into the sterile jar. "See the yellow pieces? This looks like they used cadaver tissue to support her abdominal muscles. The tissue is disintegrating and the sutures can't even hold it to the fascia. This doesn't look like any donor tissue I've ever seen. Generally, the tissue has a whitish tan look and is in one piece. From the smell alone, I'm guessing gas gangrene."

Jack, who usually had a dozen questions, finally asked his first. "How did that happen? Did the body reject the tissue?"

"No," Claire said. "This tissue either came contaminated from the donor or became infected just prior to the surgeon inserting it. Look at the tissue."

Jack bent over the surgical site. He pulled back immediately and turned his head away from the overpowering smell. "How would the donor acquire gas gangrene? Isn't it something you see in old men with war injuries?"

Claire collected the remaining pieces of tissue. "The short version?"

"Sure, that'll do." Jack removed his disposable gloves, washed his hands and reapplied another layer of Vicks up his nose before re-gloving.

If her brother Patrick had been here, he'd advise Jack not to ask too many questions, knowing how Claire could get carried away with long explanations. The thought of Patrick warmed her heart.

"Okay. Pathogens, or infectious agents, generally enter the body through a scratch or a cut after contact with feces-contaminated soil. Actually, the destruction caused by the pathogen is from the release of exotoxins and not from the bacteria itself." The distraction provided relief for Claire. She didn't want to focus on the person who once occupied the body on her table. Staying in her clinical role gave her the safety net she needed to do her best for Elizabeth.

Thomas reentered the autopsy room and laid a large envelope on the counter. "Dr. O'Shaunessy, the x-rays are online and an officer dropped off a copy of the hospital records. Thought you'd like to know, the report shows all surgical instruments, sponges and sutures were accounted for before the surgeon closed the incision."

"Thanks, Thomas." Claire turned to Ian. "Pull the OR report."

"Sure thing, Dr. O'Shaunessy." Ian flipped through the chart. "I've got it."

"What does it say about cadaver or donor tissue?" Claire asked, as she carefully placed the intestines on the scale.

"The OR report lists a donor number and tissue number. The attached medical history for the frozen tissue includes blood type. Why did the surgeon use cadaver tissue?" Ian asked as he threaded the curved needle to be used to close the "Y" incision.

"Elizabeth had six pregnancies. I imagine it took a toll on her abdominal muscles. The surgeon backed the muscles for support, to help them heal. This doesn't happen to every woman, but it's not unusual." Claire removed the kidneys and weighted them. She called out the weight in grams for Ian to write on the blackboard where all the organ weights were first recorded. Claire would transfer this information to her final report after the autopsy.

"Would you like me to close while you complete your report?" Ian offered.

"Thank you, Ian. That helps me tremendously."

The techs did the final suturing, but Claire preferred doing her own closures. This wasn't a reflection of her techs' performances. She thought of this as the final step of the case. Usually she liked the feeling of completion it gave her, but not tonight. After she'd finished, Claire removed her protective gear and washed her hands. Jack had removed his gown and stood by her at the sink. For once she didn't even care about the cold tap water. She was alive and could make do. Elizabeth didn't get that option.

A glance at the clock told her they'd completed the autopsy in the usual 45 minutes, but it felt like hours. As she sat at the small desk in the autopsy bay completing the paperwork, tears streamed down her cheeks. Even as a professional, she couldn't always tune out the human element. Especially with Elizabeth. Claire kept thinking of her with her children, bright-eyed and smiling as she listened to them talk or watched them play. What would they do without her?

"Here, I think you could use this." Jack handed Claire his pressed linen handkerchief.

She took it and patted her cheeks. "Thank you." She looked at the soft linen. "I'm impressed. Most men would hand me a box of tissues."

"My mother is a stickler for manners and proper attire."

"Tell your mother she did a great job." Claire smiled shakily up at Jack as she transferred the organ weights to the autopsy report.

"How well did you know Mrs. O'Connor?"

"We lived on the same block. In high school, I babysat her kids."

Jack sat on the edge of Claire's desk. "How could you deal with performing her autopsy? That must have been hard to do on someone you know on such a personal level."

"How could I refuse Michael? He was there for our family when our father was gunned down on patrol. I owed him. Our families go back several generations." Claire reviewed the paperwork one last time, using the mundane task to wrestle her feelings back under control.

"How much longer before you're finished?" Jack asked. "Captain Ramos ordered me to make sure you got home safe. It's late and he doesn't want you out on the street alone hailing a cab."

Claire almost laughed. "Is this the same Captain Ramos who reamed me out for crossing the line and getting involved in your last case?"

A hint of a smile appeared on Jack's face. "I think it might be the same guy. Besides, if I don't get you home safe, Patrick will box my ears off."

"Okay. I'll let you play the knight in shining armor, but I need to change and stop by Dr. Johnson's office first. Also, I want to check on Elizabeth and make sure we have her ready for the mortuary service to pick her up." Although it sounded silly, Claire didn't like the idea of Elizabeth spending the night in the cooler with three hundred dead strangers.

"Dr. O'Shaunessy, I have Mrs. O'Connor ready for pick-up," Ian said as he entered her office. "Do you need anything before I leave?"

"No, I think we have everything covered. See you tomorrow and thanks for coming in."

"Goodnight," Ian called out as he and his friend Thomas left.

Jack followed Claire to her office and waited outside while she changed.

"In case you haven't noticed, Detective Miller, this building is very secure," Claire yelled through the door.

"Following you is easier than answering to Captain Ramos or Patrick if I lose you."

Claire opened the office door. "I'm ready. Dr. Johnson's office is just around the corner."

She knocked on the Cook County Medical Examiner's door before entering. Mayor Michael Keeley sat on the office sofa with his head in his hands. As she and Jack entered, Michael got up and gave Claire a hug. Dr. Johnson wasn't aware of their family ties, and Claire expected this show of affection caught him off guard.

"Thank you for taking care of Elizabeth. I know it couldn't have been easy for you." Michael's face had aged ten years overnight. "Did you find out what caused her death?"

Claire walked Michael over to the couch and indicated he should sit down. "I don't have all the information yet. I've sent tissue samples to the lab, so I won't have an answer for several days, but I believe an overwhelming infection developed and she died of sepsis. I wish I had a more definitive answer for you now, but let's wait until we have all the lab results. Technically, we're supposed to release information only to next of kin, but I know Stephen's children need him right now. I'm sure he's fine with me talking with you."

"I'll have him call you tomorrow." Michael choked on his next words. "When can Elizabeth be picked up?"

"As soon as Claire is completely finished with the autopsy," Dr. Johnson said.

"I have everything I need, so her body is ready to be released."

Dr. Johnson nodded. "Well then, anytime you can make the arrangements would be fine."

"Michael, is the family using McDuffy's Funeral Home?" Claire asked.

He nodded *yes*. Tears streamed down his face.

"I'd be glad to call them for you."

He nodded again, giving his consent. She knew this would be the closest display of public emotion anyone would ever witness from Michael. The press and news service would analyze every facial expression he made. Asking for a moment of privacy for his family was like asking for it not to snow during a Chicago winter. But for now, he was safe and among friends.

# Chapter 3

In his dingy West Side apartment, Derek Ruger stepped into the tiny room next to his kitchen. Proud of his plumbing and electrical skills, he'd converted the pantry into his secret world of photography. In his darkroom, he'd become very proficient at developing and printing. His medium was black and white film because it grabbed emotion much more strongly than color film. It heightened joy and deepened despair.

He also preferred film over digital cards. The process of developing the film and knowing precisely when to pull the print from the developing fluid could be considered an art in itself. He believed digital was the lazy man's way of producing prints.

Derek regretted that his work wouldn't show the mystery woman's red hair. The next time she came into view, he would load the camera with color film. He'd print an eight by ten glossy of her for the Keeley Family Tree printed on his living room wall. But, he'd have to decide where to put her. He had to find her identity and where she fit in the mayor's large extended family. For now he would give her a separate branch.

If only she'd pose for him, she'd become his. He could hardly contain his excitement, his hunger for her. Some would say he didn't stand a chance, but he knew better. Anything could be done if you were willing to be patient, he thought, and he was a very patient man.

His patience had rewarded him tonight. A warm feeling surged through him as the movie reel in his mind played back this evening's triumph. The extra money he'd made working at Floyd's Funeral Home part-time paid for his new camera lens. The lens made it possible for him to see and take photos from a distance.

After he printed the last photograph, he cleaned up his work area. He was very fastidious about his dark room. Everything had its place.

He kept his entire apartment meticulous. He liked things neat and organized, a lesson taught him by a past full of chaos. His mother ran off before his tenth birthday. His father, and sole source of support, had been stabbed to death before Derek turned eighteen. At least he'd had a roof over his head, all thanks to the building manager who took pity on him and let him stay in the dirty basement. His orderly nature resulted from the years he'd lived there, and the compulsion for order had served him well. His self-discipline proved a much-appreciated asset for his full-time job as an operating room tech.

While he waited for the prints to finish drying, he made his nightly mug of warmed milk and turned on the late night news. He selected Jillian Garcia's station. He wanted to see how she reported the lead story for the ten o'clock broadcast, the death of the mayor's sister. First, he heard from a spokesperson on the front steps of Chicago General Hospital. Dr. Keith Olson, Elizabeth O'Connor's surgeon, spoke next.

"At this time," the surgeon said, "we don't have all of the facts to share with you. Our hearts go out to Elizabeth's family."

Afterwards, the station switched to a pre-recorded segment filmed outside the back entrance of the Cook County Morgue. In a somber voice, Jillian Garcia reported that Elizabeth's body had arrived for an autopsy and her brother, Mayor Michael Keeley, had accompanied her. Then back to the news station for a quick report on who must be autopsied by Illinois law. After a station break, Jillian followed up with a summary of the events and stated that the citizens of Chicago would be kept apprised of any further developments.

Derek almost dropped his mug as his picture appeared in the crowd, not near Jillian. How did this happen? How had he missed seeing the cameraman who'd panned the crowd? Panic set in. He'd been always so careful. He clenched the mug in both hands. *It's her fault, the redhead!*

Suddenly the air around him thinned and he set his mug on the table. He felt lightheaded as he dropped into the closest chair. Bracing his elbows on his knees, he gulped in air. Other than his hospital ID picture, he'd made it a point to stay away from that side of the camera lens. He couldn't afford questions. He hoped no one at work saw the news clip. If they did, they might pry. What would he say? *Think!*

It took him several minutes to compose himself. He sat up with an explanation running through his mind. Chicago's skyline had been shot at sunset from the lakefront numerous times, with the last splashes of color outlining the city's magnificent buildings. He'd wanted to try the opposite approach. He could claim he thought the effect of the light reflecting off the buildings with the darkness of night hovering in the background like a blanket would be an artistic approach. It just so happened, the area near the morgue turned out to be a perfect spot because of several vacant blocks offering a clear view of Willis Tower. Like others, he had been drawn to the morgue by the sight of the flashing police lights. But what if someone asked to see his photographs? He'd worry about it then. In reality, no one at the hospital had ever taken the slightest interest in him.

He closed his eyes and slowly began a deep breathing exercise to relax himself. He sucked the air in through his nose, then gradually released it from his mouth. His arms, bent slightly in front of his abdomen, rose and fell with each breath. He let his mind wander to this evening's spectacular sunset. The splashes of color, from brilliant reds to the palest yellow, played on the back of his eyelids. Within minutes he had started to calm down. He kept breathing slowly until his mind absorbed the red. His eyelids popped open at the speed of a runaway window shade. She had shattered his peace. *She would have to pay.*

The forgotten mug sat cooling as the timer went off. Derek immediately checked on his prints. One by one, he viewed the prints with only a red light illuminating the darkness of the small room. The light cast a glow on her picture. He dared not run his fingers over her hair for fear of damaging the print. He wanted the picture perfect, just like her.

After gathering the rest of the prints, he returned to the kitchen and spread them out on the counter to admire. He could almost caress death as he held the photograph of the transport van in his hands.

"Sorry this had to happen to you, Elizabeth," he said to the photographs. "I believe they call it collateral damage."

A slight chuckle escaped his lips. His spirits were improving after the terrible scare he had a moment ago.

Next, he held the shot he took of Michael. Carefully he ran his finger over the lines on Michael's face. He noticed the hard, set edge to the mayor's mouth. *Always in control, aren't you, Michael. How does it feel to have your world come crashing down on you?* What a shame those six children had to lose their mother. This was simply business, simply revenge.

He turned off the television and allowed the silence to engulf him. He tested the edges of the other prints. They were dry. From the kitchen drawer he removed a small box of thumb tacks. He knew with one swift move he could spackle the holes the tacks made in his walls. The adhesive on Scotch tape posed more problems for repair. He wasn't planning on moving, but he liked to think ahead and be in control.

With precision, he hung the additions to his wall. He placed the redhead's picture on the wall first.

"You will be mine," he told her.

Next his fingers roamed gently over each name, only stopping at the ones with a black line crossed through them. Smiling, he remembered with affection how each black mark had been earned. And now for his crowning glory!

With trembling fingers, he reached for the red marker he'd been waiting to use. He rolled the marker back and forth between his palms, allowing the moment to build. This was his first red 'X'. He wanted to savor every second of anticipation. He refused to rush. The movement of his hand stroking the permanent red ink over Elizabeth's photo would be imprinted in his mind forever. Something for him to replay for his enjoyment.

He stared at the photo of the happy mother of six next to the picture of the transport van. With envisioned pomp and circumstance, he raised the marker and ceremoniously drew a large red 'X' through Elizabeth's picture. Exhilarated, he moved over to Michael's picture.

"You're next!"

# Chapter 4

Claire felt drained from the night before. Her back muscles ached from tensing up during the autopsy. The emotional loss was painful enough. Even a steaming cup of cappuccino couldn't give her that extra surge of energy she needed.

Page by page, Claire carefully reviewed Elizabeth's hospital chart. Her lab results were all within normal range except for her elevated white cell count, a classic sign of infection. Her temperature had spiked twenty-four hours after surgery, which had increased her heart rate. While her respiratory rate had also risen, her chest x-ray remained clear. That only left the cadaver tissue implanted in Elizabeth's abdominal cavity to provide Claire with any relevant information.

Fresh out of answers, Claire headed to the histology lab. Within a minute, she pushed open the door and called out to the graying lab supervisor. "Hey Sam, do you have any results on the tissue from the O'Connor case?"

Sam's eyes remained glued to the electron microscope. "Now Dr. O'Shaunessy, you know how long it takes before forty-eight hour cultures can be read. I started them at ten last night. When do you think I'll have an answer?"

"You only call me Dr. O'Shaunessy when you're trying to get my goat." Claire knew Sam loved the power he held over the pathologists. Until they received his test results, they couldn't close their cases.

"I heard that while I vacationed in Wisconsin, a few weeks ago, as a token of your deep appreciation for our lab pushing *your* work through at lightning speed, a round of pizzas graced our lunchroom." Sam put another slide under the microscope and adjusted the lens, never looking up.

Claire knew she had been conned the last time. Ian had mentioned that a 'token' of her appreciation might move her specimens to the front of the line. "Well, I can't deny it. The lab has been very receptive to my requests. However, at the moment I haven't received results for any of the tests I requested." She wasn't about to hand over another fistful of twenties without getting something in return.

"Perhaps you would like to take a look at a slide from the O'Connor case?" Sam sat back on his stool with his arms crossed over his robust abdomen.

Claire didn't need a second invitation. She looked through the microscope lens. Bacteria Clostridium perfringens stared back at her. She let out a low whistle.

"What do you think?" Sam slid off his stool.

"There's nothing like having a little gram-positive, rod-shaped, spore-forming bacterium gracing the slide. I knew I smelled gas gangrene when I opened her up. The sepsis had to be from the cadaver tissue. How else could it have happened?"

"I don't envy you," Sam said. He recorded the information in the log. "The road from this microscope back to the donor could be politically very long. Not just anybody's sister died. Getting through the red tape to find the answers will be more than an uphill battle, and I don't imagine the company that sold this tissue will be cooperative. Once the company lawyers hear about the situation, they'll be circling their building."

"Thanks for your extra effort. Maybe in a few days everyone will feel up to enjoying another round of pizzas. Just remember to include Ian, Thomas, and the ancillary staff who worked extra last night. Pick the day, and I'll order the pizzas myself."

"You know Claire, you're all right. Now scoot out of here, I have work to do." Sam picked up another slide and positioned it effortlessly under the microscope.

As she left Sam's lab, Claire found the energy she'd lacked before. The information might only be preliminary, but now she had a starting point. She returned to her office and put in a call to Dr. Olson, Elizabeth's physician. The receptionist told Claire the doctor was making rounds over on the postpartum unit and would be there for another hour. Claire thanked her, grabbed the lukewarm cappuccino, and left her office.

* * *

Chicago General Hospital stood only a few blocks east of the morgue on the Illinois Medical Campus. Moments later Claire entered the elevator and pressed the button for the seventh floor. She found Dr. Olson charting on one of his patients

"Dr. Olson," Claire called from the other side of the nurses' station.

"Hi, Claire. Is this business or a friendly visit?" Dr. Olson closed the patient chart and returned it to the rack. He stood and came around the counter. She noticed he lacked his usual jovial welcome.

"Maybe we could make it a friendly business visit," Claire answered. "I'm assigned to Elizabeth O'Connor's case. I've read her chart, but I need to ask you a few questions."

"Walk with me. I'm headed to surgery."

"How are you doing?" Claire knew he had to be hurting. The OB/GYN doctor had cared for her and Michael's families for years. He had a stellar record and had never lost a patient before. She couldn't believe this had happened to him. Elizabeth's family weren't the only ones hurt by her unexpected death. Her passing took a toll on the hospital staff as well.

"I'm okay. Did you find anything during your autopsy to explain what happened?" Dr. Olson asked.

"Officially, the labs aren't back, but it looks like the cause of death is gas gangrene."

"What?" Dr. Olson stopped dead in his tracks. He ran his hands through his thick blond hair. Under the bright hall lights, the bags under his eyes looked darker. "How in the hell did that happen?"

Claire laid her hand on his arm. "I can't imagine how you must be taking this. Everyone is devastated. I promise you, I'll find out what happened."

They walked in silence to the elevator. Once alone and inside, Claire told him of her suspicions.

"I don't understand. We've used the same company for years. I've never had any incidents of infected tissue from them," Dr. Olson said.

"I brought a copy of the OR report with me. Perhaps if I could talk with everyone involved in the case, I can learn something. Sometime between Tri-State collecting the donor tissue and your placing it in Elizabeth's abdomen, something went terribly wrong,"

Claire said as they stepped off the elevator next to the surgical unit. They headed for the PACU, the post-anesthesia care unit.

Dr. Olson held the door to the PACU open for Claire to enter. "Debbie, Joan," he called out to the nurses. "Could you give us a couple minutes?" They nodded and Debbie came over while Joan admitted the next patient into a recovery bay.

"Hi, Dr. Olson," Debbie answered. "What can I do for you?"

"Debbie, this is Dr. O'Shaunessy from the Office of the Medical Examiner. She has a few questions regarding Elizabeth O'Connor."

Claire read panic on the nurse's face as her eyes widened and wrinkles appeared on her forehead. Claire offered Debbie her hand. Hesitantly, the woman took it.

"I don't know if I should talk with you." Debbie looked like she'd cry on a minute's notice.

"It's all right," Dr. Olsen said gently. "Dr. O'Shaunessy is just looking for information. We know you did your job well, like you always do."

"That's right," Claire said. The anxiety in Debbie's face eased a bit. "Were you the surgical circulating nurse for Elizabeth's case?"

"Yes."

"So you saw the donor tissue placed in her abdomen?"

"Yes." Debbie jammed her hands into her scrub jacket pockets.

"Can you think of anything that seemed different that day? Perhaps something was out of place?" Claire continued.

"No. The case went off on time. Nothing happened that I can think of."

"When I opened Elizabeth, I found the surgical site infected with gas gangrene," Claire said.

"Oh, my God! How did that happen?" Debbie pressed both hands to her mouth.

"That's what I'm trying to find out. Also, I'll be talking to the company that supplied the tissue. I'm looking for the source to prevent anyone else from getting sick." Claire fished a business card from her pocket. "Here's my card. Call me anytime if you think of something." She pressed her card into Debbie's shaking hand as the other nurse, Joan, walked over. Claire repeated the same questions to Joan, but neither nurse had anything new for her.

# Chapter 5

Claire scanned the operating room report again. She only needed to speak with the surgical tech.

Dr. Olson's cell phone rang. "I'm due in the OR now. Do you have any more questions?"

"I'd like to speak with Derek Ruger, the OR tech on this case," Claire said.

"Joan, would you find Derek for Dr. O'Shaunessy?"

"Sure thing, Dr. Olson. He should be back from break any minute," Joan answered.

"Claire, keep me in the loop. If I discover anything, I'll call you," Dr. Olson said as he left the PACU for surgery.

Claire waved a quick goodbye to him.

"Dr. O'Shaunessy, let's go see if Derek is in the break room. If he isn't, I'll page him for you," Joan offered.

He wasn't in the break room. They went to the nurses' station, where Joan paged him. He responded immediately, arriving within a few minutes.

"Derek, this is Dr. O'Shaunessy from the Cook County Morgue. She performed Mrs. O'Connor's autopsy and is investigating her cause of death."

"Hi." Claire offered him her hand, but the short, stocky tech looked reluctant and stepped back slightly. *He's probably scared about being blamed, or thinks there'll be a lawsuit,* Claire thought, *which is only natural since his name is on the OR report.*

"I don't know how I can help you," he answered in a measured tone.

"I'd like to know more about the donor specimen. Do you remember noticing anything different about the packaging or labeling on it? Did you notice if the seal was intact?"

"I checked the integrity of the packing myself," Derek said. "Everything was in order."

"What about storage? To your knowledge, were there any problems with the freezer? Any temperature fluctuations?" Claire pushed, hoping for an answer.

"I check the temperature daily and record it." Derek stood with his feet slightly apart and his arms crossed. "Everything was normal."

Claire sighed over her lack of progress. She addressed the nurse. "Joan, I think I'm done here for now. Could you get me the name of your contact person at Tri-State Bone and Tissue Services?" She turned back to Derek. "Thank you for your time. Here's my card in case you think of anything. No detail is too small."

Derek pocketed the card and walked out without even a goodbye. "Strange guy," Claire said to herself, unaware Joan had returned with the contact information.

"He's efficient and good at his job, but lacks people skills. It's probably a good thing he doesn't have to converse with the patients other than to ask them to move from the gurney to the surgical table. Here's the contact information for you."

"Thanks, Joan." Armed with the Tri-State representative's name and phone number, she headed back to the morgue.

* * *

Derek patted the business card tucked safely in the breast pocket of his scrubs. He had actually met the mystery woman with red hair, the one whose photo hung on his apartment wall. The one who captivated him, but just like Jillian Garcia, had become a threat. Garcia's broadcast might expose him, and now the redhead—Dr. O'Shaunessy—knew who he was. Why were these problems happening to him now? He'd always been so careful. His face felt flushed just before a horrible chill consumed him.

He covered his mouth as he darted into the bathroom across the hall. He almost didn't make it before his lunch revolted, spilling into the john. He couldn't remember how long he'd stood holding the sink when he heard a voice ask if he was all right.

"I'll be out in a minute," he responded, his strength gone. After rinsing his mouth, he splashed cold water on his face, but it didn't help.

When he opened the door, Debbie, his supervisor, stood waiting for him.

"You look terrible," she said. "Don't tell me you ate the chili dog from the cafeteria."

"I guess it didn't agree with me," Derek lied.

"We're on our last case in the OR. I'll send the case cart down to Central Service to be sterilized for you," she said. "Go ahead and head home. Hope you feel better tomorrow."

He could feel Debbie's gaze on him as he walked toward the men's locker room. The last thing he heard before the door closed was her mumbling something about him not thanking her. Why should he? Supervisors are supposed to send sick employees home.

As he changed out of his scrubs, he pulled out the redhead's business card. It read, *Dr. Claire O'Shaunessy*. Maybe she wasn't even related to the mayor? That could certainly put a different light on things.

# Chapter 6

After receiving clearance from Dr. Johnson, Claire scheduled an appointment with Ruth Weinstein, Director of Donor/Hospital Relations for Tri-State Bone and Tissue Services. Claire was disappointed to have to wait until tomorrow. She also wondered how receptive they'd be.

Glancing at her watch, she realized she had about thirty minutes to gulp down her yogurt and banana before the staff meeting. She'd just enough time check to see if her brother had been discharged. She'd decided not to see Patrick when she stopped by Chicago General earlier because she knew he'd jump out of his hospital bed and follow her up to surgery. Plus, he'd remind her to leave the investigating up to the police. Of course, this investigation was justifiable and approved by Dr. Johnson. The tissue specimen in Sam's lab needed a history. If Elizabeth received tainted donor tissue, then someone else out there might experience the same fate. Claire considered this medical research, not a homicide investigation.

As usual, she had a stack of charts on her desk. She grabbed the top one and completed the last few notes it needed. She was reaching for the next one when Detective Jack Miller knocked on her door.

"How are you doing?" Jack didn't wait for an invitation. He sat down in the chair opposite Claire.

*He must be making the 'brotherly' rounds for Patrick*, she thought. "Okay. What brings you to my luxurious office?"

Jack looked around, then laughed. "I think you need your eyes checked."

"You should talk. I've seen your office. All you and Patrick have are a couple of gray metal desks in a big room that looks like a homeless shelter. Speaking of Patrick, I need to call and see if he was discharged."

"I just heard from your sister-in-law." Jack yawned as he stretched. "Sylvia definitely has her hands full with Patrick. He's at home and the word 'rest' is killing him. I bet he'll be at his desk tomorrow morning, complaining about the diet Dr Wong put him on."

"The girls should be home from school soon and they can entertain him. I'll call him tonight. By the way, you didn't answer my question. You could have called just as easily with the information about Patrick's discharge."

Jack leaned forward and rested his arms on his thighs. "I've got to tell you, I can't stop thinking about that cadaver tissue you removed from Elizabeth O'Connor's abdomen. Do you honestly believe this was an accident?"

"Her death is a horrible tragedy, but accident, I don't know." Claire pulled her unruly hair back, twisted it, and attempted to secure it with a big clip. A few strands at the back of her neck slipped out.

"How could the tissue pass all the tests, be sterilized and still be infected? Could this one package have slipped through and missed the last step? Don't forget, I don't believe in coincidences."

"Jack, that's Patrick's line. I can't imagine how this occurred either. Quality control at reputable companies is tight. One mishap could destroy them."

"I hear a 'but' coming, especially after the word reputable."

"The 'but' is a lot bigger than you can imagine. The entire donor tissue system lacks a system of checks and balances. The FDA, Food and Drug Administration, is responsible for tissue safety, but their budget falls drastically short for them to institute and follow up on regulations."

"You're kidding me."

"No, I'm not. This wouldn't be the first time someone died from donor tissue infected with gas gangrene. Harvesting donor tissue, including bone, is a billion-dollar body parts business, full of shoddy practices. Though most tissue transplant companies have good reputations and do a lot of good."

"Isn't there some association that requires accreditation?"

"Sure there is. The American Association of Tissue Banks requires its accredited members to follow high standards, but hospitals can legally buy from unaccredited suppliers that offer tissue cheaper. In the future, hospitals will use more artificial mesh instead of donor tissue for specific surgeries. In abdominal cases, human tissue is used because the patient could gain weight and would need it to expand."

"I take it the risk of problems might increase when money is the focus?"

Claire nodded. "A couple of years ago a New Jersey company scavenged tissue from corpses. To start with, they didn't have the families' permission to harvest their loved ones' remains. There are unaccredited companies using cadavers rejected by accredited companies. There isn't a unified tracking system in place as the tissue travels from donor to recipient."

"So Elizabeth's death could have been prevented?" Jack asked.

"I don't know for sure, but I'm going to find out."

"It's personal, isn't it?"

"It's personal for all of my cases, and not just because Elizabeth is from the old neighborhood and her brother is the Mayor of Chicago. Not only do I care about all my cases, but it's my duty to provide the families and law enforcement the answers they seek. Yes, this case hit close to home. But it's a matter of professionalism, too."

"I thought you would say that. So, where do we start?"

"How about a road trip tomorrow?" Claire checked her watch.

Jack got to his feet. "Where are we headed?"

"Slow down for a minute. I said tomorrow. Right now I have a staff meeting to attend." Claire grabbed a pen and her notebook. "After that, I have a date with that stack of charts on my desk."

Jack slid back into the chair.

"Tomorrow morning, I've an appointment in Oak Brook with Ruth Weinstein of Tri-State Bone and Tissue Services. Want to join me? I'll have to take the lead, though. They might clam up if they think the police are looking at them."

"No problem. May I use your computer while you're at your meeting? I don't want anyone at the station catching wind of this."

Claire hit a couple keys. "Here's the Internet for you. I'll be back in about an hour. You wouldn't be researching cadaver tissue, would you?"

Jack nodded as he shifted to the seat behind her computer. "Could we keep this between us until I have something solid I can take to Captain Ramos? He wants to keep this quiet until there's more concrete information on Mrs. O'Connor's case, otherwise the public might think we're giving priority to the mayor's family over other cases."

"Okay," she answered. She knew how investigations could be twisted in the public's eye.

# Chapter 7

Derek Ruger couldn't wait until he reached the security of his apartment. His heart raced as he walked the four blocks to the quiet side street where he parked his car before daylight. A light drizzle fell on his umbrella. The wind hadn't kicked up yet, but it would by this evening when the forecast thunderstorm hit.

In the sparse afternoon traffic, he slipped down the streets to his alley parking space in record time. Within minutes, he reached the safety of his apartment, and leaned against the back of the multi-locked door to steady himself as his umbrella dripped on the front hall rug. His heart still pumped hard as his thoughts replayed the meeting with the medical examiner, Dr. Claire O'Shaunessy—his redhead. His excitement was laced with an edge of panic. She scared him. She'd performed Elizabeth O'Connor's autopsy and asked too many questions.

As always, he could be patient for what he wanted. He'd worked around harder obstacles before and he could do it again. If she got lucky with her investigation, though, time might not be on his side. He would have to be very careful, and thorough, if he wanted to secure his ultimate goal. It was almost in sight.

Derek hung his damp jacket and umbrella on a hook in the bathroom to dry. His stomach growled, reminding him that he'd vomited his lunch. He poured a can of chicken noodle soup into a saucepan and dropped a slice of bread into the toaster. A few minutes later he took his snack into the living room.

Once settled in his favorite chair, he hit the remote for the DVD player. Immediately *Silence of the Lambs* started up. He watched Anthony Hopkins elevate fear to a new level and wished he could emulate his hero, Hannibal Lector.

He barely touched the soup, but the toast settled his stomach. The movie rejuvenated him. He needed to work on his plan to destroy Michael Keeley. Then he needed to decide how to terminate Dr. Claire O'Shaunessy, the latest threat to his existence.

He no longer found the redhead exciting. He realized he didn't know anything personal about her, other than where she worked. He would need to know more to execute his plan.

He checked the weather channel. The weatherman reported rain with thunderstorms in the late afternoon and through the evening. Perfect. Quickly, he washed the dishes while he formulated his next move.

* * *

Derek parked his car kitty-corner from the morgue's employee parking area. He could see everyone entering and leaving the lot. Before he left home, he had called the morgue on the pretense of reviewing old logs for genealogical research and to ask what time they closed. Five o'clock sharp, the woman on the other end of the line told him. He had his answer now. All he had to do was wait for Claire. With the lousy weather, he didn't expect too many people would notice him. They'd assume he was picking someone up from work.

For his disguise, he wore a dark jacket and a blue baseball cap with a Bears emblem above the bill. He pretended to read a Patricia Cornwell paperback, *Book of the Dead*. How ironic, he thought, in many counties this was the name of the log where all the coroner cases were entered by hand. He assumed Cook County had their log on a computer. He envisioned the keyboard. Using one key at a time, a clerk had plunked Elizabeth's name into the system last night. He dreamed of the same fingers typing out Michael Keeley's name one day soon. The thought warmed him.

The parking lot had almost emptied when he saw Claire run through the rain to her Ford Taurus. He'd almost given up, but reasoned the doctor probably had a late case. He ducked slightly behind the steering wheel and started his car. He watched her pull out onto Harrison and drive east. He followed but kept a safe distance. With heavy rush hour traffic, they caught most lights. Claire turned onto South Michigan Avenue, then Roosevelt and east to South Indiana, which surprised him. He had thought of her as a Lincoln Park type, where the yuppie professionals lived. Over the past several years, the South Loop area had become quite trendy. Actually, this location worked better for him.

From his aging Chevy Malibu, he observed her drive into a secured indoor parking lot. He pulled into an empty spot on the street, picked up a pair of binoculars from the passenger seat, and scanned the building's lobby. He saw the doorman assisting a lady with her packages. The sign outside read, *New Condo Units Still Available*. This pleased him. New building, new tenants, new doorman! The doorman wouldn't know every tenant yet, nor know much about them. Luck was on his side for once.

He paid no attention to the large drops of rain pelting his windshield. The promised storm hit with a vengeance, hindering traffic, but it didn't faze him. He focused on his next stop, a chain grocery store west of his apartment for a flower arrangement.

In the florist department, he made sure not to handle the vase with his bare hands. It was his nature to be careful. He thanked the young girl for wrapping the arrangement, but she barely nodded at his comment. Her only interest was yakking on her cell phone. Derek doubted she would even remember the sale.

At home, he placed the flowers on the kitchen counter. He slid his fingers into a pair of disposable gloves before filling a pitcher with water. After carefully unwrapping the flowers, he transferred them to the pitcher. Then he cleaned the tell-tale barcode sticker from the bottom of the vase. He hadn't dared ask the girl at the flower counter earlier to remove the sticker. He didn't want to give her a reason to remember him. He scrubbed the vase inside and out. When he was satisfied there was nothing to link it back to him, he filled it with water and replaced the flowers, then rewrapped the arrangement and stapled the paper shut.

After preparing the arrangement, he withdrew the Stipula Vedo fountain pen from the tiny top drawer of the desk he'd salvaged from the alley and restored. Gently he stroked the pen's sleek barrel. The fountain pen had been an extravagance on his salary, but he couldn't resist its simplicity and style. *The hallmarks of classic Florentine elegance*, the tag read. The italic tip moved over surfaces like a hand gliding through water. Carefully he filled the pen from the bottled ink. No pre-filled cartridges for him. He considered himself a purist.

He selected a piece of poster board about the size of one of those magnetic signs stuck on the sides of vans. He loathed those magnetic signs. They made a statement that the business was barely surviving and the van probably doubled as the family's vehicle.

With the poster board flat on the kitchen table, he drew two half circles, one under the other. First he penciled the words *Flowers By* on the top line and *Rolph* on the inside curve, with a fake web address underneath. Next he went over the letters with his pen. Stepping back, he viewed his penmanship. He'd wanted to attend art school, but that dream fell apart the minute Timothy Keeley gave Derek's father's job to his own son, Michael. But the lack of funds hadn't totally held him back. The Harold Washington Library offered a course on calligraphy for almost nothing, and library books were free.

His calligraphy skill had come in handy at Floyd's Funeral Home. Besides preparing bodies, he penned the deceased's last name on the sign placed outside the viewing rooms. The pay left a lot to be desired, but he took personal pride in every sign he made. Often the families would ask if they could buy the sign, but he let them have it for nothing. Floyd's had already screwed them. Floyd's overpriced the caskets, and the guaranteed sealed vaults made of inferior supplies probably leaked.

Cremations were another source of easy money for Floyd's. The crematorium stood behind the funeral home. Floyd's had a practice of shoving more than one body in the oven at the same time, then dividing the community ashes. This saved on the cost of firing the ovens. The families just didn't know any better. Nor did they have any idea tissue and bone had been removed from their loved ones before cremation and sold to less reputable companies.

After he created the floral sign, he took his fountain pen into his living room. On the wall before him on his wall was his masterpiece! His precision was breathtaking. He had penned the entire Keeley family tree in a beautiful script. Photos hung next to the names. Tonight he would add Claire's name. He roughed out her name first in pencil, then took the fountain pen to the wall with great pride.

On the computer he printed a *Flowers By Rolph* delivery ticket and delivery sheet. Next, he used a common ballpoint pen to address a card. *To Dr. O'Shaunessy, Thanks for a job well done, Dr. Gregory Johnson.* He'd researched the name on the Internet.

His hands shook with excitement as he stapled the white card and delivery ticket to the arrangement.

"Tomorrow," he whispered to himself. "*Tomorrow*!"

# Chapter 8

A light morning rain blanketed Chicago as Derek Ruger waited for the bus to pass before approaching the corner. He allowed himself fifteen minutes to borrow a van from the grocery store parking lot. He thought of how others would say he had stolen the van, but he only needed it for an hour. He'd leave the van in perfect condition on a well-used street. Thinking of the puzzled look on a cop's face when he discovered it so quickly stroked Derek's ego. He enjoyed messing with people's minds.

Standing under his black umbrella, he watched the cars pull in and out of the lot. A few minutes later a young mother pulled in. He heard a child crying. The thunder and rain offered a perfect distraction as the mother quickly helped a toddler out of the van and grabbed a baby in a carrier before sliding the door shut. With her purse slung over her shoulder, she hurried the children inside.

Once the grocery store doors closed behind her, Derek walked over to the van. The SUV next to it offered him partial protection from the security cameras. Yes! In the mother's rush to get her children out of the rain, she hadn't heard her keys fall to the pavement. He pulled on a pair of gloves stashed in his pocket and snatched them up. He quickly entered the van and folded down the front window visors.

Within a few short minutes, he pulled out of the lot and headed the opposite direction from where he wanted to go for the benefit of the security cameras. A couple of blocks later he circled around and parked behind his car. The downpour had passed. He grabbed a couple of old towels from the back seat and wiped the rain from the van door. He removed the flowers and the sign from his car, and exchanged his brown jacket for a blue one. In a deserted alley he stopped for the final preparation of his plan. He taped the sign to the passenger side of the van and put on his Bears baseball cap.

The trip over to Claire's condo went quicker than expected. He thought the weather must be keeping the retired folks at home this morning. He purposely pulled into the circular drive in front of the building with the passenger side facing the doorman. He wanted the doorman to have a view of the delivery van's advertisement as he signed off on the delivery sheet. The timing was perfect. A UPS truck was already there, and the doorman was busy accepting packages from the driver as several ladies spoke with him.

Derek jumped out of the van and hurried through the rain to the front door, just as the UPS driver drove off. "Hi, I have flowers for Dr. O'Shaunessy," he said to the doorman. "Can you ring her condo?"

"I saw her leave for work early this morning," the doorman said. "I can take them for you and see to it that she gets them when she comes home."

"That would be appreciated. Could you sign here?" Derek placed the flower arrangement on the front desk and handed the clipboard to the doorman.

"Sure." The doorman glanced outside as he signed for the flowers.

"Thanks, and have a nice day," Derek said. He hurried to the van as the rain kicked in again. Moments later he was in the flow of traffic on Roosevelt Road. A few blocks down, he pulled into an alley and got out. He removed the *Flowers by Rolph* sign and threw it in a dumpster. Next, he drove around to Roosevelt Road and parked the van in front of a dry-cleaning business. A couple of blocks later he caught a bus. He'd have to transfer once before he got to work and pick up his car later this evening, but it didn't matter. His plan unfolding the way he wanted was his only concern.

# Chapter 9

Homicide Detective Patrick O'Shaunessy wasn't taking his desk restriction graciously. He had a few more days left on his medical leave, but he convinced his cardiologist if he had to stay home one more minute he'd have the big one. Everyone welcomed him back after his health scare, but he thought death would be a welcome relief over a desk job. Nor did it help that his partner was nowhere to be seen. "Working a special case," Captain Ramos said when Patrick inquired. About now he'd love to make Captain Ramos eat those very words. This wasn't like his boss, to keep him out of the loop. Even though he and the captain went back to high school boxing days when he could punch the guy out, it would do nothing for his career right now to use his right hook.

Life sucked. Jack Miller had been his partner for six years. Patrick almost had by-the-book Jack broken in. They didn't come cleaner than Jack. He saw everything in black or white, a throwback from Jack's college days. His best friend, Tad, had been murdered during a robbery and the perpetrators got off on a technicality. Patrick kept pounding it into Jack's head that sometimes life has some gray areas, too.

The case they'd just finished definitely had gray areas, namely his sister, Claire. While he and Jack were investigating the homicide of a man found in Jackson Park and the death of Claire's childhood friend, Sarah, his sister had stepped beyond her role as a forensic pathologist. She'd managed to get herself caught up in their case. Actually, that was what gave Patrick the mild heart attack. If he were being honest, he'd have to admit he'd been in lousy physical shape for a long time. But the stress Claire caused by almost getting herself killed didn't help, even though she'd solved the case. She had too much police blood in her, like three generations' worth, and it scared the hell out of him.

The next thing, which really got Patrick's goat, was that the snacks he'd squirreled away in his desk had disappeared. Only

Jack had keys to his desk. Jack had to be the culprit. The next time Patrick's wife, Sylvia, wanted him to go shopping for drapes or something equally stupid, he'd insist Jack join them for the adventure. After lunch he'd pick up refills. He'd place some of those health bars, the ones made from sticks and twigs, up front for Jack to see when he opened Patrick's desk. Jack didn't need to know what Patrick planned to hide in his cold case files. The Snickers bars would be for emergencies only. Dr. Wong had taken Sylvia's homemade buttery garlic bread and hefty helpings of pasta away, and left him with grilled chicken, and worst of all, lettuce. *Only rabbits eat green leafy stuff!*

Patrick checked the wall clock. He'd been officially back to work for twenty-five minutes. He'd sharpened his pencils, accidentally cleaned out his desk while in search of a snack and suffered through a cup of decaf coffee. Only wimps and little old ladies drank decaf coffee. There was nothing manly about it, or that flavored stuff.

He was still grumbling to himself when Claire called to wish him well on his first day back. She didn't have to remind him to behave himself, he thought. On the sly, he asked her if she knew where his partner was. Jack hadn't returned any of his calls. Claire denied knowing Jack's whereabouts, but shared the information regarding the contaminated tissue. However, she waited just a hair too long in offering the excuse that she had to run because of a full docket.

*Thank you Claire*, Patrick thought. At least he could guess why Jack hadn't picked up his calls. Pissed he wasn't out there with his partner hunting down leads on the contaminated tissue, he accepted his fate, thirty days on desk duty, per Dr. Wong. At least it was better than sitting at home.

As he sat there stringing Jack's paperclips together he thought about Elizabeth, her husband and the six kids she left behind. He knew from personal experience the death of a mother was brutal. His own mother died of pneumonia when Claire was just a little tyke, leaving him and his five sisters for his dad to raise. During Claire's senior year in high school, their dad had been gunned down while on foot patrol. Perhaps Claire would have been more ladylike if their mother had been around, but they'd never know.

Patrick kept adding more paperclips to his already lengthening chain. Hadn't the Keeleys had enough pain in their lives? He'd grown up with Michael's youngest sister, Mary Anne. They even went to the senior prom together. Unfortunately sixteen years ago, while riding her bike to work, a tragic accident shattered her life.

Mary Anne, a patent attorney, loved to ride her bike from her Lakeview condo to the small law firm in the Loop where she worked. One Monday morning, in a matter of seconds, everything changed. The doctors declared it a miracle she'd lived, considering the severity of her head injuries, but she never fully recovered. She'd lived, if you could call it that, in a nursing home ever since. She didn't know the difference between day and night, or recognize any of her family. She didn't have control over her own bodily functions or muscles.

That was a hard pill for the Keeleys to swallow. Patrick couldn't begin to imagine their pain. What if something happened to Claire? How would he face his parents in the next life? After losing his father through an act of violence, he could understand Jack's angst over his friend's murder. No one's family seemed to get a break.

As Patrick's fingers added more paper clips to the chain, he thought about when eight-year-old Reese, Elizabeth's fifth child, was hit by a stolen car. The vehicle jumped the curb, rammed into Reese, and vanished in a matter of seconds. Of course, no one remembered the make of the car, only seeing the color from a distance. A partial imprint of the license plate bruised the little girl's thigh. Thank heavens Reese only suffered a broken arm and sprained an ankle. The minor cuts and abrasions were gone within a week, but the emotional trauma scarred her for life. To this day she was abnormally terrified of traffic.

And then Michael's second oldest son, Shane, had been knocked off his bike as a kid. He didn't know the guy on the other bike who had taken his foot and shoved Shane into a brick wall. The growth plate to his right leg had been permanently damaged, leaving it one inch shorter than his left leg. No one saw who did it.

Something didn't sit right, now he thought about it. Patrick dropped the paperclip chain and reached for one of the freshly sharpened pencils as he started a list. The Keeley clan was a large family. He added two serious bike accidents, a broken arm from a hit and run, and one post-op infection resulting in death to the list. Then he remembered someone had poisoned Michael's dog while he attended law school. Other incidents came to mind. They always seemed unexplainable. None had been witnessed, and, they occurred more frequently as time went on. Patrick wondered if his imagination was getting the better of him. Had his mind become so hungry for action that it had started playing tricks on him? Or could the infected tissue that caused Elizabeth's death mean murder?

Patrick couldn't stop his blood from pulsating. Adrenaline set the pace, not sugar or caffeine. He could feel the heavy rise and fall of his breathing. It scared him a little, no, a lot. *Relax*, he told himself. Another heart attack wasn't going to help anyone, especially him. He squeezed his eyes shut and realized it hadn't been a chest pain. What made his blood race at pounding speed through his body was the realization that Claire and Jack might be looking into Elizabeth's death as a possible murder. Though he couldn't fathom who or why anyone would have it in for the Keeley family.

The desk Patrick hated thirty minutes ago had just become his command post for his own personal investigation. When he had enough facts, he would go to Captain Ramos. Until then, his captain could think he'd started working on old cases. Jack would be his leg man. Right now, he needed to talk to Michael without anyone knowing his suspicions. He picked up his cell and dialed. Not everyone had the mayor's private cell number. He and Michael were from the old neighborhood, a bond that united them forever.

Michael answered on the third ring. After a brief phone conversation, Patrick dropped the paperclip chain into Jack's desk drawer and left the squad room.

# Chapter 10

Ruth Weinstein had waited for Claire, along with one of the company lawyers, Mr. Markham, just as Sam had predicted. She escorted Claire and Jack into a conference room after the company security officer cleared them. The security officer mentioned to Mr. Markham he'd seen a Chicago detective's badge in Miller's wallet. Ruth made introductions and offered them coffee.

"Thank you," Claire said. She accepted the china cup and saucer with the company logo on them. "This is much appreciated. By the time I drank my cup this morning, it was cold."

"Detective. Miller, would you like coffee?" Ruth asked, already pouring another cup.

"Yes, thank you. You have no idea what a pleasure it is to sit down and have fresh coffee. At this hour of the day, you can literally slice the coffee back at the station."

Claire was glad Jack followed her lead. Their lives rarely included the niceties of corporate offices.

"Dr. O'Shaunessy, when we spoke earlier you had questions about how our company obtained and processed donor tissue." Ruth poured cups for herself and Mr. Markham.

"Yes. Recently, I removed infected donor tissue from a body during an autopsy. The purpose of my visit is to track this tissue back to its donor and learn how specimens are handled." Claire pulled out a copy of the OR report. "Elizabeth O'Connor received your donor tissue during a surgical procedure at Chicago General Hospital a few days ago. I spoke with her surgeon, Dr. Keith Olson, and he led me to you. He stated that he's never had any problems with any of your products." She slid the papers across the mahogany table.

Ruth read the report and passed it to Mr. Markham. "What do you want to know?"

"First, can you track the donor number back to the source? Second, can you check to see if any other recipients have had a problem?"

Mr. Markham leaned forward. "You're asking us to spend a lot of time on research. How do you know our tissue is your problem?"

Claire chose her words carefully. "In response to your question, Mr. Markham, I do know it came from your company. What I don't know is how it became infected. The final laboratory report won't be ready for a while. However, yesterday morning, I looked under an electron microscope at a sample of the donor tissue I removed from Elizabeth's abdomen. There I saw bacteria Clostridium perfringens. In layman's terms, that's gas gangrene."

"Then you have no proof we sent you a contaminated specimen. It could have been contaminated after it was opened at the hospital, or through poor storage. You're on a fishing expedition. You just want to make a name for yourself and see how much money we can be bled for." Mr. Markham stood up abruptly. "This meeting is over. Ruth, I advise you not to say anything."

*Shit*, Claire thought. This hadn't gone as planned. While a bunch of lawyers played games, more innocent people could die.

"Ruth," Jack spoke softly, "Elizabeth was probably about your age."

Claire watched Ruth shift uncomfortably in her chair and pull her jacket closed.

"Do you have any children?" Jack gently probed.

"Don't answer that, Ruth," Mr. Markham advised.

"Elizabeth had six. I've worked with Dr. O'Shaunessy before on cases, and the last thing she's trying to accomplish is making a name for herself. She's already well respected in her field. She really cares about her patients. She's been known to put her life on the line trying to prevent others from dying. You would want her to do that for you."

Claire watched Mr. Markham's facial expression relax just a hint. Ruth continued to hold her jacket tightly closed. As long as Jack could get the job done, it didn't matter to Claire how he did it. More infected tissue would make time their enemy.

Jack continued. "I understand your reaction to me because I'm a homicide detective, but I can here today as your friend. Dr. O'Shaunessy is offering Tri-State a chance of a lifetime."

"What do you mean, she's offering us a chance of a lifetime? From where I stand, she is simply here to point the finger." Mr. Markham held tightly to the back of his chair.

"Glenn, just shut up for once and sit down. I want to hear what they have to say." Ruth let go of her jacket and placed her hands in her lap.

With the same quiet voice Jack spelled out Claire's mission. "Dr. O'Shaunessy has approached you in search of the truth. She isn't out to cause harm. What she is asking you to do will undoubtedly cost you time and possibly money, but in the long run your assistance will only strengthen your reputation."

Mr. Markham sat down with his arms folded over his thin chest. "How is this supposed to make us look good?"

"Because your company is going to prove this is either not your fault, or to what lengths you're willing to go to prevent harm from coming to anyone else."

"You see, Mr. Markham," Claire said, "without treatment, gas gangrene is fatal within forty-eight hours." She prayed she could get him to understand the short time frame in which they had to work. "Even treatment can't always save people. About two out of three people with the infection to the trunk of the body die. With limb infections the death rate is one out of eight. Often the others require amputation."

"We could have gone through all the proper channels," Jack said. "We could have obtained the correct paperwork and found a judge to sign off on a subpoena, but critical time would have been lost. Dr. O'Shaunessy is concerned about other recipients from this donor, not dragging your name through court."

Mr. Markham leaned forward. "Can I have your word that you will not release the name of our company to the press?"

"That's not our style," Claire said. "If your company name is leaked to the press before the case is completed, it won't come from us. In that situation, if I'm asked by my director to make a comment, I will tell them you have made every effort to help us locate the problem because of your concern for the health and well-being of all your donor recipients."

Ruth faced Mr. Markham. "Well, Glenn, it's your call. I suggest you don't waste any more time in making this decision."

"I'm sure, Dr. O'Shaunessy, you can understand that it's my job to protect Tri-State. Normally, I wouldn't agree to anything without a subpoena, but if this woman died recently, then that forty-eight-hour window you spoke of is shrinking as we speak. We will follow up on this donor, hold any specimens we have in stock, and check on all our shipments and recipients until we're sure the problem didn't originate from us. How does that sound?"

Claire could have cried, she felt so relieved. "Mr. Markham, I couldn't have asked for more. Thank you for your help. I know Mayor Keeley will be pleased with your support."

Ruth had a puzzled look on her face. "Why would Chicago's mayor be concerned?"

"Haven't you heard or seen the news in the last day?" Jack asked.

Both Ruth and Mr. Markham shook their heads.

"Elizabeth O'Connor was Mayor Keeley's sister," Claire said.

# Chapter 11

Jack silenced his cell phone. He knew Patrick was pissed that he hadn't been there to welcome him back to work, but he had a special assignment. The more research he did on cadaver tissue, the more he became convinced Elizabeth's death wasn't accidental. He kept playing the 'what if' game. What if he and Claire couldn't find the source of contamination quickly enough? How many more innocent people would die? The cadaver tissue and organ business was a billion-dollar a year body parts industry. He'd read online how one fourteen-year-old had died from a fungus-infested heart valve. Another man lost a leg to gangrene from a bad tendon.

Meanwhile, good doctors had put their faith in their hospital's purchasing departments and used the tissue supplied for their patients. Jack's skin went cold when he learned the people who order the tissue had no idea how it was treated, or if it was treated at all. *What a nightmare*, he thought. Several years ago, authorities had caught a company buying tissue removed at funeral homes. Only licensed laboratories could harvest and process tissue and bone. The procedure was performed before the body was delivered to the funeral home. The funeral homes involved didn't have permission from the deceased or the family for the illegal procedure. Somehow, this struck him as death for sale.

Jack walked into Chicago General's legal department. Already hot under his collar because of Elizabeth's death, he knew he had to keep his cool if he wanted information. He couldn't believe his good fortune when the head of the legal team agreed to his request. The lead attorney went to law school with the mayor, but Jack never pulled that card out of his pocket. If the mayor had been his classmate, he would have done anything to help the police find the answers. However, he'd have to tread gently to get what he needed.

A thirty-something blonde greeted him. "Detective Miller, this way please."

Jack met the gazes of several concerned employees when he entered the conference room. There were no smiles, no cordial greetings. *More collateral damage*, he thought. These were good people sorry about Elizabeth's unexpected death, but probably more concerned they would be blamed for making an error.

"Good afternoon, I'm Detective Jack Miller." Jack walked to the head of the table and cleared his throat. "I know this is the end of the work day for most of you, so I won't keep you long. There isn't one of you happy to be here. This is not a fishing expedition. I'm not here to point the finger. I need your help to prevent what happened to Elizabeth O'Connor from happening to someone else, like in your family. The company that sold the tissue to Chicago General is working hard to find any remaining tissue samples from this donor, and check the progress of anyone who did receive this donor's tissue."

"Then why do you want to talk with us?" The voice belonged to a lady dressed in casual office attire.

"To see if we can find out if a break in the system exists," Jack offered. "I'd like to start with Lila Peterson."

"That's me," the same woman answered.

"Ms. Peterson, what can you tell me about how you order tissue and bone for surgical patients?"

Lila shifted in her seat, and then referred to her notes. "Right now our hospital is under contract with Tri-State Bone and Tissue Services, so I place all my orders through them."

"Why does the hospital use them?"

"Because they're accredited with the American Association of Tissue Banks and are certified through several other reputable organizations. The surgeons have a voice in the process here at Chicago General as well and have had much success with Tri-State."

Jack noticed Lila sat a little taller after she delivered her information. "Good, thanks," he replied. "Is James Blackwell here?"

A slender black gentleman raised his hand.

"I understand you're in charge of receiving."

"Yes sir, I am."

"When you receive a tissue delivery, what do you do with it?" Jack hated putting these good people on the spot.

"We sign for all packages, which may come in refrigerated containers, depending on the product. The time received is recorded in the log. Then either I or one of my employees hand-carry donor tissue packages directly to surgery. The secretary signs and times receipt of the package. If you want to see my logs, you can follow me down to receiving when we're finished, but I know you will find all deliveries were made immediately upon receipt."

"Thank you, Mr. Blackwell, but that won't be necessary at this time. Cindi Wu, I understand you're the secretary in surgery?"

"Yes, I am," a small-built woman answered. "After Mr. Blackwell or one of his employees brings us the tissue, I record the time in our log. Then I give the package to one of the surgical techs for proper storage."

"Do you keep a record of who received it for storage?" Jack had a feeling this might be a crack in the system.

Cindi Wu looked five shades whiter as she practically swallowed her response. "No."

"You're doing fine, Cindi. Please try and relax. How many surgical techs do you have?" Jack already knew the answer, but he wanted to calm her down so she would open up to him.

Cindi folded her hands on the table. "We have five surgical techs total. They're staggered from five in the morning to nine at night. Everyone takes his or her turn on call for nights and weekends."

Jack made a note to see who was on the schedule when they received the shipment in question. "Cindi, do you order specifically for each surgical case?"

"Yes. After the doctor schedules the case, I'm notified to request what the surgeon needs for the patient. Then I place the order with Tri-State and contact Lila Peterson to initiate a purchase order. Since they're based in Oak Brook, we can get immediate delivery even for emergencies." Cindi had definitely become more relaxed.

"Is the patient's name on the order?" Could someone at Tri-State have targeted Elizabeth?"

"I give the patient's name to Tri-State and to Lila Peterson. That way we can match the delivery quicker," Cindi said.

"Are any of the surgical techs present?" Jack couldn't read the name tags on the employees at the far end of the table.

One of them, a short and stocky man, spoke up. "I'm a surgical tech. Derek Ruger."

"Derek, how do you store the donor tissue?" Jack asked.

"Each package is clearly marked if it needs to be kept frozen or in a controlled environment. All of our refrigerators and freezers are checked daily and the temperatures are written in the log."

Jack checked his watch. He only had a few questions left. He was anxious to hear if Claire had an update on the labs. "Who removes the tissue and sets it up for the surgeries?"

"My name is Kumar, and I can answer your question." The man sitting sat next to Ruger answered, in a thick Indian accent. "Whoever is assigned as the scrub tech for the case is responsible for setting up the specimen and checking the donor and tissue numbers with the scrub nurse and circulating nurse. The accompanying history of the donor is attached to the surgical record."

"Why does the tissue have a donor and tissue number?" Jack knew the answers to all the questions he'd asked. He'd designed the questions to see what the employees might say.

"That is simple," Kumar replied in his stilted English. "The donor number refers to the person the specimen is removed from. Since many specimens can be collected from each person, the specimens are individually numbered as well."

"What happens to the packaging?" Jack knew there'd be little chance they still had it.

"I can answer that also. We dispose of it in our hazardous waste container."

That was the one piece of evidence Jack would have loved to get ahold of. His best guess was it held a major part of the answer to the puzzle. Three women at the table hadn't yet spoken. One he had talked with on the phone, the Director of Surgery, Amy Cook. The other two were undoubtedly the circulating and scrub nurses, Debbie and Joan.

"Is there anything any of you can think of that might help me?" Every face in the room looked sad as Jack looked at each one of them. He handed out his card. "If you think of anything, no matter how slight, please call me. If you aren't comfortable talking to me, please tell Ms. Cook and she can contact me. Thank you for your time."

The employees got up and left. "Amy, before you go, could I run something by you?" Jack called out.

"What do you need?" Amy asked as her cell phone rang. She held up her finger as she answered it and listened. "I'll be up in one minute," she said into the phone, then turned to Jack. "One of the cleaning ladies found a screw under a surgical table and she's convinced the table will fall apart if we don't find out where it goes. If this is the worst issue of the day, then I'm in good shape. Now what can I do for you?"

"I'd like to find out when the tissue for Elizabeth arrived, which techs were on duty at the time, and who was assigned to the O'Connor case."

"For those first two questions, I'll have to check the log for the date and time received, against the time each tech worked that day. The answer to your third question is Derek Ruger. Could I get back to you tomorrow on the rest of the information?"

Jack handed Amy his card. "Just call me on my cell. If I can't answer for some reason, you can leave the information and I'll check back with you."

"That works for me."

"Thanks for your time and help. This really does give me a better feel for the system." Jack wanted to say he had a better feel for the break in the system had occurred. Of course, the problem may have come from the source – Tri-State. Elizabeth's name had been on the order. For now, he decided to keep this to himself. His cell phone vibrated in his pocket. He looked at the number. Claire. "Now it's my turn. Thanks again." Jack waved goodbye as he answered the call. "Detective Miller speaking."

"Jack, I think I pissed somebody off."

# Chapter 12

Jillian Garcia spotted Patrick first. She shoved the mike in front of him. "Can you tell us why homicide is here to see the mayor?"
Patrick hated the press. He thought of them as a necessary evil. He especially hated seeing them camped out on Michael Keeley's front lawn. "Well, Jillian, homicide isn't here to see the mayor. Mayor Keeley is an old neighbor and I'm simply paying my respects. Our families grew up on the same block in Bridgeport."

"Cut," Jillian called out to her cameraman as she made a slicing motion across her neck. "Sorry, Detective O'Shaunessy."

"That's okay. You're just doing your job." Patrick knew how to play the diplomat. No sense in Captain Ramos getting a call from the local alderman saying one of his detectives was throwing his weight around. Shit. There was that word again, *weight*. As Patrick passed a local beat cop on guard at the mayor's home, he made a conscious effort not to think about his weight.

Laura, Michael's wife, answered the door and directed him into the study. The roaring fire was perfect for the damp late October afternoon. Michael shook hands silently as he motioned for Patrick to sit opposite him in the wing-backed chairs in front of the fireplace.

"How are you holding up?" Patrick asked.

"I'm still in shock. I can't believe Elizabeth is gone. It just doesn't seem fair. Stephen is barely keeping himself together, but having six kids will help. I know this touches close to home for you, too."

"This does bring back some hard memories," Patrick replied, fighting the lump forming in his throat. Moments like this reminded him of the loss of his parents.

"Seems you're running around awfully soon after your heart attack. Laura ran into Sylvia at the grocery store yesterday and she said you just got out of the hospital."

"The heart attack was mild. If I stayed home any longer, I would have welcomed the big one. I've been assigned to desk duty for a month, which may be a mixed blessing."

"What do you mean? I've never known you to sit still except for a Sox or Bears game." Michael threw another log onto the fire. The dry wood caught immediately, sending sparks up the chimney.

Patrick leaned forward, hands clasped with his elbows resting on his legs. He turned his eyes toward the crackling fire as if lost in thought. "Michael, I know the Keeley clan is large. No, *huge* would probably be more accurate, but have you ever entertained the idea that the family has had more than its share of bad luck?" He looked up and met Michael's eyes.

"Are you comparing us to the Kennedy family?"

"No, but you have to admit, some of your relatives have had some serious misfortunes. Forget what I said. I'm probably way off base here. It must be the drugs they gave me in the hospital." Patrick waved his hand in front of his face as if to dispel his thoughts as he rose to leave.

"Wait," Michael said. He crossed the room, took a sheet of paper from a desk drawer, and handed it to Patrick. "I've been keeping a record of these events for some time now. My father and brothers scoffed at the idea that our family was being targeted. Between the family's liquor distributorship and politics, I'm sure we've made a few enemies. I can't imagine any of them doing physical harm to any of us, but there are a lot of crazy people out there."

Patrick sat back down and reviewed what Michael had given him. Many of the items were on his list, too. Others he wasn't aware of, like the demise of some family pet rabbits, found in the alley with their heads bashed in. "Did someone leave the rabbit cage door open?"

Michael had reclaimed his chair in front of the fire. "The cage sat inside the garage. The doors to the garage were locked. Even if the rabbits escaped from the cage, how did they end up in the alley?"

"Good point." Patrick rubbed his chin as he proceeded down the list. "I remember hearing something about your brother Timothy's tires being slashed."

"Make that a double slash. Two days after he replaced the tires on his new Pontiac Grand Prix, someone cut them again." Michael sighed and rubbed his face. "I don't know. It sounds kind of nuts, when I think of somebody doing all this stuff. I mean, who would?"

"What's this about your mother's dog?"

"That one really hit my mother hard. Mom had tied Sweetie's leash to the front porch table and went back in the house to get her coffee. She'd only been in there a minute. When she returned, Sweetie had disappeared. The collar was still clasped and hooked to the leash. None of us ever believed the dog pulled her head through the collar and ran off. My mother couldn't move five inches in the house without Sweetie being right under her feet. Why are you bringing this up now?"

"Michael, there is no easy way to say this, but Elizabeth's death may not have been accidental." Patrick had purposely tap-danced around the word *murder*.

Michael stared at him. "What are you saying, Patrick? *Is* someone after my family? Why?"

Patrick crossed the study and placed Michael's list on the desk. "I think stalking is the correct word. Come look at the timeline. The time frame between each episode is shorter than the one before." He tapped the paper as Michael came over. "Check the last item on your list. Your son was knocked over and his backpack stolen five weeks ago, around 7:00 p.m. near the UIC Pavilion. No one saw anything. Why? Because the day students had left or had gone to the library. The evening students were in class. Think about it, someone knew when the streets might be empty and knew your son's routine."

"What does Claire think?" Panic edged Michael's voice.

"I haven't shared my idea with her. Currently, she's trying to find the source of the infection for the tissue the surgeon used. She's concerned other tissue specimens may have come from an infected donor and the death toll will climb. The tissue donor company is researching from their end. At this point, I don't know which is worse, Claire discovering gangrene caused by an infected donor putting others in jeopardy, or someone targeting your family."

Patrick saw the distraught reaction play out over Michael's face. There was a possibility of more victims no matter what the final outcome.

Moisture formed in Michael's eyes. He closed them and rooted his head against the back of the upholstered chair. "So at this point, you don't know if Elizabeth's death was accidental or intentional, or a result of the family being targeted?"

"Personally, I think someone has been stalking your family for a long time, but until Elizabeth's death it hadn't dawned on me."

"But how could a stalker cause Elizabeth's death? It just doesn't seem possible." Michael shook his head.

"Who hates your family that much?"

"When you're the mayor you always have political enemies, but I can't imagine anyone taking it to this level. Elizabeth was a stay-at-home mother and started several programs to help the less fortunate children of Chicago. Stephen works for the family business, which you know I'm not a part of to avoid any conflict of interest."

"Anyone ever had a serious beef with Keeley Liquor Distributors?"

"Not that anyone has mentioned. Sometimes a local bar might not have the money for their order, but generally the company tries to work with them. I haven't worked for the family business since my college days." He ran a hand through his hair. "Maybe someone from back when I was with the D.A.'s office . . . but I couldn't tell you who."

"Michael, I think you need to take this seriously. Whoever relishes hurting your family has taken it to a new level. The incidents are becoming more dangerous and they're getting closer to you."

"What do you suggest, then?"

"Usually a stalker feels rewarded when he gets attention. I want to keep this out of the news. Let him think we haven't figured it out, but you have to tell your family. Have you decided on funeral arrangements yet?"

"We're waiting for an aunt to arrive from Ireland. Everyone else is local except for a few cousins. I talked to Stephen a little while ago, and he would like the wake and funeral the beginning of next week. Our parents are so devastated. They can't even talk about Elizabeth."

"Michael, you do realize you could be the ultimate target? The department needs to have time to prepare so we can protect you and your family. The exposure of a wake, church service and cemetery burial could make you prime targets. My guess is this is one person working alone, but he could do a lot of damage."

"I'll get you the final arrangements in a day or two. The family is meeting here tonight."

"Good. I want you to put it out to everyone that they need to be extra careful. Make sure the kids are always with friends and don't go anywhere alone. This is just a thought, but have your dad think about who might still be at the warehouse who worked there when all the incidents started. See if they remember any incident that could have caused this type of repercussions. Also, have him look into whoever was fired around that time." Patrick stood. "Make sure everyone has mine and Jack's cell numbers."

"I will. I'll let you know if Dad comes up with anything."

"Also, this must stay within the family, which means the kids can't tell their friends about this or make their activities public. We don't want to give this person any edge. Be careful." Patrick shook Michael's hand. "I'll be in touch."

"I'll walk you out and do the mayor thing. The news crews have to make a living, too."

The sun broke through the clouds as they stepped outside. Patrick managed to sidestep and get out of the cameras' line of fire. The last thing he needed was Captain Ramos seeing him on the six o'clock news at the mayor's house.

# Chapter 13

Claire guessed Jack was in his squad car from the sound of traffic in the background of his cell phone.

"What happened?" he demanded.

"I decided to take a late lunch and run home to pick up my gym bag. The doorman handed me a floral delivery. When I got upstairs I read the card."

"What did it say?" A horn blared over the cell phone.

"The card caught me off guard. The flowers were from our ME, Dr. Johnson. I thought it seemed a little strange for him to send them, but I called to thank him anyway."

"Why did he send them?"

"Jack, he didn't. I checked the name of the florist in the phone book and on the web. No such business exists. The phone number on the delivery ticket and the web address are bogus."

"Have you checked to make sure no one is in your place?"

"No."

"I'll stay on the line while you look."

"Okay." Claire didn't realize how tight she was holding the handset until she saw how red her fingers were turning. She checked closets, the bedroom, under the bed and the bath. She felt like a fool holding her breath as she looked behind the shower curtain.

"Claire, are you still there?"

"Yes. Nobody's here. I even checked behind the shower curtain." Of course, she didn't tell Jack the movie *Psycho* was running through her head at the time.

"Okay. I'm just a few minutes away. Please don't touch the vase or packaging again."

Claire wanted to tell Jack that once she realized something was wrong she hadn't touched the floral arrangement. After all, she wasn't born yesterday. As a matter of fact, once she learned that

Dr. Johnson hadn't sent them, she treated the arrangement like a bomb.

A few minutes later the doorman buzzed and told her he'd sent up a Detective Miller. She debated how long to make Jack wait for her to answer the door, but thought twice since he would only cause a scene. She opened up before he could knock and stood in the doorway. "Good afternoon, Detective Miller."

"Are you crazy? Why didn't you wait inside?"

"I didn't want you banging on the door and drawing attention to me."

Jack followed her in. "Well, it's a little late for that. The evidence tech will be here any minute, and Sergeant Perchowski will be taking the doorman's statement and pulling the security tapes. So where's the delivery?"

"On the side table." Claire pointed to it.

Jack put on a pair of disposable gloves. "Where's the card?"

Claire started to reach for it when Jack's hand stopped her. "Don't touch it."

"Aren't you being a little melodramatic? I've already touched the card." She almost regretted having called him, but who else could she call? She certainly didn't want to worry Patrick. Of course, that had been a silly thought. He'd hear about it anyway. She knew Patrick would have gone all police ape on her, but Jack, she'd expected to remain calm.

"I know, but there's a slim chance the lab can raise other fingerprints. We'll need yours to rule out the ones we collect."

The doorman buzzed again. This time Jack talked with him and cleared the next person.

"Jack, this is all very interesting, but I have to get back to work. I'm already late," Claire said.

"You're staying put for now." He handed her his cell phone. "Dial Dr. Johnson's number. I'll talk to him."

"Jack, this is probably just a stupid joke or I inadvertently pissed someone off and now they're messing with my mind." She gathered her purse and keys, but Jack blocked her exit.

"Dial the number." He pointed to his cell phone. The doorbell rang, but Jack beat her to the door and let in the evidence tech.

Claire caved and dialed Dr. Johnson. When he answered, she promptly handed Jack the phone. She listened to Jack speak with her boss as the evidence tech fingerprinted the outside of the vase. When he finished, he took her fingerprints. Then the doorbell rang again, but this time Claire got to the door first.

"Hi, gorgeous! Did you miss me?" Frankie Biaggi, the wild Italian from Claire's old neighborhood, stood in the doorway. He gave her a bear hug and planted a kiss on her cheek.

Claire noticed he kept his eyes on Jack. *Not the male testosterone war again*, she thought. On their last case, Frankie did his best to unnerve Jack, and it worked. Claire had hoped they were past it by now.

"How could I forget you after the five pounds you put on my hips from your wonderful meals." Claire cringed at the thought of the number of miles she would have to run to remove those unwanted pounds. "What's in the bag?"

"Hey, when Detective Jack calls and says he needs my services, I come prepared."

Claire turned to Jack. "You called Frankie?"

"He can cook. Of course if you prefer carry out, you can do that instead."

"Did I miss something here?" Claire's tone of voice had gone from fear at discovering the flowers weren't from Dr. Johnson, to annoyance that Jack and Frankie thought they could corral her.

"Dr. O'Shaunessy, could you sign here? I have to take the arrangement and packaging with me," the tech said.

Claire signed the form and the tech gave her a copy. She turned to face the remaining two males in her living room. With her arms folded, she said, "For both of your information, I intend to go to work and go about my life as if this were just a sick joke. I appreciate your concern, but the Police Department has more important things to worry about, like finding out who is responsible for Elizabeth's death."

"Slow down there, gorgeous. If Detective Jack's concerned, then I'm concerned. If you want to go somewhere, you've got me. He can't be everywhere. Let's make this easy on Patrick."

No fair, Frankie had used the Patrick card. Of course he was right. This would only add to Patrick's stress and Jack didn't have time to drive her around. Well, this did say something; Jack finally trusted Frankie.

"All right, but I still need to get back to the morgue."

"Dr. Johnson said to take the rest of the day off," Jack answered.

"I'm going to lose my job."

"No you won't," Jack replied. "Dr. Johnson asked that you try not to get yourself killed because there's a hiring freeze."

Claire laughed. "Now, that sounds like Dr. Johnson."

Jack approached her. "Claire, I want to go over a few things with you, and then I'll be out of your hair. If you want to go somewhere, take Frankie or one of his brothers with you. I know the classic stalker is a white male in his late twenties to early forties, but this could be anyone—even a woman. Skip the showers at the gym for now. I want you to give some thought to these questions. Have you had a run-in with anyone at the morgue? Did anyone ask you out who might have gotten upset when you turned him down? Also, don't forget our cadaver tissue case. Maybe we struck a nerve. I'll catch up with you later." He turned to Frank Biaggi. "Thanks again, Frankie."

"Sure you don't want to stay for dinner?"

"I would love to, but I have to face Patrick."

Frankie winked at Claire. "Okay gorgeous, I guess it's dinner for two.

* * *

Jack stopped in the lobby to check on Sergeant Perchowski's progress. "Did you learn anything?"

Perchowski flipped through his notes. "The doorman said the delivery was pretty straightforward, but two things about it bothered him. First, the driver wore gardening gloves, and second, he kept his head down so the doorman only saw the bill of his Bears cap."

"I could understand the gloves if he'd delivered soil or mulch, but not a floral arrangement. Where are the security cameras located?" Jack asked.

Perchowski pointed them out. "We've pulled the tapes. Most delivery men want the doormen to recognize them, to make their job faster and easier the next time they come. This guy doesn't want to be remembered. I'll let you know if we find anything."

Jack let out a low whistle. His gut told him someone wasn't trying to be funny with Claire. He was looking for Claire.

# Chapter 14

Jack heard Patrick call out as he entered the squad room. It appeared Patrick was the only one there.

"Well, it's about time you showed up for work. I thought you had gone AWOL."

Jack shook Patrick's hand and gave him a pat on the back. "You doing all right?"

"Sylvia's new menu has too much green food on it, but I'll live. By the way, my desk was noticeably lower in calories when I came back to work. You weren't trying to help me out?" Patrick pulled out the lower desk drawer, which doubled as a stool for his feet.

"Not a chance. So what did you do today?" Jack grabbed his desk chair and threw his jacket over the back before sitting down. His desk faced his partner's.

Patrick looked around. "I think we have a stalker on our hands."

Jack was amazed. "How did you hear about Claire so fast?"

Patrick's feet were off the drawer and on the floor as he leaned across his desk. "What do you mean, Claire? I was talking about Mayor Keeley."

"I'll go first," Jack offered, knowing Claire trumped the mayor at the moment. "Claire received a floral arrangement today. The card said it was from Dr. Johnson at the morgue. When she called to thank him, she discovered he didn't send them. The floral shop was bogus, along with the phone number and web address. Sergeant Perchowski pulled the security tapes and interviewed the doorman. The only things the doorman noticed out of the ordinary were the driver wearing gardening gloves and keeping his face down so the doorman only saw his Bears cap. The arrangement is in the crime lab right now."

"Who did she piss off this time?"

Jack laughed. "That's exactly what Claire asked."

"What's your take on the situation?"

"It could be a disgruntled employee at the morgue, a driver for one of the mortuary services, someone she turned down for a date, or maybe we hit a nerve on the case we're covering. Hopefully, the latent fingerprint guys can lift a usable print. One thing is for sure, this guy knows where Claire lives and works. I've got Frankie covering her right now."

"I take it you have Frankie on your speed dial?"

Jack flashed a quick smile.

"Smart choice. He and his brothers will stick to her like glue." Patrick relaxed, sinking back in his chair. Vince, Frankie and Sol Biaggi worked for the family automotive repair service and had helped them on their prior case. Meanwhile, the youngest brother Joey, who was in high school, couldn't comprehend cars to save his life.

"When you think about it, other than our last case, Claire's life is fairly predictable; work, family, a few good friends, an occasional trip to the gym or a run along the lakefront. If this guy went to the trouble to make it look like he delivered flowers from a floral shop, then it's very personal for him. We just have no idea how long he's been watching her. What has Claire gotten herself into?"

"I don't think she did anything. Someone crossed her path and became infatuated with her, or angry with her and wants to mess with her head. I bet it's work-related. Now it's your turn," Jack reminded his partner. "You said something about a stalker and the mayor?"

Patrick nodded. "This morning while I sat here thinking about Elizabeth, other Keeley family tragedies came to mind. I grew up four doors down from them. So I started a list. By the time I finished it, I had a half a dozen incidents over less than twenty years. By themselves, they all looked like accidents. My gut tells me Elizabeth's death wasn't an accident, though. I went over to see Michael. He added another half dozen incidents to the list, and the time line is getting shorter between each."

"What kind of incidents?"

Patrick handed over the list he and Michael had made. "Missing and dead pets. A couple kids with broken limbs from a hit-and-run, and being shoved off a bike. Tires were slashed, a backpack stolen, and a car keyed in the family driveway. Until Elizabeth's death, Mary Anne sustained the worst injury. Approximately sixteen years ago, she had a serious bike accident. No witnesses. She's been in a nursing home ever since, and doesn't recognize anyone. The scariest incident happened last year, to Michael's niece. Someone tried to take Brittany's car just after she'd strapped her son into his car seat. She caused such a scene by screaming that the thief took off."

Jack reached into his desk for a pen and came out with a paperclip chain. He stared at Patrick, who smiled.

"Just a little something I whipped up for you today."

"You need to get back on the streets. When was the last incident prior to Elizabeth's death?"

"Five weeks ago, Michael's son was knocked down and his backpack stolen near the UIC Pavilion. I think the stalker's taken his actions to the next level: murder. My personal guess is that Michael is the grand prize. Whoever this guy is, he knows the Keeley family well. Over the years he's hurt Michael's siblings, children, nieces and nephews, and pets."

"It could be someone within their close personal circle; maybe a handyman, a maid, or a lawn service. What about the funeral?" Jack tried to undo the paperclips but gave up and stuffed them back in the drawer.

"Michael said the plans should be finalized this evening. The family is meeting tonight at his home. Michael will fill everyone in on my suspicions. We decided to keep this away from the press for now. We don't want this maniac reveling over his adventures on the ten o'clock news."

"I think we should look at people who might have had a close connection with the family when the Keeleys started having problems. It could be as simple as someone who thought the Keeleys contributed to the failure of their business, or a family member seeking revenge for something Michael isn't aware of. Maybe someone thought the Keeleys fired them unfairly. The bottom line is, the stalker had to have access to personal information about Elizabeth. Whoever this is, he knew she'd been scheduled for surgery and he had access to the donor tissue." Jack got up and walked over to the coffee pot. He sniffed the carafe. "Do you want a cup?"

"Thanks, but I've been downgraded to unleaded." Patrick removed his tie and dropped it in his desk drawer.

"Somewhere along the path from ordering the tissue to the surgeon placing it in Elizabeth, the tissue became contaminated. How many people do you think knew about her surgery?" Jack took a swig of the coffee.

Patrick leaned back in his chair and rubbed his eyes. "That could be a dozen people, but the person responsible either had to have access to the tissue or knew someone who would."

"I spoke with the people who cared for Elizabeth in the OR today. The only time someone wasn't responsible for the donor tissue was from the time the OR tech stored it to the time it was retrieved."

"How long was it at the hospital before it was used?"

"I don't know. I'm waiting for the director to get back to me with that information." Jack finished his coffee. "You know what's bothering me?"

"What?" Patrick asked.

"If the tissue didn't come contaminated from Tri-State, how did it acquire gangrene? Maybe the lab report will be able to explain it." Jack stood and stretched. "You look bushed. We can't do anything more tonight. Do you think Sylvia has enough green food that I could swindle an invite out of you for dinner?"

"You can have my share," Patrick said as he shoved papers into his desk drawer and locked it. "Besides, when did you ever need an invite for dinner?"

Jack laughed. "You're right." Glad to see his partner back, he unplugged the coffee pot as they left. He didn't know how he would have handled losing him. Patrick had become more than a mentor, he was the father and brother Jack never had. Patrick had filled a horrible void in Jack's life. Ever since his best friend Tad was murdered, Jack's emotions often wavered from emptiness to anger.

# Chapter 15

"Thanks for the information, Sergeant Perchowski," Jack said. "I'll pass it on to Patrick and Claire. She felt sure the delivery came from a bogus flower shop." Jack hung up and faced his partner across the desk.

"Here's the part you didn't hear. They found the van parked on Roosevelt Road in front of a dry-cleaners. The owner reported the vehicle stolen from a grocery store parking lot on the west side of the Loop about thirty minutes before the flower delivery to Claire. The license plate on the van matches the partial on the security tape.

"The driver threw the sign and gardening gloves in a dumpster two alleys over. Sergeant Perchowski took the items to the Latent Fingerprinting Lab himself. They aren't holding out much hope for prints inside the cotton gardening gloves because of the rough texture of the fabric. They're processing the van right now."

Patrick tapped his pencil on the edge of his desk. "This doesn't make any sense. Someone went to a lot of trouble to upset Claire. I don't like the feel of this. What did she do to annoy someone for this type of response?"

"Just wanted you to know Captain Ramos pretty much gave me carte blanche on Claire's case. I have Frankie acting as her bodyguard, with Sol and Vince as backup. She should be safe, and the morgue is secure. Do you want some coffee?" Jack asked as he headed to the coffee pot.

Patrick shook his head as he let out one of his famous laughs. "Well, I wouldn't want any of those dead people escaping."

Jack wadded up a sheet of scratch paper and threw it at him. "Okay, partner, where are we on Michael's funeral plans for Elizabeth?"

"He called me this morning. He's contacted headquarters for the official police detail, but wants us involved because of our suspicions that Elizabeth was murdered. He believes his family has been stalked, too." Patrick emptied his water bottle. "I have to bring Captain Ramos up to speed on the case and funeral plans."

"What about Claire? Do you think she'll attend everything—the wake, funeral and burial?"

Wild horses won't keep her away. Having her there'll be like adding fuel to the fire. If anything happens, we might not be able to tell who the real target is—Claire, Michael or his family. Thank heavens Frankie has a couple of brothers."

"Do you have the rundown on all the locations?"

Patrick checked his notes. "The wake is at McDuffy's Funeral Home. Elizabeth's husband selected St. Patrick's for the funeral service because it was her favorite church. The family plot is at Mt. Carmel Cemetery in Hillside."

Jack clasped his hands behind his head and leaned back in his chair. Frankie could get Claire in and out of the wake through a back door. The same for the church service, but the burial in that large, old cemetery could be a nightmare.

"Will we get support from the Hillside Police Department?" Jack asked, leaning forward with his elbows on his desk.

"They're providing traffic control and will secure the perimeter of the cemetery. Our officers will do the rest. I'd better go talk to Captain Ramos."

Jack picked up his phone. "While you're with the captain, I'll give Claire an update. Because of the issues with these cases, I think we're going to need undercover and possibly SWAT."

"My thoughts exactly," Patrick answered as he headed for Ramos's office.

# Chapter 16

Ian greeted Claire after Frankie dropped her off at the front door of the Cook County Medical Examiner's Office and watched her go in. "Got a new man in your life, Dr. O'Shaunessy?"

"No," she answered. Claire hated rumors. The office grapevine spread faster than any documented virus. Tomorrow she would drive herself even if she had to hog tie the Biaggi brothers to the hydraulic lift in their father's garage. She needed freedom to move around, the ability to get her job done.

"Dr. Johnson wants to see you."

"Thanks, Ian."

Claire stopped by her office first to drop off her damp jacket. Chicago, scheduled for one of its famous raw, wet and windy days, had already dropped its temperature to the low forties. The mild, breezy fall weather was history until next spring. How she missed those days when a sweater was enough.

A few minutes later, she knocked on Dr. Johnson's office door. She dreaded seeing him even though she knew yesterday wasn't her fault.

"Come in," he called out.

"You wanted to see me?" Claire asked, holding her breath.

"Yes, take a seat." He motioned to the chair opposite his desk.

Before Dr. Johnson could speak, Claire blurted out, "Is my job in jeopardy?"

A smile as wide as the Mississippi River spread over her supervisor's face. "Good heavens, no." His robust abdomen jiggled with his laugh.

Relieved, Claire eased back into the chair.

"I wanted to alert you to some security measures we have in place for you. I won't tolerate my staff being threatened at work or home. We don't know the root of the threat, but I have informed Detective Miller that since we have a police presence here at the morgue, all outside mail, deliveries, et cetera for you will be handled by the duty officer. I know we rarely have anyone stopping by asking to see our pathologists, but your visitors will be screened."

"I'm sure yesterday's incident was just a bad joke. You don't need to go through all this trouble for me."

"Nonsense. Now I understand from Detective Miller that he has someone assigned to work undercover as your bodyguard until this issue is resolved." Dr. Johnson shuffled through some papers on his desk. "Here he is, a Mr. Frank Biaggi. We have his picture at the front desk and back door."

Claire almost burst out laughing. Jack had Frankie working undercover? She wondered how much Jack had shared with Frankie regarding his new status. She wasn't even going to ask him if Captain Ramos knew of Frankie's elevation to undercover status. No matter what, Jack knew Frankie would stick to her like glue.

Grateful that Cook County Morgue's full docket kept her mind off yesterday's flower scenario, Claire dug right into the cases. She needed her life back.

Sadly, last night's gang activity provided her with four more shooting victims. They ranged in age from eleven to nineteen. The eleven-year-old tore her heart out. Lamar Wilson had sustained a fatal gunshot wound to his chest from a stray bullet through his kitchen window while doing his homework. Secretly, she hoped the police found the person responsible and inflicted deep pain. In reality, unless someone squealed, the murder would go unsolved. Besides, even if the police did luck out, they'd never risk doing anything to jeopardize the case.

Lamar's mother came to view the body of her only child with her pastor and several church members. They prayed and she wailed. Claire wasn't surprised to learn money didn't exist for a wake or funeral. The county would bury him. A tag with his case number would be his marker. The only flowers to grace his grave would be a bunch of fresh cut blooms from a local supermarket placed by his grieving mother.

Claire put her unfinished charts in her desk drawer and locked it as she envisioned Miss Wilson performing a last act of motherly love. The thought of flowers made her mind jump back to yesterday's flower arrangement. What was going on? Just a short time ago she'd learned of her childhood friend's murder, and now this? If bad things came in threes, what was next?

More emotionally than physically exhausted, she reached for her office phone to call Frankie for a ride home. Before she could dial his number, it rang.

"Dr. O'Shaunessy," she answered. No one responded. "Hello, this is Dr. O'Shaunessy. Can I help you?"

Then the notes began to play, very softly at first, until the sound increased to a deafening level. Claire dropped her phone as if it were on fire as the Buffalo Bill theme song from *Silence of the Lambs* played.

"No," she cried. "Stop this!"

Covering her ears, she turned to run out of her office. A large figure blocked her door. Her scream filled the hallway.

"Claire, it's me, Jack. What happened?" His arms embraced her, but they couldn't stop the tremors or screams.

"No," she cried.

"Claire, open your eyes," he commanded.

It took a moment for Claire to do that. She could hear footsteps pounding in the background.

"What happened?" Jack asked again.

Ian called out from behind him. "Is she okay?"

Claire pointed with a trembling finger at her phone. The song still played, loud enough to be heard across the room.

Jack looked grim. "Ian, take Dr. O'Shaunessy to Dr. Johnson's office and stay with her."

"Sure thing, Detective Miller. Come on, Dr. O'Shaunessy." Ian held out his hand for her.

She looked over at her office phone one last time. The words fought to get out of her mouth. "Someone's playing the theme song from *Silence of the Lambs*."

Jack immediately called for an evidence tech. With luck they would be able to trace the caller, but he didn't really believe that for one minute. Whoever placed the call would have been smart enough to use a burner phone.

He watched Ian guide Claire down the hall. It scared him to see her like this. She was tougher than many of the female cops he knew. Without hesitation, he called Frankie and told him to bring backup. Somehow he would have to figure this out without worrying Patrick. But who was doing this and why?

# Chapter 17

After the evidence tech arrived to examine the phone system, Jack headed to Dr. Johnson's office. He found the director pacing the floor. Claire sat on the couch sipping what smelled like hot chocolate. Ian stood dutifully nearby.

"Detective Miller, what is going on?" Dr. Johnson asked. "I can't have one of my best forensic pathologists scared out of her wits."

Jack stood with his hands shoved deep in his pockets, wishing he could pull out the winning card. "I wish I had an answer for you. For some reason, Dr. O'Shaunessy is being stalked. I believe her safety is at risk. At the moment we don't know who's doing it or why."

Dr. Johnson stopped pacing and faced Claire. "Maybe you should stay home until Detective Miller gets this worked out." He returned to his desk and unceremoniously plopped in his chair.

Jack could read the worry and frustration on Dr. Johnson's face. Heck, he felt the same, only many times stronger.

"No." Claire put the mug down and stood up with her arms crossed. "I will not allow anyone to interfere with my personal or professional life. I'm sorry I lost it for a minute back there, but I can assure you, it won't happen again. No one, and I mean no one, is going to keep me from my job."

"I think you should listen to Dr. Johnson," Jack said. "He needs you in top shape. Who knows which cases of yours may end up in court?"

"I don't think either of you are listening to me. I refuse to allow some sicko to dictate my life. Now if the two of you don't mind, I'm going back to my office, collect my things and go home. Ian can escort me."

Dr. Johnson stood and slammed his hand on his desk. "Whoa, Claire. I insist you remain right here until Mr. Biaggi arrives to take you home. Are we clear on that issue?"

Just then Jack's cell phone rang. "Excuse me.

He stepped out of the chief medical examiner's office before he answered. "Detective Miller."

"It's me," Frankie answered. "I'm downstairs at the main door. Sol's in the car. What happened?"

"Stay put. I'm bringing Claire down now. I'll explain when I get there."

"Okay."

Jack returned to the ME's office. "Dr. Johnson, Claire's ride is here. Thank you for your support, and you too, Ian. The department will set up a recording device so all her calls are taped. For now she's not to answer any incoming calls unless she recognizes the number on the caller ID. If the caller is unknown or the number is blocked, then Ian can answer and offer to take a message. Maybe Claire will recognize this guy's voice. We should have the system in place by morning." He turned to Claire. "Okay, let's go."

Jack kept his hand on Claire's elbow all the way to her office. "Frankie's downstairs."

"You never told me why you're here," she said.

"I almost forgot. Sergeant Perchowski phoned to let me know they recovered the van on Roosevelt Road. The theft occurred shortly before the flowers were delivered. The police found the gardening gloves your security guard mentioned and the sign from the side of the van in a dumpster several blocks away."

"What did the security tapes show?"

Jack waited while Claire grabbed her jacket and purse. "The only other piece of information we have is a partial license plate number, which matched the van's plates."

"Someone is going to a lot of trouble to upset me. I can't think of anyone or any reason for this. When is this going to end?"

"Hey gorgeous," Frankie called out as they arrived in the waiting room, "How was your day?"

# Chapter 18

What a perfect day, Derek thought to himself as he sat down to enjoy the fried chicken strips and mashed potatoes from his favorite carryout restaurant. He reveled in his accomplishment. Hannibal Lector would be proud of him. Sure, he knew Hannibal was a fictional character, but if he were real . . .! He hit the remote to watch Hannibal enjoy his dinner as Derek popped a chicken strip into his mouth, but Claire kept invading his thoughts.

He assumed Claire had her car parked in the condo's secure indoor garage. He'd seen someone else drive her to and from work. That eliminated one opportunity. There had to be another way to let her know he could knock her off her game plan without her realizing from where the threat originated. He felt compelled to do it soon. Dealing with her might distract the police from his ultimate target.

He didn't know why the thought came as he savored the mashed potatoes, but it did. She needed a gift. She should receive something that would blow her mind and terrorize her for weeks to come. Something so frightening she wouldn't even be able to whisper the name of the object, and he had just the thing. After dinner he'd research the best place to have it shipped from. This time his disguise would require more than a baseball cap and a dark jacket.

At Floyd's Funeral Home they kept donated clothing for wakes for the less fortunate. He'd check the closet tomorrow after he'd made the sign for the upcoming wake. The family had requested cremation, which offered him the opportunity to obtain Claire's gift. The deceased wouldn't require the item any more.

Satisfied he'd planned the next step, he leaned back to watch his favorite movie. Never comfortable with loose ends, his mind strayed to Jillian Garcia, the television reporter. She didn't appear to be a threat any longer. No one at work had commented on seeing him in the background of the television footage from the morgue. For now, he'd let Jillian live.

# Chapter 19

Claire felt like a kindergartener with Frankie escorting her to the door of the county morgue where Ian waited to take her to her office. She went along with their routine because she knew better than to argue with either of them and Dr. Johnson had demanded it. Besides, Jack had better things to do than referee small battles and she couldn't waste her energy. Sleep had evaded her for the last couple of nights, and the stack of files she'd locked in her office drawer had to be completed this morning. At least Frankie could make a hell of a cappuccino. He'd even filled a thermos with her favorite poison to get her through the day.

"You look like you've lost your best friend," Dr. Sam Nicholson said as he entered her office waving a sheet of paper. "The grapevine rumor has it you're being stalked."

"Talk is cheap. What do you have?" Claire answered, then indulged in another sip of cappuccino.

"I have one culture report for you. Your assessment of my slide from Elizabeth was 100 percent accurate. She died of gas gangrene." Sam handed her Elizabeth O'Connor's lab report.

Claire looked it over. "Now the million-dollar question is, how did she come in contact with the infection?"

"Did you have any luck at Tri-State Bone and Tissue Services?" Dr. Nicholson asked.

"Sort of. Would you like some cappuccino?" Claire offered as she refilled her cup.

"Thanks, but the doc has me on unleaded."

His remark brought a smile to Claire's face. "Now you sound like my brother Patrick. He's been downgraded to decaf since his heart attack. Back to your question regarding Tri-State, they've promised to research the donor and all other tissue recipients to make sure everyone is all right. I expect a progress report from them today."

Sam rubbed his chin as if in thought. "If not Tri-State, then who? Was it accidental or intentional?"

"I would prefer for it to be accidental and not murder. Chicago General could undoubtedly be sued, but murder    I can't fathom why someone would hurt Elizabeth."

Sam leaned against the doorframe. "Maybe this isn't about Elizabeth. What about her brother, the mayor? Did she take the hit for him?"

Claire put her cup down. Michael! Why hadn't she thought of that before? Probably because her life had been turned upside down since the flower incident. Was Elizabeth the stepping stone to the main target? A chill passed through her. What better way to place the mayor out in the open than at a large family funeral?

"Sam, the thought makes me sick. I know politics can be vicious. Not everyone is going to be thrilled with the person in charge, but to kill a family member as their only way to get to Mayor Keeley is beyond horrible. I can't imagine anyone on the city council or the opposing party stooping that low."

"I agree, but I can't see how Elizabeth could have been infected, either. Well, I see you have a stack of charts, and I have plenty of specimens to test. Let me know if I can do anything else for you."

"Thanks. By the way, let's look at a day next week for a pizza lunch."

"I'm sure everyone will enjoy the pizza more by then." Sam waved as he left.

Claire dialed Tri-State Bone and Tissue Service and asked for Ruth. "Ruth Weinstein's office," a cheerful voice answered. After Claire identified herself, the secretary put her through.

"Hello, Dr. O'Shaunessy. You were on the top of my list of calls to make. We have good news for you. The donor died of a coronary and all his labs were negative for everything. Plus, all recipients of his tissue and bone donations are doing great."

"That's wonderful. I'm greatly relieved," Claire answered. "I can't thank you and Mr. Markham enough for going to all this trouble."

"We feel pretty good about the results, but I know you still don't have an answer."

"True, but no one else seems to be at risk from your end. That's a start. The laboratory results proved gas gangrene caused the infection. We'll find the source, it may just take some time."

"I hope you do. Please let me know if there's anything else I can help you with. I wish you the best of luck."

"Thank you."

Claire hung up and emptied the thermos of Frankie's gift. Slowly she savored the last few ounces as her emotions ran from relief for Ruth's donor recipients to disappointment. Was Sam on to something? Did Elizabeth take a hit for her brother? Could this all boil down to some political rage? It just didn't seem realistic for someone to kill Elizabeth because of their hatred for Michael. Why did they think Elizabeth's death would work in their favor? Were they trying to punish the mayor for a ruling that didn't produce the result they wanted? She shook her head. No one would be that crazy. Would they?

At least she could share confirmation of the results with Dr. Olson. She put the emptied mug down and dialed his cell. Jack would be her next call.

# Chapter 20

"Detective Miller, Homicide," Jack said as he answered the phone.

"Jack, it's Claire. I have good news and bad news. Which do you want first?"

Jack rubbed his forehead, hoping to relieve his headache. His gut told him no matter what Claire had to say, he and Patrick were a long way from solving Elizabeth's murder. "Give it to me however you think best."

"Okay, then, first the good news. I just spoke with Ruth Weinstein. The donor died of a coronary and all the other tissue recipients are doing great. Bad news is, I still don't—"

"Yeah, I know," Jack interrupted, "we don't know the source." His headache pounded mercilessly.

"Hey, don't give up on me so quickly," she argued. "I'm more certain than ever the source had to come from within the hospital. There is no other answer. Dr. Nicholson suggested that perhaps Elizabeth was a stepping stone to the intended target, Mayor Keeley. If it's the mayor, then is this an issue of revenge for political reasons, or a Keeley family matter?"

Jack had had some of the same thoughts. "I don't buy the political angle. No matter who the mayor's political adversaries are, they aren't going to risk doing life in a state penitentiary because they couldn't convince the mayor to vote their way on an issue. There has to be more. Murder is the ultimate act of hate."

"I agree," Claire answered.

Jack grabbed a pad of paper and a pen. "Tell me what you know about the Keeley family. I don't just mean the mayor's immediate family."

"Where's Patrick? You should ask him. He probably knows more than I do."

"He's in with Captain Ramos, going over our part in the funeral arrangements. He'll probably be tied up for a while." Jack glanced over toward the captain's office and could see them in deep in conversation while Patrick took notes. "I thought I could do some research in the meantime."

"Okay, here's the abbreviated story. Michael's father started the Keeley Liquor Distributorship back when Michael and his brothers and sisters were kids. Along with a bunch of siblings, Michael has a ton of nieces and nephews. Several of his siblings run the company today, and I believe some of their offspring also work there. Because of his political ambitions, Michael had nothing to do with the family business.

"Originally, the company was mostly a mom-and-pop operation, but it grew rapidly and now has locations all over the Midwest. So, if you ask me if someone could be pissed at the Keeley family for some reason, I would say yes. Did they put someone else out of business? Did they fire an employee who thought he'd been treated unjustly? I think there could be a dozen reasons. But I don't buy the idea they'd murder Elizabeth to balance their idea of the scales of justice."

"I'm at the same place as you," Jack answered. "Maybe they didn't mean for murder to be the final outcome. It just happened."

"I don't agree. Gas gangrene is a deadly infection. They knew what they were doing and had to have access to the donor tissue. You don't order it online or at your local pharmacy."

"You're right, but where would anyone get their hands on a specimen other than the one the hospital ordered from Tri-State? There can't be that many possibilities."

"Jack! The answer is right in front of us," Claire replied. "Try a hospital or a morgue. You could put a doctor's office or a clinic on the list, too. I'm going to talk with Dr. Johnson and see if he can help me penetrate the system. He'll know if we've had any victims lately. Also, I can check with the infection control nurse at Chicago General Hospital and see if they've had any recent cases of gas gangrene."

Speaking with Claire relieved some of the pressure from his headache. Funny, but he always felt better after talking with her, even when they were at odds. *Focus,* he told himself as he filed his last thought away for now. "If Chicago General had recent cases, we have to figure out how it got to the donor tissue and why."

"Which means we're back to the issue of who knew Elizabeth was going to have surgery and if the specimen would be available at the same time. Maybe this involves more than one employee. I hate thinking a hospital employee did this, but it might be the reality. Listen, I've got a couple of ideas. I'll let you know what I find out."

"Claire, don't cross the line. If you mess up our investigation, Patrick will be more than upset. Captain Ramos will hang both of you out to dry."

"Don't worry. The lecture Captain Ramos gave me after our last case is still fresh in my mind. I'll stay on my side of the street."

# Chapter 21

"Come in," Dr. Johnson's voice boomed.

Claire entered her director's office. "Just thought you'd like an update on the Elizabeth O'Connor case."

Dr. Johnson pointed to the chair directly opposite his desk. "Grab a seat and fill me in."

Claire sat and shared the Tri-State information and her conversation with Jack.

"Okay, how can I help? I assume you're here because you need a favor."

"I need information." Claire moved to the edge of the chair. "First, have we processed any deceased here in the last couple of months diagnosed with gas gangrene? If so, did they come from Chicago General Hospital?"

Dr. Johnson flipped his computer screen on. Slowly he moved his fingers across the keyboard. "Give me a minute. I flunked typing in high school. I didn't think it was going to be a concern with the career choice I made."

Claire smiled. "There're days I would love to toss my computer out the window when the system is down. Thank heavens pen and paper still work."

She waited, trying not to let her impatience show. A moment later, she heard him say, "I got it." He glanced over at her.

"This may not be good news, but we haven't had anyone with gas gangrene in thirteen months. The last patient came from a sewage disposal plant on the far south side of the county, west of Matteson. The guy had a good-sized burn on his thigh from hot coffee. He must have caught the infection from his soiled work pants."

"Strike one, "Claire said. "Could you arrange for me to speak with the infection control nurse at Chicago General? If the hospital hasn't had any cases in a long time, then it eliminates them as a source. If they have, then there's a slight possibility the infection came from them."

Dr. Johnson reached for his phone. "I'll do you one better," he said as he dialed a number. "My second cousin once removed on my mother's side runs the show at Chicago General." As he informed Claire of this, he hit the speaker button. A sweet voice answered.

"Gregory, is that you?"

"Hi, Maddie. How've you been?" He mouthed to Claire, "That's short for Matilda."

"You'd know the answer to that if you came around more often," his cousin replied.

"You're right. The job practically has me cuffed to my desk. If I try to leave the building, alarms go off."

Claire listened as Maddie came back with an irrepressible laugh.

"I take this is not a social call even though you owe me one," Maddie said.

"You're one smart lady," Dr. Johnson answered. "One of my forensic pathologists, Dr. Claire O'Shaunessy, needs some information. I'll tell you what, if you can spare a few minutes to speak with her, I'll take you out for brunch this Sunday."

"Make it the Atwood Restaurant in the Hotel Burnham, over by the Art Institute, and you have a deal. Now what can I do for Dr. O'Shaunessy?"

"Thanks, Maddie. Here's Claire to explain the situation."

Claire gave Maddie a brief rundown on Elizabeth O'Connor's case.

"I wish I could help you, but our last documented case of gas gangrene occurred at least six or seven months ago. Dr. Olson came down to see me a few minutes before Gregory called. I gave him the same information. However, I'm pleased to hear that Tri-State researched the donor for you."

Discouragement made Claire's shoulders sag. *Another dead end.* "Thank you for your time. If you hear of anything, could you please call Dr. Johnson?" she asked.

"I'd be happy to do so. Now you tell my cousin I'm making the reservations for eleven in the morning. I'll meet him there and I don't care if the Queen herself is in town, he'd best be on time."

Claire knew Dr. Johnson could hear the entire conversation. "I'll pass on your message."

"She might be built small, but she sure can pack a wallop when she wants." Dr. Johnson leaned back in his chair and smiled. "She was a spitfire when we were kids. I'm not surprised she never married. There isn't a man alive who could have handled her."

"Then you'd 'best be on time'. Thank you for your help," Claire said as she got up to leave.

"If it wouldn't be too much trouble, could you drop these charts off for me downstairs for filing?" Dr. Johnson asked.

"Not a problem, since I'm heading down to the front office to check on my autopsy schedule anyway." Claire took the stack from him.

"Thanks, Claire."

A few minutes later she dialed Jack to share her latest news, or more honestly, lack of news. As she descended the back stairs, her call went to voice mail. Claire placed the files in the front office bin, checked her schedule and opened the door to the receiving area where bodies were weighed. At that moment, Claire thought she recognized a funeral home driver taking a body out of the back bay.

"Thomas, do you know who that driver was?" Claire asked.

Thomas looked down at the signature on the Permit for Disposition of Dead Human Body. "Shoot, I can't read the handwriting. The guy drives for Floyd's Funeral Home on the southwest side. Woody checked the toe tags for identification against the paperwork. I can ask him when he gets back from lunch. Maybe he'll remember the name from checking the guy's driver's license. I'll let you know what I find out, Dr. O'Shaunessy."

"That would be great. Thanks." Claire headed to the autopsy area. Even though she didn't get a good look at the driver's face, a sense of familiarity about him gnawed at her. She just couldn't place where she'd seen him before.

# Chapter 22

"Detective Miller, this is Fred Drake. I'm the doorman at Dr. O'Shaunessy's condo. You said to call if she received any packages."

Jack grabbed a pad of paper from his desk drawer. "What do you have?" he asked.

"It may be nothing, but a FedEx package just arrived. The return address is from a FedEx office out in Rockford, Illinois. I noticed a light dampness at one of the bottom corners."

"Fred, put the box in a secure area and don't touch it again, and wash your hands. If Dr. O'Shaunessy should come home before I get there, don't tell her about the package."

"No problem. Consider it done," Fred replied.

Jack was out of his desk chair before the doorman had finished answering, knocking on Captain Ramos's office door.

"Come in, Jack." Captain Ramos set aside the papers in his hand. "What can I do for you?"

"Captain, we might have a situation." Jack explained the call he'd received. "I don't want to concern Patrick with this. He's at the doctor's office for a follow-up appointment. Could you detain him if he gets back before I do?"

"No problem. Take whomever you need. Do I need to call the Bomb and Arson Squad?"

"I hate to say yes, but the doorman said one corner was damp. Could we do this quietly so it doesn't make the evening news? Between Claire's current problem and the mayor's situation, we're trying not to stroke this person's ego."

"Smart decision. I'll tell them to use unmarked vehicles and try not to call any attention to their activities."

"Thanks, Captain," Jack yelled as he ran out of the homicide office.

* * *

In spite of the cooperating light traffic, Jack couldn't get to Claire's condo fast enough. He didn't want to use his lights and sirens. Yet, if the package contained a bomb, the well-being of more than Claire was at stake.

He darted around cars and received several fingers. A few minutes later he pulled into the circular drive with an unmarked van right behind him. One of the men jumped out of the van and slapped a fake "Joe's Electrical Company" magnetic sign on the side of the vehicle. *Nice touch*, he thought as he walked inside the foyer with the team on his heels. He found Fred Drake at his post.

"This way, Detective Miller." Fred led them to a door that blended into the wall at the back of the lobby.

Jack and two men in dark protective body suits followed Fred into a locked room just off the main entryway. "You should wait outside," Jack said. "Don't encourage the ladies to linger in the hallway."

"Not a problem," Fred answered, standing a little taller.

After the door shut behind Fred, Jack turned to the two men from the Bomb and Arson Squad. "What do you think?"

One of the officers, a tall African-American, sniffed the damp corner. "Can't really say without further examination. However, the damp corner doesn't smell like an accelerant I'm familiar with. There's a slight iron scent. Is there another way out of the lobby?"

"Yes," Jack said. "The door next to this one goes to the garage. What do you have in mind?"

"Since our orders are to maintain a low profile, I'd like to pull the van into the garage. Shut the door and place a 'Temporarily out of order' sign on the door. In the meantime, we bring in the bomb retrieval container through the garage, package the parcel and slip back into the garage as undetected as possible, and leave."

"Sounds good to me," Jack answered. "I'll fill the doorman in on the plan while you pull the van into the garage."

No sooner had Jack spoken with the doorman when he heard a familiar voice.

"Was the sign your idea?" Claire stood waving the cheap magnetic sign from the van, with Frankie racing in on her heels.

"What's happened, Detective Miller?" Frankie asked.

Jack grabbed Claire's wrist and pulled her into the back room before she could draw attention to them. Frankie followed. Jack spun her around and pointed to the package the officer guarded. "This came for you today."

Claire reached for it, but Jack pulled her back. Frankie stayed against the back wall. "The sign was a cover for the Bomb and Arson Squad. We're trying to avoid making the five o'clock news. Before we pack it up, I want to take a photo of the label so we can put a trace on it." He pulled out his cell phone and took several shots of the label and package. Then he noticed the damp corner was dripping.

"If I didn't know better, I'd say that smells like formaldehyde." Claire bent down for a closer look. "There appears to be some blood mixed in the solution. Notice the brown edging at the rim of the leak."

A second later the other Bomb and Arson officer knocked. Jack let him in. "Who are these people?" the officer asked.

Jack introduced Claire and Frankie to the men as the package recipient and her bodyguard. "Dr. O'Shaunessy is a forensic pathologist over at Cook County Morgue." He shared Claire's assessment of the dripping fluid with the officer.

"Well, doctor, I hope you're right and this isn't an incendiary device. However, my orders are to secure the area as needed and return to base with the package." Wearing protective gloves, he lifted the package into the container he'd brought in, and his partner secured the top. "We'll report our findings to Captain Ramos as soon as we have them." Carefully, the two officers opened the door to check the lobby. They gave Jack a thumbs-up sign and left. Jack, Claire, and Frankie followed them as far as the lobby.

Claire opened her mouth to speak, but Jack put his hand up to stop her. "Frankie, take her up to her place now. I'll be up in a few minutes. I have to interview the doorman first." Claire gave him her strongest frown, but entered the next elevator with Frankie.

Jack questioned Fred and thanked him for his quick response to the situation. Then he headed up to Claire's, dreading the argument they were about to have over her safety.

# Chapter 23

Derek Ruger glanced at the clock from his position at the operating table next to the surgeon. As he handed him the closing suture, he stared at the gallbladder resting in the sterile basin on his surgical mayo stand. Behind his mask, no one could see the slight smile forming on his face. The bloody fluid swarming around the organ made him think of the present he'd sent Dr. O'Shaunessy yesterday.

The trip to Rockford, Illinois, had been uneventful. For the benefit of any security cameras, he'd dressed as an older lady from clothes and a wig stored in the closet at Floyd's Funeral Home. He'd carefully prepared the package after removing the heart from the old man headed to the crematorium after his wake. The glass specimen jar he'd brought home from the hospital worked perfectly. He'd sealed it in a plastic bag before wrapping the jar in several layers of bubble wrap.

After placing it in the FedEx box, he'd added a personal note: *I want you to have my heart.* This should really throw Dr. O'Shaunessy off her game. Even though the Chicago Police would trace the package back to Rockford, they wouldn't be able to identify him. He'd purposely paid in cash, including the extra fee for guaranteed delivery by noon the next day. By now his package should be in her doorman's hands. Hopefully she would go home for lunch. Sending a chocolate heart never would have had the same effect on her.

The surgeon passed the needle holder back to him after cutting the last suture. Per procedure, he attached the used needle to the safety magnet and closed the packet. While the surgeon left to speak with the family, Derek and Joan, the circulating nurse, removed the sterile drapes now coated with blood and bodily fluids, and disposed of them in the bio-hazard waste container. He changed his contaminated gloves for sterile ones, washed the betadine soap and fluids from the surgical site, dried the area and taped a sterile pressure dressing over the incision.

With each step, he reminisced over the emotions he'd felt when he finished Elizabeth O'Connor's case. The hope, the promise, the vision that his family's pain would be forever erased. He'd be finally free of his past, which soothed him.

He helped anesthesia and the circulating nurse transfer the patient from the operating table to the cart. The patient stirred a little. While they moved her to the recovery bay, Derek disposed of the garbage and placed all the instruments in the heavy metal tray in the case cart, then pushed the case cart out and down the hall to the elevator. Just before he reached it, he noticed Debbie, the charge nurse, in the supply room. He watched her place the sterile glass specimen containers from the shelf into a box on a small cart.

"What's going on?" he asked.

Debbie turned at the sound of his voice. "Oh hi, Derek. I got a recall notice from the vendor . . . they found hairline cracks in a specific lot number for the jars. Apparently they're leaking." She checked the lot number stamped on the bottom of two more jars and then placed them in the box.

Derek felt his stomach lurch and the color drain from his face. He nodded and immediately left the area, pushing his cart on to the next elevator for sterile processing in the basement. He leaned against the cool metal elevator wall, trying to slow his breathing and heart rate before the doors opened.

His mind raced through all the possibilities, but it kept coming back to the one that scared him the most. What if the jar had leaked, making the package undeliverable? Would the police be notified, since he'd used a phony address? Would it make the Chicago news? Would the nursing supervisor hear the news? Did she realize the jar count was off by one? Would she put two and two together and question him? He was known for being anal about the supply count. His count always matched the documents, but the room wasn't kept locked. Anyone could have removed a jar. Comforted by the thought, he left the cart in the designated spot for processing and returned to the unit.

Unaware the charge nurse was watching him, Derek clocked out on the computer and went home.

# Chapter 24

"Claire, are we clear on this?"

"But . . ." she started to say.

"We aren't having a discussion on this. You're grounded. Frankie, see to it that she doesn't leave her condo until I give the all-clear sign, even if you have to call in your brothers and tie her down. I don't know what was in that package, but my gut tells me it's bad."

Jack watched Claire stuff more of the buttery popcorn Frankie had made her into her mouth. At least that kept her quiet for the moment.

Jack ran one hand through his hair. The other rested automatically on his gun. *What is going on,* he thought. He almost didn't want to know the contents of the package. He'd notified Captain Ramos and sent him the pictures from his phone. It wouldn't be long before the Rockford police received the information and checked the FedEx location. He felt like his brain was short circuiting, just as his cell phone rang.

"Detective Miller speaking." For several minutes he didn't talk, just listened. He turned his back to Claire because he didn't want her to see his reaction to Captain Ramos's news until he composed himself. He'd been right. The news was bad. No, it was *sick!*

"What about Patrick?" He paused for a moment as the captain continued speaking. "Sounds good. Thank you." He tapped the screen and ended the call.

Claire had stopped eating popcorn. "What's wrong with Patrick?"

"He's fine. Captain Ramos sent him home after his check-up, which went well. The captain told him he needs Patrick rested because the next few days are going to be draining with the wake, funeral and burial." Jack read in her face the same relief he felt.

He checked his watch. Officially he was off duty. "Frankie, you wouldn't have a cold one in the fridge, would you?"

Frankie reached in and grabbed a beer for Jack. "The rest of the news must be pretty bad if you're asking for a beer."

Jack took a couple of swigs before setting the beer down. "You're too perceptive. The good news is, the box didn't contain a bomb."

"What's the bad news?" Claire stood up.

"Sit back down, Claire." She did what he asked, only now he saw her clutching her hands tightly.

He held his breath before he delivered the information. "You were right about the formaldehyde and blood. Someone sent you a human heart. The jar had a crack, that's why it leaked."

She stood again with as much reaction as if he'd told her he was picking up Chinese for dinner, then grabbed her purse and started to leave. He stopped her as she reached for the front door knob and turned her around. Tears were streaming down her face. Whoever this evil person was, his determination to break Claire would not be tolerated. Jack pulled her tight into his arms. "Just let it all out," he said.

"Do I need to give you two some privacy?" Frankie said.

Jack and Claire separated. "No," they responded at the same time, then laughed.

"Okay, I know I said I wouldn't break down again, but I think it's been an accumulation of everything from Patrick's health to this." She wiped her cheeks with the linen handkerchief Jack offered. "This is becoming a habit."

"I'm running out of clean handkerchiefs. Let's all sit down so I can finish going over the rest of the information."

Frankie brought over a fresh bowl of buttery popcorn and napkins. He grabbed a beer for himself and Claire.

Jack spoke first after they all sat. He turned to Claire. "I have no idea why someone is fixated on you, but it's scary. The note in the box read, 'I want you to have my heart'." He heard her take a deep breath and saw her clutch his handkerchief as if holding a lifeline. "At the moment, with all the plans for Elizabeth's wake through to her burial, the captain agrees with me that we should keep Patrick out of this current loop. There's nothing to be gained by worrying him more. I doubt he has any idea who it is, either.

"In the meantime, we have to look at where someone could even get a fairly fresh heart. The item in question could have been purchased from someone who has access to it."

"That leaves only a couple of possibilities," Claire said. "It has to be a morgue, a funeral home or a crematorium. How are we ever going to solve this? Where did it come from?"

"Rockford," Jack answered.

"Rockford? That doesn't make any sense. I've never been to Rockford, nor do I know anyone out that way." Claire took another sip of her beer.

"What's your take?" Frankie asked.

"Personally, I think we have one very sick individual on our hands." Jack got up and picked up a pad of paper from the kitchen counter. "Let's start at the center of the problem." He wrote Claire's name and circled it. Next, he drew a second circle around the first one. "Okay, Claire, thinking of your life, who or what would you put in the next perimeter?"

"Obviously, family and friends, but they didn't do it. So I guess I would put the morgue and maybe the health club as a wild card."

"We probably can rule out the health club," Jack said. "I think the morgue has more possibilities." Quickly he jotted down a list and passed it over for Claire and Frankie to read.

Frankie scanned the list. "There's nothing about Rockford on it."

"Exactly," Jack answered. "At this point, I think Rockford is a red herring, designed to throw us off track. Of course we'll have to wait to see what the Rockford police discover. Hopefully, something will show up on the FedEx security cam, but I'm not holding my breath. Captain Ramos is having all recent autopsies checked, not only at the Cook County Morgue, but the six collar county morgues around Chicago. This heart hasn't been laying around for a couple of weeks.

"He's also having all crematories in the same area questioned for any cases that might have seemed suspicious. There could be more than one person involved, but I doubt it because this guy's actions lead me to believe it's personal and his next move won't be any more rational." Jack took another sip of his beer.

"What do you want me to do next?" Frankie asked.

"Just what you've been doing. Stay right with Claire until we catch the guy."

Claire got up and walked over to the sliding glass balcony doors, and looked out at the city before turning back to Jack. "And what if we don't stop him soon? I can't expect Frankie to suspend his life forever. This isn't fair to his father, who expects him to be working at the family garage servicing cars."

"Dad said I'm to cover you as long as needed, and Sol and Vince are available at a minute's notice." Frankie removed the empty bottles and popcorn bowl to the kitchen.

Jack heard him open the oven door. Whiffs of something incredible penetrated the air. "Frankie, by the time this is over, we're all going to be deeply in debt to you. Not only do you take Claire's safety off my mind, but this'll keep a big worry away from Patrick. Okay, let's get back to my list.

"Claire, is there anyone you've had a run-in with at the morgue? This includes staff, grieving families, funeral home drivers, transport drivers, and the supply truck drivers."

"No, but something strange did happen yesterday."

"What?" Jack noticed this caught Frankie's attention also.

"Dr. Johnson asked me to drop off a couple file folders in the main office. On my way back through the area where the funeral home drivers pick up the bodies, I got a side view of one of the drivers. There was something familiar about him, only I couldn't place where I'd seen him before. Only that it was recent. I had Thomas check the log for his name, but he couldn't read the signature. Woody signed the body out. Thomas promised to get the name of the driver for me. Wherever I've seen him before, it had nothing to do with the morgue."

"Which funeral home does he drive for? I'll go check him out myself," Frankie said.

"Frankie, you can't. I need you with Claire. I'll check with Woody and follow up."

Claire tapped her fingers on the table. "You're going to keep us in the loop, correct?"

"I will on one condition—the two of you won't go off on some hare-brained sleuthing adventure like you did on my last case. If I find out you have, then I'll have to tell Patrick."

"I think Detective Miller has us over a barrel," Frankie replied.

"You've got that clear, Frankie. What about you, Claire? Can I trust you to stay out of my investigation?" Jack prayed they'd keep their word.

"Oh, all right, but you better play fair with Frankie and me. I'll behave. Just let me catch you lying to either of us and all bets are off. Is that understood?"

Before Jack could answer, his phone rang. Patrick's number appeared on the caller ID.

"Where are you?" Patrick asked.

"I'm with Claire, at her place," he answered.

"Is there something I should be aware of?"

Jack rolled his eyes. He knew Claire and Frankie couldn't hear Patrick laugh after his last comment. This wasn't the first-time Patrick had mentioned this thought. "No, I was telling Claire, we'd figure out how to get her in and out of the wake and funeral safely in case the flower guy is hanging around."

"Right," Patrick replied. "It's after seven. Do you need me to come over and chaperone?"

"No, and Jack was just leaving," Claire called, loud enough for Patrick to hear. "Good night, big brother."

Jack hung up. Frankie's smile widened. "That was close!"

"I was going to mention the plans for the wake and funeral, so I didn't really lie to Patrick. I'm not sure how we'll manage the burial, though."

"I'm going to the burial. You can't stop me," Claire said.

Frankie intervened. "Claire, let's give Detective Miller some time to work out the logistics before we get all crazy. The man has a lot on his plate without us adding to it. Speaking of plate, my lasagna is ready. Can I offer you some, Jack?"

"I thought you'd never ask."

# Chapter 25

"Nice of you to drop by the department," Patrick called out as Jack entered Homicide. "I feel like I have to make a date with you, just so I can see my partner."

"Good morning to you, too," Jack answered as he slung his jacket over the back of his chair. "What's the game plan?" he asked, heading to the coffee station. "Want a cup?"

"Already had one, but thanks. It's decaf for the rest of the day. Getting down to business, Michael will have the family's wishes for Elizabeth's services today. We're supposed to meet him in his mayoral office at two this afternoon." Patrick glanced at his watch. "A few minutes ago, I spoke with Michael's brother, Paul, over at Keeley Liquor Distributors. He can see us in a half hour. I have a gut feeling the family business is connected in some way to all the Keeley mishaps."

"Why do you think so?" Jack sipped his coffee.

Patrick tapped his pencil on the top of his desk and passed a sheet of paper over to his partner. "Here, look at the list of events that have plagued the family for roughly the past fifteen years. The timeline between them has consistently diminished. Also, the last few incidents have increased in severity until we have a human death. No one witnessed any of these events, which tells me they were carefully planned. During this period, the only fact that hasn't changed is the ownership of the family business."

"In other words, the timeline doesn't match because the criminals Michael Keeley sent to prison during his stint with the District Attorney's Office were incarcerated when the events started, and they began before he became mayor," Jack answered.

"Exactly. The family business goes back at least thirty years," Patrick answered.

"We've just one little problem," Jack said.

"What?"

"You're still on desk duty for health reasons."

Patrick looked around the homicide office. The place was empty, including Captain Ramos's office. With a smile, he said, "Hey, I can take an early lunch break just like anyone else in the department."

Patrick wasn't happy that Jack insisted on driving, but his partner had a point. His presence behind the wheel would give the illusion that he'd gone back on full duty. No sense inviting trouble. He directed Jack to a set of commercial buildings on the west side of O'Hare International Airport, in Elk Grove Village. Keeley Liquor Distributors, a massive glass, chrome and concrete building, had a line of truck bays the length of the backside of the warehouse area. Jack parked in the visitors' lot out front.

They went in, and Patrick introduced them both to the perky brunette receptionist. Her name badge said *Amanda*.

"Mr. Keeley is waiting for you," she said. "Please follow the security guard."

Out of nowhere the guard appeared and led them up in the elevator to the fourth floor and down the hall to Mr. Keeley's office. "Thanks, Ted," Mr. Keeley's secretary said. She announced their arrival over the intercom, said, "Yes, sir," and then rose. "This way."

They followed her to the office door. Upon entering, Patrick noted this office had to be the size of the entire first floor of his home.

Paul Keeley came around his desk to greet them. "Good to see you, Patrick." As he shook hands, Patrick introduced his partner.

"Can Chris get you something to drink?" Paul offered. He motioned for them follow him to a sitting area with a soft leather couch and several wing-backed chairs. Paintings of Chicago and the lakefront graced the walls.

"No, thank you. Wish this was a social call, Paul, but I need some history from you on the business."

Paul took the chair directly opposite them. "I know Michael mentioned something about the possibility of our family being stalked. The idea seems so farfetched I almost couldn't wrap my mind around it until Michael went over the list the two of you prepared. Do you believe this is for real?"

Patrick pulled a piece of paper from his jacket pocket. He leaned over, resting his elbows on his knees as he scanned the list.

"Yes, I do. I called the District Attorney's office early this morning and requested they take a look at Michael's convictions, but I doubt they'll match the timeline of the events. I've pretty much dismissed the idea of the attacks being tied to his mayoral office for the same reason. That leaves the family business as the only constant during this period." Patrick handed Paul the list. "I believe the inciting incident goes back before Mary Anne's bike accident. Whatever happened set this person on a personal mission of revenge."

"What's your take on this?" Paul directed the question to Jack.

"I'm afraid I agree with my partner. This guy, and I'm assuming it is a male, isn't finished. We both think the grand prize is Michael," Jack said. "If you read over the list, not all the events are tied directly to Michael's immediate family. They include your mother's dog, Michael's siblings, nieces, nephews and various other family members' pets. He wants the entire Keeley family to suffer. I wonder if whatever happened to this person had a profound effect on *his* family, or he believes it did, whether true or not."

"Do you believe Elizabeth was murdered?" Paul asked.

"Yes," Patrick answered quietly. "We don't have definitive proof yet, but there's no logical reason for the infection that killed her."

"Michael said gas gangrene contaminated the donor tissue? Isn't it possible the tissue came infected from the donor and this master plan to destroy my family really doesn't exist?"

Jack took the floor. "I interviewed the company the hospital ordered the tissue from. They were more than cooperative. The donor died of a coronary and all other recipients of anything from him are doing fine."

Paul rubbed a spot between his eyebrows. "How in the hell do we find this maniac before he hurts another family member? My parents are beyond grief-stricken. Stephen and his kids are devastated, while the rest of the family is wondering who's next. Now you tell me you believe Michael is the prize? With the rest of us, what—collateral damage?"

"In the past this person has managed to upset Michael through the previous incidents, but this time he hurt him a lot by causing Elizabeth's death. My guess is he wants Michael to feel the ultimate pain and be crushed before taking his life," Patrick said. "There might even be a personal connection between this guy and Michael. Maybe a slight one, but real."

Paul got up and walked over to a mini bar at the opposite end of the office. "Can I get either of you a bottle of water?" he asked as he reached for one for himself.

"That would great. We'll each take one," Jack said.

Paul returned to the sitting area and tossed them their water bottles before claiming his chair. "What I really want is about two fingers of my favorite bourbon."

"Tell me about it," Patrick said.

"Okay, what can I do to help?"

Patrick took a sip of water before he spoke. "On our drive over I thought about the span of time involved. Let's pick a range five years before Mary Anne's accident and look at who worked for your dad. Include employees who were angry because they didn't get a promotion or a raise they thought they deserved, or were fired. Don't forget to add any vendors your dad had to cut off deliveries to for any reason. If you could point us to where the old records are stored, I can have Captain Ramos send over some police cadets to start checking them."

Paul closed his eyes and leaned his head against the chair back. A moment later he looked at Patrick. "That's not possible."

"Why not?" Jack asked, putting his water bottle on the glass coffee table.

"Because we lost all those records in a warehouse fire about ten years ago. We're lucky all the financial records had been scanned into the computer at our old office, but not the employee records you want."

Patrick thought he saw Paul's eyes fill with tears. "Okay. How about current and prior employees who worked during this period? Someone might remember something." Patrick prayed a few were still alive.

"Twenty years ago, we were spread out in several locations. We stored the hard liquors in a warehouse in Bensenville, while the drink mixes and non-alcoholic beverages were either in Schiller Park or Addison. After the fire, Dad decided we needed a new facility with everyone under the same roof."

Patrick could read the frustration on Paul's face as the lines in his forehead deepened.

Jack spoke up. "Wait a minute. You're a family business, correct?" he asked Paul.

Paul nodded. "What are you getting at?"

"Do you also extend the family plan to other employees, like hire their relatives?"

Paul got up, went to his desk, and pushed the intercom button. "Chris?"

The secretary's voice sounded in the room. "Yes, Mr. Keeley. What can I get for you?"

"Grab a pad of paper and come in." He disconnected. Before he reached his chair, Chris appeared. "Come sit down with us." He motioned to the other wing-backed chair and made introductions.

"Chris has been with Keeley Liquors for almost twenty years. Her grandfather ran the Bensenville warehouse until he retired, and passed away a couple of years ago. Her dad worked at both of our old locations. Chris is like a walking encyclopedia on the history of the company."

Patrick grinned. He explained to Chris what he needed. "I imagine some of the old employees have retired, but if you could find out where they are, that would save us a great deal of time. Right now we only have a short time before Elizabeth's services."

"I can do better than that. Some of our retired employees still have family working here, like Mary in accounts payable and Bill down on the loading dock. They may have heard stories from their family members. Also, if any of our old employees are in nursing homes, I'll try and arrange meetings, with their families' approval, of course."

"Thanks, Chris. Use anyone you need to gather the information." Paul turned toward Patrick. "Should Chris contact you directly?"

Patrick handed Chris his card and Jack's. "Yes," he answered. "This'll save a lot of time. I have to ask you to be discreet, just in case this person still has a contact working here. We don't want to tip our hand."

After Chris left, Patrick and Jack made their goodbyes with Paul.

"We'll find him, Paul, don't worry." Patrick crossed his fingers behind his back, praying no more Keeleys would be harmed in the meantime.

# Chapter 26

Captain Ramos was standing with his arms folded over his chest in the middle of the Homicide department when Patrick and Jack returned. "I thought we had you on desk duty for a couple more weeks?"

"We went for lunch," Patrick said.

"And?" Captain Ramos asked.

"Okay, we went for lunch and stopped to pay our condolences to the mayor's brother, Paul, over at Keeley Liquor Distributors."

"Is that what they call detective work these days? While you paid your respects, did you gather any good leads?" Captain Ramos didn't budge from his spot. Even the crease in his uniform pants didn't buckle in the slightest.

Jack jumped in. "Actually, Paul's secretary seems to know everyone and a chunk of the company history. We're looking at a specific window of time, approximately fifteen to twenty years ago."

"Why that period?" Captain Ramos waved his hand, indicating they should follow him to his office as other detectives entered the room and the noise level went up. Once seated behind his desk, Captain Ramos said, "Okay, let's hear it."

Patrick gave the captain a rundown on the initial event and showed him the list of all the incidents involving harm to the Keeleys. "Elizabeth was the first death, which we believe the murderer planned. I'm sure we have a serial stalker turned killer on our hands and no one in the mayor's family is safe, least of all Michael. I wouldn't be surprised if he is the ultimate goal."

"Why zero in on the family business? Why not Mayor Keeley's current job, or something from when he worked for the District Attorney?" the captain asked.

"The timing doesn't work, sir. It's gone on too long, and the people he put away during his DA stint were incarcerated when a lot of these things happened. The only thing tying these incidents together is the family business. For whatever reason, someone is really mad and has shown he'll stop at nothing to seek revenge. But who he is, and why he's driven to cause the Keeleys pain, remains unknown. We're hoping Paul's secretary comes up with a couple tips and fast."

"Captain, if you could excuse us, Patrick and I are scheduled to meet with the mayor at two o'clock regarding Elizabeth's services," Jack said.

Ramos nodded. "Okay. Keep me abreast of what you find out regarding the family business and the funeral plans."

"Yes, sir," Patrick answered as they left the captain's office.

Twenty minutes later, Jack pulled into a designated parking space for the Chicago Police at City Hall. By the time they'd cleared through security, they were only a few minutes early for their designated appointment. Jack noticed that Patrick's face appeared slightly flushed. "Are you feeling all right?" he asked in a quiet voice.

"It's been a long day, that's all. After this I'm headed home. Can you hold the fort, Kemosabe?"

"No problem. Do you have to call Sylvia for a ride?" Jack asked.

"Yes, her car is in Biaggi's Garage for a tune-up, so she has mine."

"How about I drop you off at home, since I want to stop at the morgue and see if Woody identified the signature on the release form yet. I don't want Claire deciding to go off on a scavenger hunt looking for the guy she thought she recognized."

"Good idea. I don't trust Claire to stay put. I'm sure Sylvia will appreciate you saving her a trip down to the station in afternoon traffic."

"The mayor is ready for you" the receptionist called out.

Mayor Michael Keeley stood to shake their hands as they entered his office. "Thanks for coming, Patrick. And Jack, I appreciated your support the other night."

"No problem," Jack said. The mayor looked like a thousand-ton weight lay on his shoulders, and Jack doubted he'd slept well since his sister's death. Amazing the guy could still function, considering.

"Have a seat." Mayor Keeley indicated the chairs opposite his desk. "Usually the Chicago Police Department wouldn't have such an active role with a funeral for a Chicago employee's family member. However, after discussing the possibility that Elizabeth's death wasn't natural causes, and the other events that indicate my family has been stalked, the chief believes it's necessary." He handed Patrick and Jack each a sheet of paper. "I think we have the framework for the services. I don't have all the specific times nailed down just yet. Headquarters will provide security at McDuffy's Chapel in Bridgeport, and accompany Elizabeth the next day to Old St. Patrick's Church at Adams and Des Plaines in Chicago for the funeral. A reception will follow at St. Francis Xavier Warde School next to the church." He swallowed hard, as if fighting back grief, and continued. "A Chicago Police escort will lead the hearse and family cars from the church after the reception for a private interment at Mt. Carmel Cemetery in Hillside. The Hillside Police will provide security at the cemetery."

Patrick addressed his old friend with unspoken sympathy. "Mr. Mayor, no matter how quiet we try to keep the plans, word will leak out and we can expect crowds. I'm very concerned about your safety."

"Never mind the 'Mr. Mayor,' Patrick. We've known each other far too long to be formal behind closed doors."

"Thanks, Michael."

"Patrick," Jack said, "I've an idea regarding crowd control."

"Go for it," Patrick said.

"We should announce the plans for the services, for a couple of reasons. First of all, people who live near the funeral home and church are about to have their lives disrupted with increased traffic and police barricades. This way they can plan different routes. Also, the public will expect to be told. Many of them thought the world of Elizabeth, and they'll want to pay their last respects. I've been to McDuffy's Chapel. They have several large rooms. It'll be easy to guide everyone through if we use ropes like they do at movie theaters. Also, entrances and exits can easily be monitored. I think the Secret Service has portable body scanners so we can check for weapons."

The mayor frowned. "We can't use the scanners at the church. Father O'Malley will never approve."

"We won't need them at church because the only way you can get in is if you have an invitation or your name is on the list," Jack said. "That part we won't make public. The invitations will be numbered. You and your family can provide us with a list of names and addresses. The invitation is also their ticket to the reception.

"Also, Heritage Green Park is directly across the street from the main doors of St. Patrick's and I believe it has a wrought iron fence around its perimeter. This is a perfect place to have the public view the church. Just north of the park is a good-sized parking lot for the guests." Jack loosened his tie slightly as he sat back in the office chair.

"Sounds perfect," the mayor said. "I'll have my wife Laura prepare the invitation list. This'll give the family something to do. We can mail the local ones and hand-deliver the few we'll have to the suburbs."

Patrick spoke up. "Michael, I'd limit the number to 200 total with a separate, shorter list for the burial. The chapel at Queen of Heaven Cemetery won't hold that many."

The mayor nodded slowly. "Elizabeth mentioned once that she wanted a graveside service at the family plot, across the street from the Queen of Heaven Cemetery in the Mt. Carmel Cemetery. But who knows what kind of weather we'll have, and my parents wouldn't be physically able to attend. Using the chapel over at Queen of Heaven is a smarter idea."

"I agree," Patrick said. "Plus the police will be able to provide better security. Family members can visit her grave the next day."

"Will the family be going back to your parents' or another family member's home after the chapel service?" Jack asked.

"Probably, but we haven't decided yet." The intercom buzzed. "I'll be right with you. I have another meeting with a couple of aldermen regarding funding for summer events in their neighborhoods."

Patrick and Jack stood.

"I'll be in touch with Laura for the list. She can call me with the correct timing of everything, to free you up, and contact Sylvia if she needs anything," Patrick said.

A thin smile flitted across Mayor Keeley's face. "Thanks, Patrick."

Patrick shook the mayor's hand. "We can see ourselves out."

# Chapter 27

Jack dropped Patrick at his front door before heading to the morgue. He pulled into the back parking lot on the west side of the building where only a few cars remained. The late afternoon sun broke free of the clouds as he got out. What a different feel the place had now than on the night he brought Claire over to perform Elizabeth O'Connor's autopsy. He vividly remembered the flashing lights and the television camera crews. Everyone wanted a piece of the tragedy, but only because of the woman's relation to the mayor. Where were they when the innocent lost their lives to a stray bullet? Sure, those stories made the news, but not with the same intensity.

Jack locked his unmarked vehicle, went inside the building, and entered the room where the staff weighed the recent admissions. He saw Thomas pushing a covered cart into the x-ray room. "Hey, Thomas, is Woody around?"

"Sure," Thomas answered. "I think he's in the front office. I'll call him for you."

"That's okay. I can find him. Thanks." Jack walked into the front office where the back room aroma didn't seem to penetrate. "Woody," he called out.

A short, slim man with thinning dark hair responded. "Yes?"

Jack introduced himself and described what he'd come for.

"Let me pull the record."

Jack followed Woody to a file cabinet and watched him dig through it.

After a moment Woody found the file. He opened it, found the release form, and pointed to the signature. "This one's a sloppy writer. I had to ask him to spell his name since I couldn't read it. That's why I wrote it down in pencil under his signature. I checked his name against his license, and it matched."

Jack took out his notebook and wrote down *Craig Floyd* and his information. "Is he related to Floyd's Funeral Home?"

"I think he told me once he was a nephew. He doesn't come here very often. He's really an odd sort."

"In what way?"

"His affect is flat, for one thing. Most drivers for the funeral homes ask a concerned question or two about the folks they bring here. Craig couldn't care less if it was a body or a bag full of potatoes. I know this sounds strange, but his eyes have this dark, almost empty look to them. I've seen dead bodies with more life in their eyes than his." Woody took in a deep breath and let it out, like he was trying to cleanse himself of the memory.

After getting a fuller description of the driver, Jack thanked Woody and headed to Claire's office. Halfway down to the second floor hallway, he ran into her.

She grinned at him. "What brings you to my humble abode?"

"Just checking out the name of the driver for Floyd's Funeral Home."

"Shoot. I meant to do that this morning, but I had a full docket and this is the first time I've stopped all day. So, who is he?"

Jack scratched the back of his neck. "Craig Floyd. According to Woody, he's the owner's nephew and as cold as a dead fish."

"Maybe he doesn't want to work for the family business. That still doesn't tell me why he looked so familiar."

Jack checked his watch. "Are you done for the day?"

"Just about. Why?"

He took her elbow and directed her to her office. "Call Frankie and tell him I'll bring you home. The guy deserves a break."

# Chapter 28

The ride back to Claire's condo took them less than twenty minutes with light traffic and decent weather. After they arrived, they settled in around the kitchen table for a pow-wow with Frankie while they waited for a local Chinese restaurant to deliver her favorite orange chicken.

"Okay, Jack, I agreed to wait until we got here so you didn't have to repeat yourself, but you better start talking fast because I know Chinese torture tricks."

"I wouldn't cross her," Frankie said as he gathered the tableware for dinner and placed the items on the counter.

"You've got that right, Frankie. Okay, here's the latest," Jack said.

Claire took notes while Jack gave them the rundown on his and Patrick's visits, first with Paul Keeley, then with Michael. "When do you think they'll have everything finalized?"

"My guess, within a day or two. They're waiting for one relative to arrive from Ireland. We have the locations for each phase. We just need the final times approved. I suspect headquarters will give the okay based on staffing needs for the assignment plus their work schedules."

"So, what's the plan at this point?" No matter what argument Jack or her brother came up with, they wouldn't keep her away.

"You already know the wake will be at McDuffy's Funeral Home in Bridgeport. We'll let that be open to the public, but probably have a private wake for family and close friends beforehand. I'm thinking the public wake will be from two in the afternoon to seven in the evening. Family won't be greeting people at the public viewing because it will slow the line down considerably. We'll set up the ropes for the public viewing and cut off the line at the door at six o'clock. Also, I think we can get a body scanner for weapons from the Secret Service. Captain Ramos is working on that.

"Usually there's a family room with refreshments, but this'll be closed to the public. All exits and entrances will be secured. Elizabeth's family will arrive in private limos and enter through the garage, so they aren't exposed. A policeman will be posted on the inside and outside of the funeral home and garage for the entire wake."

"I'm impressed the department would go through all of this," Frankie said. The door buzzer announced the food delivery. "I'll be right back."

Jack handed him a couple of bills. "I insist, so don't argue." Frankie nodded and left.

"I take it the department agrees with our concerns about the Keeley family being stalked and the possibility of Elizabeth being murdered?" Claire asked. She set the table and retrieved serving bowls from the kitchen cabinet.

"You're correct, but don't think you're off the hook for one minute. Patrick and I have two cases going at the same time, Elizabeth's murder and your stalker."

"Did I miss anything," Frankie asked as he walked in, carrying a delivery bag that smelled like heaven to Claire.

"No," Claire answered. "How about the funeral mass? Will it be at Old St. Patrick's?" She filled the serving bowls, placed them on the table and gave everyone bottles of water before she sat down.

Jack passed her the rice. "Yes, with the reception right next door at the school. Admission will be by invitation only to both."

"Did you know Old St. Patrick's Cathedral is the only church left standing from the 1871 Chicago Fire?" Claire passed the rice to Frankie and then scooped a big mound of the orange chicken onto her plate.

"No, I didn't. How do you know so much Chicago trivia?" Jack asked as he took a bite of his dinner.

"I volunteered the summer between my junior and senior years in high school at the Chicago Historical Society to earn community service hours for graduation. Back then I didn't know how lucky I was to spend that summer at the museum. Maybe someday I can do it again. Chicago really has the coolest history."

Claire and Frankie listened to Jack describe the rest of the arrangements before she spoke again. "Did Patrick tell you our parents are buried in Section Q, one section over from the Keeley family graves at Mt. Carmel?" She took another bite of the delicious entree.

"My family has several mausoleums over in Section 24. The Italian sections look like row houses. There're at least 400 at Mt. Carmel alone," Frankie said.

"I don't need the two of you going off visiting family graves on the day of the funeral," Jack said. "You have to stay with the funeral party for security reasons."

Frankie offered Jack more helpings, but he shook his head. "I like the idea of the invitations. My youngest brother Joey isn't worth beans in the garage, but he's a wiz on the computer. He always prints my mom's Christmas cards."

"Michael's wife should use Joey to print and distribute the invitations. That way we'd feel secure that none of them will fall into the wrong hands," Claire said.

Jack took out his phone and dialed Patrick to relay Frankie's information. They spoke for a few minutes, and then he put Patrick on hold. "Frankie, are you sure Joey would take the job? He'll be paid, of course."

"Let me find out." Frankie called Joey and explained the job, including the issue of complete security. "He'll do it for only the cost of the supplies."

"Joey should take the money," Claire insisted.

"He'd prefer to use the Keeleys as a reference and give them a few business cards to hand out."

Jack relayed this to Patrick. They finished their conversation before Jack took another bite.

"What did my brother say?" Claire asked.

"He's all in favor of security regarding the invitations. He's sure Laura will be glad to have Joey use her for a reference. He's calling her now. He had one additional idea, that Laura come over and have Sylvia help address the envelopes. The stalker could be watching the mayor's home but chances are he won't think of Patrick's house."

"They'd be welcome to use my condo, but we still don't know about the creep who's harassing me," Claire said.

# Chapter 29

Derek sat in his parked car about a half block from Claire's building. The shorter November days worked in his favor. With the main entrance all lit up, he could see everything. Silently he watched the doorman greet the residents coming home. He recognized the man as the same one from the day he'd delivered the flowers. He assumed this man covered daytime hours. But *what about his package?* He hadn't seen anything on the evening news or in the next day's paper. Derek felt frustration build up inside him. He'd tired of seeing her escorted to and from work by that Italian or that detective, laughing at their remarks. He didn't know the name of the Italian, but he recognized the cop from their meeting at the hospital.

The one thing he knew for sure, she was a definite threat to him. The Italian was simply a nuisance, and the cop wasn't worth the prison time. The best target would be the doorman. He was expendable, if necessary.

About fifteen minutes later, at seven o'clock, Derek noticed a different doorman relieve the daytime employee. They spoke for several minutes, and then the day doorman left the front foyer and returned with his jacket on. He waved goodbye to his relief and exited the building.

Derek gave the doorman a head start, then left his car and followed on foot. About a block down, his prey crossed the street mid-block and Derek seized his opportunity. Removing a pipe from under his jacket, he ran up and pressed it into the guy's back like a gun barrel, pushing him into the narrow, pitch black alley. The doorman sucked in air to scream, but Derek threatened him.

"Shut up or you're dead." He pushed the pipe harder into the man's back. "Now put your hands on the wall and don't turn around." Shaking, the man complied.

"I won't hurt you unless you force me to. I want information. Do you understand?"

"Yes." The man's voice quivered.

"Did Dr. O'Shaunessy receive a package a couple days ago?" Derek kept sweeping his gaze out to the sidewalk and back down the alley. A dog walker might come his way, or someone taking a shortcut, or a garbage picker scrounging cans.

"Yes."

Derek could hear the man gasp for air, but he didn't care. "What happened to the package?"

"I don't know," the doorman cried.

"Not good enough." Derek pushed the end of the pipe even harder into his victim's back.

"The police came and took it away," the man whimpered.

Derek mulled the answer over. "How did the police know she received a package?"

"I don't know."

"Liar! If you don't want a couple of busted kneecaps, you'd better come up with the correct answer right now." Derek whacked the side of the man's right knee and listened to him cry out in pain as he slumped to the ground. "I'm only going to ask you one more time. After that, you'll never walk again in this lifetime. Do you hear me?"

"Yes," the doorman answered, gripping his knee. "The police told me to call them if she received any packages."

"Idiot! You ruined everything!" In a surge of fury, Derek clubbed his victim over the head and left. He stopped at the edge of the building and peered out before leaving the alley and stepping onto the sidewalk. He had to force himself to walk at a normal pace to his car. Once inside, he pounded the steering wheel, struggling to regain control. As he pulled away from the curb, his pager went off. *Damn, of all nights to be on call.*

# Chapter 30

Jack's radio squawked as he stepped out into the chilly November night air. "All units in the area of Roosevelt and South Indiana, please respond to a man down in the alley."

"What?" Jack realized the location was just down the street. He ran toward the alley and saw a man and his dog hovering over a body slumped on the ground next to the wall of a building. Jack flipped out his badge and yelled, "Police. What happened?"

The man, sixtyish and African-American, turned toward him. "I was walking my dog when he stopped by the alley and kept barking. He wouldn't go past it, so I turned my flashlight down the alley and saw this man on the ground. That's when I called 911."

Lights and sirens filled the night. "What's your name?" Jack asked as he bent down, feeling for a carotid pulse. The aroma of prior dog visits reached his nose.

"Greg Steiner. I live across the street, about a block down." The dog walker petted his German shepherd, who lay down next to the injured man. "Good boy, Duke," he said, as Jack rolled the man over.

"Oh, my God!" Steiner said. "That's Fred Drake, our new doorman! Fred, are you okay? Please talk to us. Help is on the way."

Jack froze for a split second. This couldn't be a coincidence. Quickly he hit Frankie's cell number. He didn't give Frankie any time to answer. "Is Claire okay?" he yelled above the sirens.

Frankie sounded puzzled. "Yes, why?"

"Don't have time to explain. Don't let her leave until you hear from me." He clicked off.

Fred began to moan in response to Mr. Steiner talking to him as Jack placed his rolled-up jacket under the doorman's bloody head. "Duke will keep you warm," Steiner said, as the dog pressed his body against the doorman. "Fred always has a dog biscuit for him."

An ambulance pulled up, and paramedics raced down the alley with their stretcher. They tried to question the man on the ground as they checked him over, but he drifted in and out of consciousness. Jack gave the doorman's wallet to the responding policeman after identifying himself. An officer in the street controlled traffic as another paramedic backed the ambulance down the alley. They put Fred on a back board and lifted it to the stretcher, then slid him into the ambulance.

Jack climbed in beside the doorman. "Which hospital?"

"Chicago General," the paramedic answered. "Why are you coming with?"

"Long story short, this attack is related to one of my cases. The person who did this has been stalking my partner's sister."

"That's hitting pretty close to home." The paramedic cut Fred's jacket sleeve and started an IV. His partner placed an oxygen mask on Fred's face and checked his pupils with a penlight to see if they were equal and reactive to light. Then he took the patient's vital signs. "Fred, can you hear me? Squeeze both my hands if you can." He turned to Jack. "I feel a slight response, but it's not equal," he said. Then, to the doorman: "Hang in there, Fred. We're almost at the hospital."

Jack held his breath while the ambulance raced down Harrison Street. Traffic lights changed for them at every intersection. Jack's first thought strayed to Fred and the package with the human heart. Did that make Fred a target?

Within minutes, the ambulance pulled into the emergency bay at Chicago General. The bay door opened and a team of two nurses, a doctor and an orderly stood ready to assist. They whisked Fred to the trauma room and switched him to an emergency cart, cut off his clothes, applied electrodes, and connected him to machines that would monitor his vital signs.

Jack stood outside the trauma room. Fred had become another innocent victim of this monster. He didn't care who he hurt. What had brought on such horrible, destructive actions with no respect for life? He had to find this person before any more people were hurt, or worse.

"Detective Miller, what brings you to our emergency room at this hour of the night?"

Jack turned to see Amy Cook, one of the nursing directors, standing behind him. Quickly he brought her up to speed on Elizabeth's case and how he'd come across the injured doorman. "Did you have any luck finding out when the tissue for Elizabeth O'Connor arrived and which techs were on duty then?" Tri-State would at least have the delivery time.

She scowled, looking deflated. "I don't know how to tell you, but the assignment schedules for that two-week period are missing. I spoke with Joan, the circulating nurse. She said Derek Ruger was the assigned OR tech for the O'Connor case, but we can't find the other records. This has never happened before. We might be able to check with payroll to see who punched in and out during that time frame. Right now they're going through an audit, so my request isn't at the top of their list. The hospital administrator and the legal department have been notified of the issue. They might be able to push my request to the top of the pile in a day or two."

"Thanks for all your efforts. If you find out something, give me a call."

Before he could say more, the nurse came out of the trauma room.

"Detective Miller, Mr. Drake is coming around a little, but the doctors believe he sustained a concussion. Is it really necessary that you speak with the patient now?"

"Yes. It's important I see him as soon as possible. This attack is connected to a case I'm working on."

Her eyes widened. "Here comes the doctor. You can ask him yourself, and I hope you get the idiot."

Jack turned to see the ER doctor leaving the trauma room. He stepped up and asked if he could speak with Mr. Drake for a few minutes.

"You have about two minutes before we send him to X-Ray. With his head trauma, he might not remember anything about what happened to him."

"Thanks." Jack entered the trauma room and introduced himself to the nurse who was recording vital signs into a computer. "The doctor gave me permission to ask Mr. Drake a question."

She glanced up from her work. "Of course, but don't push him too hard."

Jack nodded. He approached quietly and gently placed his hand on Drake's shoulder. "Fred, it's Detective Miller. Do you remember me?"

Drake's eyes opened slowly. "Yes," he whispered with effort.

"Did the man who hurt you ask about the package you received for Dr. O'Shaunessy?"

"Yes."

"Can you tell me what he said? Did you see his face?"

"Didn't see his face." Drake took a labored breath. "He said I ruined everything because I called you. The police."

The monitor alarm shrilled as the blood pressure reading climbed. The nurse hurried over. "I'm going to have to ask you to leave," she said.

"Okay." He squeezed Drake's shoulder once more. "Don't worry about anything. You just get better. I'll have a 24-hour guard outside your room so you'll be safe."

The alarm sounded again. The nurse frowned. "Detective Miller, I insist you leave now." At that moment the doctor raced back in with an orderly and told the team to move the patient to X-Ray and CAT scan immediately.

Jack stepped out of their way and headed to the nurses' desk. He showed his badge and asked the secretary to page Amy Cook. When she answered, the secretary handed him the phone.

"Jack, what can I do for you?" Amy asked.

"This wasn't a robbery. Mr. Drake was targeted because he's involved in another case of mine. The individual we're after is really one sick guy. Mr. Drake has seen him twice and might be able to identify him. Do you have a room close to a nurses' station so there are more eyes on Mr. Drake?"

"Excuse me. I have to answer this other call." Amy clicked off, then back a minute later. "They're taking him to surgery. The CAT scan revealed some damage and clots. Mr. Drake will go directly to ICU, but you can still post a guard."

"Is he going to make it?" Fear hung on his every word. After all, he was the one who'd asked Drake to call if Claire received any more deliveries. If anything happened to him, it was totally on Jack.

"He should do okay, but we'll keep him sedated for a while. He may not have any memory of the incident after he comes around."

"As long as he's all right, I can live with it." But if anything happened to Claire, well, that would be a different story.

"I'm being paged again. I have your cell. If there's any change, either way, I'll call you."

# Chapter 31

Jack stared at his cell sitting in the palm of his hand. He almost wished someone would call with a wrong number, so he could delay making the calls he needed to make.

Patrick was his first call. They ran through all the possible scenarios and his partner agreed Fred Drake needed a 24-hour guard.

"I hate to say it, but he'll be safer in ICU. With fewer patients, strangers will be more noticeable," Patrick said. "Have you told Frankie and Claire what's happened?"

"No. I only called Frankie long enough to make sure he stayed with Claire when I discovered it was Fred in the alley."

"How about I call Captain Ramos and arrange the 24-hour detail, while you check on my sister and our Italian friend? Also, you need to check with the building manager in case Fred has family we need to call."

"Consider it done. If he isn't all right, it's my fault. I'm the one who suggested Fred call me if Claire received a package."

"Jack, you're not to blame," his partner answered. "First of all, let's give him a chance to recover. You know as well as I do, in this business shit happens and we have no control. I need to reach Ramos so we have the guard in place when Fred comes out of recovery. Keep in touch. I'll call you with confirmation on the guard."

"Okay. I'll head back to Claire's building and find out what I can about Fred's family. I'll see if they've been notified. Amy Cook is one of the nursing directors. I can give her a heads-up that a guard is on the way. Catch you later."

Drained, Jack headed downstairs. His reserve hovered near empty. *Where did this night go wrong?* The thought sickened him as he realized this horrible person had staked out Claire's building and intended to injure the doorman, or worse.

He walked out of the hospital's front lobby, then remembered he'd left his car at Claire's. *Oh, what the hell*, he thought and hailed a cab.

When he arrived at the condo, he obtained the name of the building manager and told the night doorman what had happened to Fred Drake. He kept to himself the part about the heart and his conviction that Fred had been targeted. Once upstairs in Claire's apartment, he called the building manager and asked about Fred's family. Fred was single but had a brother in Wheaton. Jack contacted him and explained what had happened, including what time Fred went into surgery, then gave him the hospital phone number along with his own cell number.

After the call, Jack closed his eyes and let out a sigh of relief as he faced Claire and Frankie.

"Do you want a beer before you fill us in?" Frankie asked, standing with his hands on his hips.

"Thank you, but no," Jack answered. "This'll sound strange, but I'd love a glass of milk."

Claire laughed. "I don't believe you. You want milk?" She reached for a glass and set it on the counter. Frankie grabbed the container out of the fridge and poured.

"I find it calming, and calm is exactly what I need right now." Before he could go any further, Patrick called.

"Ramos has the detail all set up and he contacted the hospital. Did Fred have any family?"

"A brother in Wheaton. I just spoke with him. He has all the contact information. I expect him to arrive at the hospital within the hour."

"Where are you now?"

"At Claire's. I haven't had time to give them any details yet. Once I have, I'll head back to Chicago General to check on Fred and make sure the detail understands he's still vulnerable."

"Don't stay at the hospital too long. Get some sleep and I'll see you in the morning," Patrick said.

"Okay, partner." Jack dropped into a chair. In front of him on the kitchen table were the glass of milk and a bonus of fresh-baked brownies. "Thanks for the snack. Give me a minute and I'll tell you everything."

Claire sat opposite him with her hands folded on the table. "We're giving you one chance to come clean before I start with the Chinese torture."

"I'm so mentally exhausted you probably could take me out with one swing," Jack replied, then indulged in a bite of the warm brownie. "Okay, here it goes."

Revenge

# Chapter 32

Derek didn't consider himself a violent man. However, he believed his actions were justified. The Bible said, "An eye for an eye," and that was good enough for him. He reviewed the simple facts. His father had lost his job with Keeley Liquor Distributors so Michael Keeley could have a summer job. His mother left with another man because his father couldn't support them. And to top it off, his father died before Derek completed high school. Sure, he had some luck, if you could call it that, when the apartment building manager offered him the storeroom in the basement for free and helped him get public assistance for food.

But did the Keeleys experience anything other than a privileged life? *No*, he answered himself. *They had to pay.* Losing Elizabeth might be hard on them, but no harder than him losing both his parents and his home. *Bet they couldn't survive that*, he thought as he pushed the used surgical case cart into the elevator and touched the down button for sterile processing.

Debbie, the charge nurse, approached him. "Derek, could you run these papers over to the ICU? The surgeon forgot to put them with the patient's chart because he had an emergency case in OR Number 7."

"Okay," he answered as she handed them to him. Just another example of people thinking they're so high and mighty that someone else should clean up after them. He knew how the OR worked. The surgeons acted like everything was life and death as they raced to the scrub sinks outside the surgical suites, only to stand there and trade stock tips with their peers while they took their own sweet time performing a sterile scrub. He could take a complete bath in the amount of time they spent at the sinks and he wouldn't have to worry about trading one damn share of stock.

Derek put on a cover gown and walked next door to the ICU. Alarms blasted and staff were running back and forth to the supply area and the Pyxis, an automated medication dispensing system.

115

He entered the nurses' station and placed the copies in the correct patient's chart. He started to leave when he noticed the police guard outside the room across the hall. "What gives?" he asked the ICU secretary, pointing to the police guard.

She looked like she couldn't wait to share the gossip. "The patient was attacked and the police are concerned whoever it was might try to come back and take Mr. Drake out. He's a doorman at a condo building over on Indiana, near the lake."

Cold swept through Derek. It took effort to keep his shock from showing in his face. "He must be important if he has a guard."

"Have no idea. I heard he drifted in and out of consciousness in the ER prior to the surgery. They have him sedated at the moment. That's all I know."

"Hope he makes it," Derek said and then left. He hadn't made it past the ICU automated doors before he felt his heart bouncing from one side of his ribcage to the other. *What if the doorman could identify him? Another threat!* The doorman had to be eliminated. Derek needed some breathing space to work on a plan.

Back in the PACU area he yelled to the clerk that he was taking a break. He grabbed a can of pop from a vending machine near the locker room and sat on one of the benches for a long moment, rolling the can back and forth in his hands while his mind raced through all the possibilities. Just as he rose to return to work, Kumar entered the locker room. He saw Derek and frowned in concern.

"Are you okay?" Kumar asked.

"Yeah," Derek replied. "The cafeteria food hasn't agreed with me lately."

"Do as I do, bring your own food. Much healthier and less expensive," Kumar said in his stilted English. "Are you done for the day? I'm headed home."

"No. I'm off in another hour. I think you're right about the food. Thanks for the tip." Derek entered one of the stalls, waiting for Kumar to leave. When he heard the locker room door close, he exited the stall. As he turned from using the sink, he glimpsed a small rectangular object under the bench. Kumar had dropped his hospital ID. Quickly, Derek grabbed it and slid it into his back pocket.

Then he remembered seeing the pharmacy tech unloading the IV bags, personally mixed for each patient, on top of the Pyxis waiting for the nurses to hang them. A plan began to unfold in his mind.

With renewed energy, Derek made his final rounds. His job was to place the correct case cart in the right surgical suite for the first cases in the morning. Diligently he checked the surgical schedule and double-checked the tag on each cart to make sure the instruments matched the doctor and the procedure, and pulled each doctor's preferred sutures. As he made his way around the unit, he opened the lid on the large floor container for syringes and unused medications.

In the fifth suite, he found what he needed: a half empty bottle of Propofol, a medication used to sedate patients during surgery. It rested on top of the pile of discarded medication vials and syringes. Using his hemostat, which looked a little like a fine pair of pinched nose pliers, he carefully reached in and removed the medication. The bottle was double the usual size he saw in operating rooms. Perhaps pharmacy substituted this size because they'd run out of the smaller size normally used by anesthesiologists.

His next step would be a dangerous one. He had to get the medication into one of the doorman's IV bags without getting caught. He knew from his years of listening to anesthesiologists training new residents that an overdose of Propofol could cause seizures, a drop in blood pressure, an irregular heart rate and cessation of breathing. Any one of those side effects would work for his purpose.

Once he'd finished in the operating room, he grabbed a large syringe. In a bathroom stall, he filled the syringe with Propofol. The he stuck it his back pocket and pulled his scrub top over the pocket to hide it. Next, he clocked off the unit. He exited via the main entrance to the OR, then used Kumar's ID to re-enter the unit. He slipped into the storeroom and took a couple IV bags for props, then walked into the back area of the ICU. Checking the area first, he discovered the nurses were either busy or in the conference room having dinner. Pretending to restock, he looked on the Pyxis for an IV bag marked with the same bed number as the room with the guard. He removed the IV bag, walked into the ICU storage room, and emptied the syringe into the port. He held his breath as he came back out, leaving the other IV fluid bags on the shelf and replacing the contaminated one on top of the Pyxis. Now all he had to do was wait.

A few minutes later, he cleaned Kumar's ID badge with an alcohol wipe and placed it back on the floor in the locker room. Then he fled the unit.

# Chapter 33

Frankie pulled his black SUV behind the west side of the morgue because the front lot was barricaded off for repairs. Police cars filled the area. "What is this, a convention? I bet you get to cut up more dead people today."

Claire lightly socked him in his right arm. "They're called autopsies. Why can't you say that?"

Frankie laughed. "Because it's more fun to mess with you. My guess is more business has arrived, but I didn't hear anything on the morning news."

*Neither did I,* Claire thought. *This isn't good.* "I'll call you when I'm done."

"I don't see Ian. You can't go yet."

"Frankie, half the district is here. I think I'm safe. Besides, Patrick and Jack's car is parked just outside the west fence." She opened the car door and stepped down onto the pavement.

"What, no goodbye kiss or 'Have a nice day, dear'?" Frankie crossed his hands over his heart.

"Frankie, you're so full of it. Okay, have a nice day." She turned and blew him a kiss just for fun before heading into the morgue for what she feared would be one hell of a day.

"Dr. O'Shaunessy, over here," Ian yelled from the other side of the huge scale used for admissions near the morgue's back entrance.

"Hi, Ian. What's happening?" she asked.

"Let's get out of the way, then I'll tell you." Ian guided her down the back hallway.

Once they were clear of the chaos, she said, "Okay, now spill the beans."

Before Ian could answer, Patrick walked up to them. "There you are," her brother said. "Let's go to your office."

"Now wait just a minute," Claire said. "I get the feeling you don't want me to see something. I'm not moving until one of you talks."

Ian bent his head.

Patrick sighed. "It's about Fred Drake. He had a cardiac arrest last night and the staff was unable to revive him. I'm sorry, Claire."

The news hit her like a punch to the stomach. "What? You've got to be kidding. He was stable last night. Was it because of the head trauma and surgery?"

"Hopefully we'll have some answers after Dr. Shah has completed the autopsy. Dr. Johnson assigned him the case. Thought you'd done enough autopsies on people you know."

Claire fled to the stairs and ran up to the second floor. She was knocking on Dr. Johnson's door before Ian or Patrick could catch up with her.

"Come in," Dr. Johnson called out. He glanced up from some papers, and a wary look crossed his face. "Good morning, Claire."

She stayed in the office doorway, arms firmly crossed. "I'm perfectly capable of performing Fred Drake's autopsy. My feelings don't need to be protected."

"Claire, I know that, but Dr. Shah was here and offered to get the case started. Why don't you join him?"

"Thank you." Claire spun around and was out of his office, heading for the stairs as Patrick and Ian arrived.

"Where are you going?" Patrick asked.

"To do my job. Come on, Ian, we have work to do."

Patrick tried to intervene. "But Dr. Johnson—"

"We discussed it and I won. Did you ask him to have someone else do my cases? By the way, where's Jack?" she asked, stopping for a moment.

"Back at the crime scene," Patrick replied.

"What crime scene?"

"Fred Drake's ICU room."

"How could someone murder him? I thought Captain Ramos assigned a 24-hour detail to his room. Where was the guard?"

"The room was always guarded. Even when the detail had to use the bathroom, hospital security covered for him. It's all documented. And before you say anything about coincidence, you already know how Jack and I feel about that issue."

"I'm with you on that. Are you sure the attack on Fred wasn't a random robbery? I know my neighborhood is relatively safe, but street robberies have occurred."

"Fred was targeted. When Jack tried to interview him for a few minutes in the emergency room, Fred said the guy asked about the package for you. Then he told Fred he'd, quote, 'ruined everything'."

For the first time since her father's murder back when she was in high school, she wanted to sit down and cry. Had her stalker murdered Fred Drake? The package with the human heart was ghoulish enough, but to kill Fred? What did this guy want? Who had she upset that much, that he was taking this to such extremes? Why didn't he just face her like a man so they could settle the problem?

"When Jack came by last night, he didn't mention what Fred told him in the emergency room," Claire said.

"He probably didn't want to upset you any more than necessary."

"When will you guys learn I don't need to be protected from all the evils in this world. I'm going to assist Dr. Shah. Are you joining me, Ian?"

Ian looked over to Patrick first.

"Go," Patrick said.

"I'm coming Dr. O'Shaunessy."

# Chapter 34

Because Fred Drake's case possibly resulted from murder, Claire knew Dr. Johnson had ordered the autopsy set up in a separate room from the other autopsies. Per protocol, the body and the immediate perimeter were treated as a crime scene. Next to Drake's autopsy table sat an additional table draped with a sterile cover. On it lay all the equipment connected to the victim. This included IV bags, tubing, tape, IV catheters, urine collection bag and electrodes. These items would be sent to the forensic lab for testing.

Chicago policemen guarded the two entrances to the room to prevent anyone from wandering in. Often students were present for rotation from local mortuary services, pathology residencies, and physician assistant programs. This area was off limits unless preapproved.

Claire flashed her ID and the policeman gave permission for her and Ian to enter. While they gloved, gowned and each put on a protective mask, Dr. Shah ran over his findings and discussed the labs sent. He'd just finished the abdominal cavity and was examining the heart and lungs.

"Do you see any signs of heart disease?" Claire asked as she approached the table.

Dr. Shah held the heart in his hands. "No, none." He turned the heart over and checked it carefully. "I don't doubt that he flat-lined and the staff coded him, but not because of coronary artery disease." Next he examined the lungs while Claire watched. "Nothing here, either."

"Maybe there was a medication error or he suffered a reaction to one of the medications they administered."

"We'll have to wait for the labs to come back to see what they say." Dr. Shah weighed the heart and lungs. "Both organs are the appropriate weight. I'm doing the cranium next. Do you want to assist?"

"Of course I do. I want to know what caused his death. He should be alive and recovering in ICU, not being autopsied."

Ian removed the body block from under the victim's back and placed it under the neck to provide support for the head. He handed Dr. Shah a scalpel to release the scalp and soft tissue.

Once the scalp had been pulled back, Claire could see the bore holes made during surgery to relieve pressure from the intracranial bleed. Also, she could visualize the indented fractures as a result of a hard object hitting the back of the head.

Dr. Shah took photos at each step for further analysis. Next he used the electric Stryker saw to open the skull. He manually removed the brain and placed it on the scale. Afterwards he put it on a surgical towel on the mayo stand for further investigation.

"Now you can really see the fractures. Would you like the honors?" Dr. Shah asked Claire.

"Thank you." Claire delicately turned the brain over, examining every centimeter thoroughly. She owed it to Fred to do the best job she could. She knew the brain as well as she knew the streets of Chicago, but nothing stood out. Expected bruising appeared where the fractures occurred.

"I don't see anything other than what we anticipated from the injury. You take a look," she said to Dr. Shah, and watched him perform the same examination.

"I agree with your assessment," he said. "Perhaps the labs will hold the answer. Since we have a full docket today, I'll have Ian finish closing for me while I record the information in the chart. This will free you up to get ready for the next case."

"Sounds like a plan. Thanks, Dr. Shah."

At the first break she could get, Claire returned to her office and called Patrick. He picked up immediately. She relayed the tentative results of the autopsy and mentioned it would be several days before the lab completed the preliminary tests. "Whatever this man hit Fred with caused a round indentation in his skull, more like from a tube, not like a baseball bat. Also, Dr. Shah and I didn't find any coronary disease. Did Jack turn up anything?"

Patrick shared the latest developments on their end. "Right now it looks like an employee named Kumar re-entered the surgical area after he clocked out last night. Housekeeping found his hospital ID on the floor of the OR men's locker room. Also,

Central Supply found discrepancies in the IV solution bag count in the OR and the ICU when they came to restock this morning. The OR was short, while the ICU was overstocked."

"That's weird. Could this guy Kumar have taken some IVs over to ICU, claiming he was restocking in hopes of getting close to Fred?" Claire asked.

"That sounds plausible, but Jack met this guy before and doesn't think he had anything to do with the IV bags or Fred. He's thinks Kumar is being set up, but we don't know why or by whom."

Suddenly she felt angry. And sad and exhausted, but mostly angry that someone was hurting people and she couldn't stop him. "Patrick, it's my fault Fred is dead. Someone out there really has it in for me. In the meantime, he's taking his revenge out on others. Maybe we should set a trap for him to get close to me so you and Jack can take him down before anyone else gets hurt."

She could hear the scowl in Patrick's voice. "I don't like the idea of using you as bait."

"Well, do you have a better idea?"

"Not at the moment, but I definitely don't like your suggestion.

# Chapter 35

"Detective Miller, when do I get my ICU unit back? Recovery is backed up with fresh surgicals waiting for ICU beds while we have patients we need to transfer out to the floors."

Jack turned to find Amy Cook standing in the middle of the ICU nurses' station with her arms crossed over her chest, looking none too pleased. He couldn't blame her. The evidence techs had taken over a good piece of real estate outside Fred Drake's former room. They'd spread their equipment cases and their labeled collection bags in rows.

"Let me check with the techs and see how close they are to being done," Jack said. "Sorry we created such a scene."

She sighed. "It's okay. I'd appreciate the techs finishing up as soon as possible."

"Consider it done." Jack returned to the ICU room. "Jerry, how close are you to packing up?"

The tech, a fortyish guy built like a fullback, waved a hand. "Ed went down to our van for some larger containers. Once he's back we'll be out of here in no time at all."

A few minutes later, Ed returned and Jack helped them pack the collected evidence. Housekeeping stood by ready to clean the room. They looked surprised when they discovered not a drop of trash remained.

Back in his car in the hospital parking lot, Jack had just turned the key in the ignition when he got a call from hospital security. "The employee who reentered the operating room after his shift last night just arrived for work. We're holding him in the security office."

"I'll be right in." Jack immediately called Patrick. They decided to meet for the interview since Patrick was only a block away.

A short while later, Patrick met Jack in the hospital security office. After a brief exchange of information about the crime scene and the autopsy, they entered an inner room where Kumar sat with a security guard.

Jack nodded to him. "Kumar, I'd like you to meet my partner, Detective O'Shaunessy."

Kumar bowed his head slightly and said hello. He looked confused, and more than a little nervous.

"We'd like you to start with the beginning of yesterday's work day and walk both of us through everything you did." Jack said it casually, like it was no big deal. The calmer people were, the better they remembered things—and he felt sure Kumar wasn't their guy. "Include co-workers' names and times, when possible."

Kumar rested his folded hands on the table. "My day was much like any other," he began. Slowly he listed his activities as Jack made notes. He referred to the cases assigned to him and his particular duties for each, and listed who he worked with and his other assignments on the unit. He'd taken his lunch of chicken and rice in the break room, and he named other employees who were present. At the end of his shift, he'd clocked out on the computer, changed his clothes and left the hospital. He hadn't realized he'd dropped his ID in the locker room until this morning. When he reported it to security, they told him housekeeping had found it and he could pick it up in their office with identification.

"Can you explain how your ID was used to reenter the unit after you left?" Jack asked.

Kumar shook his head. "No."

"At any time yesterday, did you go to the ICU?"

"No."

Patrick broke in. "Kumar, I know this is a busy unit, but did anything strike you as out of place or different during your shift?"

The OR tech paused for a moment to reflect. "Nothing that I can think of, except I ran into Derek Ruger in the locker room when I went to change to go home. He told me his lunch from the cafeteria wasn't agreeing with him. I suggested he bring something from home, which would be healthier and cheaper. Other than that, everything seemed normal."

Jack glanced at Patrick, then nodded. "I want to apologize for the disruption in your schedule today. Your charge nurse, Debbie, tells me you're very dedicated and efficient. I don't think I'll have any more questions for you, but if I do, I'll contact Debbie to notify you to call me. Here's my card. If something comes to mind, no matter what time of the day, please call."

Kumar took the little cardboard rectangle. "I will take this one home with me. I taped the one you gave me at the meeting inside my locker."

"Thank you for your time," Patrick said. They exchanged pleasantries, shook hands, and then Kumar left the room.

The minute the door closed, Jack spoke. "The name Derek Ruger seems to be popping up a lot recently. He was the operating room tech for Elizabeth's case. I met him when I arranged a meeting with some of the staff regarding the handling of donor tissue. He seemed a little . . . I don't know, different, but I really didn't spend much time with him."

"I thought the name sounded familiar. I remember Claire telling me she spoke with him," Patrick said.

Jack scowled. "We're missing something. I can feel it. It's right here in front of us. What was it Fred Drake said to me in the ER?" He thought for a moment. "I remember now. I asked Fred if the man who hurt him asked about the package for Claire, and he said yes. Fred also told me his attacker said Fred had ruined everything because he called the cops."

Patrick stared hard at the table before meeting Jack's eyes. "How many different people have made deliveries to Claire lately? I'm guessing it's the same guy. This scares the hell out of me."

"She's safe at work and with Frankie. Let's pick up lunch and head back to the office. We have a wake and funeral to get through."

# Chapter 36

Grateful Jack hadn't commented on his choice for lunch, Patrick took a bite out of the first hamburger he'd had since his heart attack. He'd skipped the fries and milk shake and opted for bottled water. The crisp lettuce and sliced ripe tomato on top of the handmade beef patty were pure heaven. They'd picked up their lunch from Ralph's Fine Dining, a small hole in the wall restaurant near their office, which always had a line for lunch. Actually, they had two lines. One for the men in blue and one for the lunchtime customers. Ralph's son served in the 23rd District.

Jack pulled out his cell phone.

"You're not sending Sylvia or Claire a picture of my lunch, are you?" Patrick opened his desk drawer, ready to slide his prize burger into it for protection.

"No." Jack laughed. "After what we've been through the last few days, I think you deserve one of Ralph's burgers. I wanted to check in with Claire to see if she learned any more about Fred's death." Jack's call went to voice mail. "She must be in the autopsy suite. I'll try her again later if she doesn't return my call. Where are we on the plans for Elizabeth's services?"

"McDuffy's Funeral Home will have the private wake for family and selected close friends tomorrow at noon. Captain Ramos is concerned about the family's safety. So we need to have them out and gone by one-thirty, before the public wake begins at two."

"I bet Michael and Claire's names were on the top of Ramos's list," Jack said. He ate a mouthful of his Italian beef sandwich and washed it down with a gulp of coffee.

"Even though the two cases aren't connected, the anticipated attendance at these events, we could bring out two different crazies." Patrick chowed down another bite of burger. "With all the distractions they may be willing to take a shot at their respective targets, while others end up as collateral damage."

"Have you told Claire what time she's to attend the wake?" Jack asked.

"Not yet, but I notified Frankie and asked him to have his brother Sol assist. He'll drop them off at the wake and be waiting with the car to take Claire back to work and Frankie to the condo."

"What about the funeral at St. Pat's?"

Patrick grabbed a napkin and wiped burger grease from his lips. "Could you call Father Murray and explain the situation? Again, we need Sol to drop Claire and Frankie off for the service, but enter the church through a rear door. Headquarters is coordinating the family gathering at McDuffy's first. Then a police escort will follow the funeral procession to the church. Some streets will be temporarily blocked that morning."

"Are Claire and Frankie skipping the reception at the adjoining school?"

"Do you think Claire would agree? No, but we can put them in the funeral procession from the church to the cemetery. They should be relatively safe. I spoke with Captain Ramos early this morning and he wants us out there in the crowd. Headquarters is assigning a special undercover detail to mix with the attendees. They're aware of not only the potential threat to the mayor, but of Claire's problems as well. They're working with local TV stations covering the events, asking the stations to assign an extra cameraman to scan the audience in hopes of identifying any threats." Patrick sipped water. "Of course, the deal includes the stations being allowed to carry the story once we have the person or persons in custody."

"I wonder if any of the new facial recognition software would help," Jack said.

"My guess, old-fashioned police work will solve the case. I suggested to Captain Ramos that we review copies of the footage filmed the night they brought Elizabeth to the morgue. Maybe we'll recognize someone in the background hanging out to admire his work?"

Jack's phone rang. *Claire*, he mouthed over to Patrick before he answered. "Hi, Claire. Can I put you on speaker so Patrick can hear?"

Patrick looked up from finishing his burger.

"Give me a second," Jack said. "Okay, I'm ready. Shoot."

While Claire filled them in, Patrick drank his water and Jack finished his Italian beef. She hadn't learned much more, but felt confident the perpetrator struck Fred with a tubular-shaped object. Of course the labs weren't back yet. She'd found one interesting mark the size of a large muzzle or maybe a gun barrel on the back of Fred's jacket. She'd sent the jacket to have it analyzed.

"Thanks, Claire." The noise level rose as several officers returned from lunch break, so Jack took her off speaker. "By the way, Sol and Frankie will pick you up tomorrow at about eleven-forty in the morning to take you to the wake. We've cleared your attendance through Dr. Johnson. There's a private wake before the public viewing."

Claire must have asked about the funeral, because Patrick heard Jack tell her he was working on the arrangements before he said goodbye. "Did she give you any argument?"

Jack laughed. "Nope. Should I take her temperature?"

"Just count your blessings. I'm sure she's not done."

# Chapter 37

Claire closed the last chart after calling Frankie. She was tired of being told what to do by her brother, his partner and her long-time good friend and current bodyguard. She'd play along until after all of Elizabeth's services were over. If nothing else happened by then, she'd go back to her old life, making her own decisions. This nut job hadn't made any new attempts to contact her. Surely he'd moved on by now. She almost believed it, except for this big 'but' that stuck in the back of her mind.

The flower delivery was eerie, but not threatening. The leaking box with the human heart had been the game changer. As before, she knew there were a limited number of places to obtain a fresh heart. But had he been the one who attacked her doorman from behind? Did his sick plan include murder? If so, she'd never forgive him for that.

She questioned whether Fred's murder had ended the problem . . . or had her stalker sent a deranged message with an even darker ending?

Since receiving the heart, Claire had quietly contacted coroners and the offices of medical examiners within a six-hour drive of Chicago. So far, her search had turned up no leads. They were all horrified at what had happened, but no one had seen any bodies with missing hearts.

Yesterday, she'd started on the list she'd prepared of hospital pathology departments. Again, she turned up empty-handed. Next, she'd target funeral homes. The deceased arrived either intact or previously autopsied. If autopsied, the internal organs were contained in a red bag inside the abdominal cavity. If someone removed a heart at a funeral home, he'd risk getting caught in the act unless guaranteed privacy. If he removed the red bag for the heart, there'd likely be a mess and again, the threat of being exposed. Where did he get that heart?

With no answers at hand, Claire took her completed charts down to Dr. Johnson, but discovered he had left for the day. She returned with the stack and slid them into the file cabinet. Checking her watch, she noticed it was after six. She gathered her personal items and hurried down to the back bay entrance to wait for Frankie. The construction on the front parking lot wouldn't be complete for another week.

Stuck inside the building since early in the morning, she opened the door and stepped outside to enjoy the crisp fall air. The sun had already gone down and the street lights cast an enchanting glow against the clear, dark sky. A few strides took her to the center of the parking lot, where she stood listening to the fall leaves scurrying across the pavement in the early evening quiet.

"What are you doing out here?"

Claire jumped as Frankie's harsh voice penetrated her mental vacation. Turning around, she said, "You scared me half to death, Frankie Biaggi! I was consuming some much needed fresh air. Even I tire of the smells of the morgue."

"Be glad it was me. Get in the car. Jack's going to have a fit when he hears about your lack of concern for your safety."

Frankie slammed the driver's-side door so hard, Claire was amazed the latch didn't break. She climbed into the black SUV, shut her door and connected her seat belt while Frankie squealed out of the lot and around the corner onto East Harrison Street. "Please don't be mad. I just needed some peace and quiet, and fresh city air."

"I can't help it if you cut up dead people for a living, but I'll request they tie your butt to your office chair if you ever do that again. Wait inside for me, got it?"

She caught Frankie expressing a sigh of relief about three blocks down as they waited for the light to turn green. "Okay. I promise to wait inside from now on. I had a hard day. We autopsied my doorman. Maybe he'd be alive if he hadn't been asked to hold my packages. I can't get it out of my mind that I'm responsible for his death."

"Jack had your packages held after the flower delivery incident to protect you. He's concerned for you. He didn't know this crazy person would go after Fred," Frankie said. "None of this is your fault."

"I don't need Jack's protection," Claire responded quietly. "The only reason I'm agreeing to Jack's plans is to spare Patrick the stress."

"Sometimes I think you're blind," Frankie murmured. "You don't see Jack has feelings for you."

Exhausted from her day, Claire chose to ignore Frankie's mumblings and focused on the full moon rising directly in front of them. She caught glimpses between the buildings as they drove down Harrison Street, and prayed this nightmare would end soon.

# Chapter 38

"Good evening and welcome to the nightly news for WTLV Chicago. I'm Scott Christie.

"And I'm Jillian Garcia."

Derek watched the news from his favorite chair with a mug of warm milk.

"Jillian," Scott said, "you reported from the back of the Office of the Medical Examiner for Cook County the night Elizabeth O'Connor's body was transported there from Chicago General Hospital. What was the mood of the observers?"

"Sobering, Scott. Elizabeth O'Connor was loved by many Chicagoans. Her death has been a blow to all of us. This will be a great loss for all the programs she chaired for the children and the underprivileged of our city. I hope the community will step up and carry on her work."

"Jillian, you made a good point. Mrs. O'Connor gave so much of herself to the people of Chicago. If our viewing audience would like to help, they can contact the mayor's office or go to the mayor's web page. The phone number and web address will run continuously at the bottom of our screen for the remainder of our broadcast. You can also find them on our website, WTLV."

Jillian Garcia spoke again. "There will be a public wake tomorrow at McDuffy's Funeral Home, from two in the afternoon to seven in the evening. Because of the anticipated crowd, the Chicago Police urge attendees to take public transportation if possible. The funeral mass will be by invitation only on the following day. WTLV will be broadcasting live the arrival of Mrs. O'Connor at St. Patrick's Church. Also, our viewers are welcome to watch the funeral procession from Heritage Green Park, across the street from St Patrick's Church on the corner of Adams and Des Plaines streets. A private burial service is planned for the family at Mt. Carmel Cemetery, in Hillside. The family requests that instead of flowers, donations be made to any one of the programs Elizabeth O'Connor chaired.

"On a happier note, Ted Donaldson is going to give us a rundown on Chicago sports."

Derek turned the news off. He didn't care about sports. Why should he? They'd never had money for such extravagances. His father never took him to a baseball game like other dads did for their sons. The emptiness and pain of his childhood never quite left him.

*Focus,* he reminded himself. The evening news had given him the information he needed to make his next move. If the wake was public, the family wouldn't be present. The crowds outside St. Patrick's Church posed too many problems, but the burial had potential. He had just the right ticket to get in to what would be a well-guarded cemetery.

After returning his empty mug to the kitchen sink, he researched Mt. Carmel Cemetery on the Internet. The cemetery had a lot of Italians, with an Irish section just off to the northwest of the Bishop's Mausoleum. It was easy to pick out the Irish graves from the satellite view. Headstones marked those graves, while the Italian families used the small mausoleums that looked like miniature row houses. A freshly dug grave would be easy to find on a quick drive through the cemetery.

He bided his time and prepared the final details. In a few days, his mission would be complete. Derek had considered the possibility that he would have to leave Chicago. A few months ago he'd arranged for fake identification, opened a new bank account, rented a small apartment and purchased a used car in Little Rock, Arkansas. He'd parked the new car with the out-of-state plates safely in the garage space he'd rented and left his old car on the street. His long-term plan was to head to California. It was foolproof.

His last detail was deciding what to take with him and packing the car. He would have to do it one piece at a time so as not to draw attention. No more long Chicago winters for him. He envisioned warm sunny days enjoying the Pacific Ocean, satisfied that he'd achieved his ultimate goal.

# Chapter 39

Jack checked his watch before dialing Father Murray. The pastor should be in the rectory office after saying morning mass and having his breakfast.

"Good morning, St. Patrick's Church. This is Mary O'Brien. How may I help you?"

"Good morning, Mary. I'm Detective Jack Miller. I've been assigned to Elizabeth O'Connor's funeral. I need to speak with Father Murray regarding the final arrangements for the funeral and cemetery service."

"One moment, please. I'll get Father Murray for you."

A few minutes, later Father Murray picked up. "Sorry to keep you waiting, Detective Miller. You caught me giving final instructions to our maintenance staff. The public is unaware of all the behind-the-scenes preparations that go into a funeral of this magnitude."

"No problem, Father."

"What can I do for you and the Keeley family?"

Jack relayed tomorrow's plans for the wake at McDuffy's Funeral Home through the burial service on the following day at Queen of Heaven Cemetery Chapel, located across Roosevelt Road from Mt. Carmel Cemetery, where Mrs. O'Connor would be laid to rest.

"One of our main concerns is always the safety of everyone in attendance, but more to the point, the mayor and his family. Everyone coming to the funeral and post reception must be on the approved list. The invitations will be numbered. How many altar boys will you need for the burial service at Queen of Heaven?"

"Usually two, but I can use Mr. McDuffy's son, Daniel. He's helped in the past."

"Everyone at McDuffy's Funeral Home is already on board. We'll have you ride in the hearse with Daniel. Also, the family will be having a private wake tomorrow at noon, two hours before the public wake. Because of the volume of expected cars, I'll drive you over." Jack didn't share his other main reason, which was to check on Claire. He'd learned from experience, if she got something in her head, she would take off on her own, no matter what the risks.

"If there's anything else you need, please call me at any time," Father Murray said.

"Thank you, Father. One last detail—is the exact time for the funeral on the following day at ten in the morning?

"Generally our funerals are at that time. So far the Keeleys haven't requested anything different. I'll have Mary call you if there're any changes. In the meantime, I'll pray for everyone's safety."

No sooner had Jack said goodbye to Father Murray than his phone rang. Patrick's cell number came up on his caller ID.

"Sorry my lab draw took so long. Flashing my badge didn't get me to the front of the line like I'd hoped. Do you mind if I take Sylvia over to pick up our car from Biaggi's garage?" Patrick asked.

"Go for it." A beep sounded on phone. "Have another call. Bye, Patrick." Jack clicked off, then switched to the incoming call. "Detective Miller speaking."

A deep, gruff voice sounded in his ear. "Just the person I wanted to talk to. I'm Detective Jim Garrett, from the Rockford Police Department. I have the results from the surveillance tapes you requested. However, it's not what you're hoping for. Per the tracking number, the package was sent from a site near Rockford College. The sender appears to be an older woman wearing a dress and hat, but our IT Department couldn't get a visual on her face. Also, the sender used a fake address. My guess is the person knew exactly what she was doing and may not even be from my area."

"I wonder if this was a disguise, because of a previous incident." Jack relayed the flower episode and shared the information that the target was his partner's sister.

"I'll keep you informed if we come up with any other footage from area security cams. Give my best to your partner and his sister."

Jack thanked the detective and disconnected. Now for that cup of coffee. Halfway across the room his cell rang. Several four-letter words ran through his mind. He put his cup down and answered. "Detective Miller speaking."

The voice on the other end was female this time. "This is Chris from Paul Keeley's office. Would you and Detective O'Shaunessy be available sometime this afternoon? I've set up an interview by Skype with Bill Stevens' father. You might remember I mentioned, Bill manages the loading docks. His father retired to Florida. Would two o'clock work for you?"

Jack checked his watch. Patrick should arrive soon and they could catch a bit of lunch on their way over to Keeley Liquor Distributors. "We'll be there. Thanks for setting this up, Chris. If the mayor is available, may he join us?"

"By all means, yes. I'll put a fresh pot of coffee on and scare up some snacks. There's a bakery to die for only minutes away."

"That would be most appreciated, but if the mayor comes with, you might want to drop that last line."

"Not a problem. I'll confirm with Bill, his father and Paul. See you at two."

With the promise of decent coffee later, Jack skipped the office lead and phoned the mayor's office. After he identified himself and the purpose of his call, the secretary put him right through.

"Mayor Keeley speaking."

"Mayor, this is Detective Jack Miller, Patrick's partner. Your brother Paul's secretary set up a Skype appointment with retired Keeley employee, Gary Stevens, this afternoon at two. Would you like to attend with Patrick and me? We could pick you up at one-thirty."

"Yes, I would. I have a couple of meetings scheduled this afternoon, but this takes precedence. I'll be ready. Just phone my secretary when you're about ten minutes away and I'll come down."

"Not a problem," Jack answered.

"Thanks for including me. See you in a couple of hours."

As Jack slipped his cell phone in his pocket, a familiar voice asked if anything special was going on. He turned to see his missing partner enter the squad room.

# Chapter 10

Chris ushered Michael, Patrick, and Jack into Keeley Liquor Distributors' spacious meeting room. Jack was impressed with the large rosewood table, accompanying soft leather chairs, and photo prints of Chicago. A sideboard held several carafes of coffee and hot water for tea, cups, condiments, and two large platters that should have come with a warning sign: *These items will require two hours of power walking or one hour of intense jogging.*

Paul and Bill entered a few minutes after Jack's group had settled into the chairs with their coffee. After they exchanged greetings and handshakes, Chris pushed the controls and a large screen slid down from the ceiling. *No fifteen-inch monitor screen for Keeley Liquors*, Jack thought.

"Is everyone ready?" Chris asked. "Okay, Bill, work your magic." She poured herself a cup of coffee before taking a chair at the far end of the table.

Bill ran his fingers over a keyboard and within seconds the screen lit up. An older-looking version of Bill appeared, sporting a Florida tan. "Hi, Dad," Bill said. "How's the weather?"

The older man's broad smile filled the screen. "Eighty degrees and sunny!" Gary Stevens answered.

"Everyone, I'd like you to meet my dad, Gary Stevens." Introductions went around the table. Then Bill cleared his throat. "Dad, I know you're aware of Elizabeth O'Connor's passing, but like I said when we spoke a couple days ago, there's a concern about how she died. Detectives O'Shaunessy and Miller are working her case. Would you be up to a few questions?"

Gary was looking somber now. "You better believe I am. The Keeleys are good people. I'll do everything I can to help. Mayor Keeley, please give my condolences to your family."

Michael nodded in response.

Patrick addressed Gary. "My partner and I have some questions that may take you way back in time. I don't know if Bill told you, but we think the Keeley family has been stalked for the past fifteen years or more. Historically, I understand Keeley Liquor Distributors operated out of several locations. Which ones were you employed at?"

"Actually, I worked at all three warehouses, Bensenville, Schiller Park and Addison."

"Okay," Patrick replied. "I want to go back to fifteen to twenty years ago, approximately the five years before Mary Ann Keeley had that devastating bike accident. Where were you working at that time?"

"That's easy. I'd only been with the company a few years. I started out at the Bensenville warehouse, where they stored all the hard liquor, and some beer and wine. I was young and could still lift those heavy cartons of booze."

Patrick moved to the edge of his chair. "Did anything happen that stuck in your mind?"

"In general, no." Gary looked thoughtful. "We had the usual competition among the drivers regarding who could fill and deliver the most orders for the week. Each Monday we'd tally the past week's orders, and Paul's dad put an extra fifty in cash in the winner's pay envelope. Anyone caught cheating, threatening fellow workers, or getting involved in a push and shove match was forever disqualified. Also, you could only win two weeks in a row."

"Back then fifty bucks was worth a lot more than today," Patrick said.

"It kept the drivers from slacking off, too. That incentive built the company."

"Of course Keeley family members weren't allowed in on the game," Paul said. "Dad felt we already had enough advantages in life."

"What about bad feelings?" Jack asked. "Maybe someone who never won."

"Actually, Dad's plan kept everyone on their toes," Michael said.

"Did anyone get fired during this time for cheating to get the bonus? Or for anything else—a bad evaluation, theft?" Jack asked.

"I'd almost forgotten," Gary said. "When I started working for Keeley Liquors, I heard one of the drivers had been fired for theft.

Not only did he steal booze, he sold the cases for half price to some unsavory bars the Keeleys refused to do business with."

Jack could see everyone in the room on the edge of their seats waiting for the name of the corrupt driver.

Dad, what was his name?" Bill said. "How did they catch him?"

"I think his name was George Ryder, or something like that. One of the other drivers stopped for a beer after work and saw him handing over a case of gin. The guy reported the incident to his supervisor and they set up a sting. They caught him red-handed."

"Do you know if a police report was filed?" Jack asked.

"I don't think so. I heard the guy was a jerk. He had a wife and son, and knowing Mr. Keeley, I'm sure he felt bad firing a man with a family to support."

"Maybe this guy has a record. Is there anything else you can think of that Jack and I should know?" Patrick asked.

"Not at the moment, but if anything comes to mind, I'll let Bill know."

"Thanks for your help. You never know where this might lead us."

"Give my love to Mom, and thanks for your help, Dad," said Bill.

"I will, and you take care."

Bill broke the connection.

For a brief moment everyone sat back and took a deep breath. Patrick spoke first. "Michael, Paul, I know this is a bad time for your family, but is there any chance you could approach your father and see what he remembers? It might be easier on him if you spoke with him first. Then he can make a formal statement to the police."

"The family is coming to dinner at my house tonight," Paul answered. "I'll make time to speak with him. The word *murder* hasn't come up between us, but my parents feel this was deliberately done to Elizabeth. We just can't figure why."

"I don't think she has—had—any enemies. They're after me." Michael headed for the door, his shoulders sagging. "I have a meeting. Jack, could you drive me back to the office?"

Patrick and Jack thanked Paul, Bill and Chris again for their help. "We'll keep you posted, but please have the family be careful," Patrick said.

After they got into Jack's car Patrick turned to Michael. "Does that name, George Ryder, mean anything to you?"

"I wish it did. Maybe Paul will have some luck with Dad tonight. I had to push my meeting with the aldermen to this evening, so I won't be there."

Minutes later, Jack dropped Michael off at his office. "Patrick and I will be in touch," Jack said.

# Chapter 11

Once Jack pulled into traffic, Patrick spoke. "I think we need to visit Finch." Finch was the department computer whiz, and the geek knew it. All the detectives relied heavily on his skills.

"What did it cost us on our last case?" Jack smiled. "One extra-large meal from the Golden Arches and you gave him a pair of tickets to a Chicago White Sox game."

"I hate to say it, he's expensive, but he's good," Patrick answered.

"Do you think this George Ryder would have carried a grudge all these years? By now he's probably past his late fifties. And remember, he'd have needed access to Elizabeth while she was in Chicago General. What skills could he have that would be useful in a hospital?" A second later, Jack yelled at a driver for cutting him off. If he hadn't had so much on his mind, he'd have written the jerk a ticket.

"Maybe it's the wife. What if her husband never got another decent job or left her to raise and support their child by herself? She'd be plenty mad. She'd have the ability to move around on the GYN floor, considering all the patients are women. She might be a nurse, an aide, a housekeeper, a ward secretary or a dietitian. As a woman, she could hold any number of jobs and have access to patients and supplies. Anything that'd give her the ability to infect Elizabeth with gas gangrene."

"You're forgetting all the other incidents, though. When the mayor's son was attacked on campus and his backpack stolen, he reported a man assaulted him. And when the niece, Brittany, was threatened in the parking lot, she reported a man tried to take her car with her son in the back seat."

"Okay. What if the wife paid someone to attack them?"

"The stakes must be worth it, or this person wouldn't have hung in there for all these years. The statute of limitations has to have run out on several of these attacks by now." Jack pulled in behind the station and grabbed the last spot.

A few minutes later he dropped his jacket off at his desk, and then he and Patrick headed upstairs to see their favorite computer geek. Finch was engrossed in a search for a fellow detective when they arrived. He motioned for them to take a seat, but kept his eyes glued to the screen.

"Do you believe this?" Jack asked his partner. "Now Finch practically has his own waiting room. I have a feeling his price will be more than one extra-large meal this time. Next it'll be prime rib with a baked potato and all the trimmings."

Patrick had to suppress a laugh. "If he finds George Ryder, I'll buy it for him. Heck, Michael would probably have it gift-wrapped and personally delivered."

Jack knew how much they had riding on this lead. It wasn't just a matter of finding the person responsible for Elizabeth's death, but preventing anyone else in the Keeley family from being a target. Meanwhile, he had Claire's safety on his mind as well. Of course he'd be concerned about his partner's sister, but was that all? She had a way of getting under his skin, which wasn't always bad.

"Okay, you two dicks, you're next," Finch called out.

Patrick and Jack didn't need a second invitation. They were at Finch's side in less time than it took to dial 9-1-1.

Jack wondered if Finch had eyes in the back of his head just like Jack's mother and cousin Irene had when he was a kid. Man, they were good. They caught him every time he stepped out of line, even if it involved a forbidden cookie before dinner. How he missed those days.

"Hey, how about showing some respect for this badge," Patrick said with a tinge of laughter as he eyeballed Finch's computer station. Finch had decorated it with prints of past missing persons.

Finch didn't look up from his computer. "Do you want my help or not?"

"What's the going rate for searching a name?" Patrick asked.

"My dad said to tell you thanks for the Sox tickets the next time I saw you. He'd be really excited about going to another baseball game. So what do you need?"

"Could you research a George Ryder, starting twenty years ago?"

Jack was impressed with Finch's skills as his fingers skimmed over the keyboard bringing up various sites. He knew the guy could be a jerk on occasion, but Jack had a deep respect for the help Finch provided them. Sure, Jack knew his way around various screens available to the department, but he could never dig through the lingo for all the sites as fast as Finch could.

"He's not in any of the state or federal prison systems. Also, I don't see an Illinois driver's license or state ID issued to him for twenty-three years. I'm checking death records now."

Jack watched Patrick try not to lean over Finch's shoulder, but he understood how anxious his partner was to solve this case for his old neighborhood friend. This was personal for Patrick and for Claire.

Finch sat back. "If I have the correct George Ryder, he died in what appears to be a drug deal gone bad about fifteen years ago, according to the police record. Looks like he's buried in a massive grave for unclaimed bodies at Homewood Memorial Gardens in Thornton Township, in southern Cook County. The county contracts out for graves for the indigent in many cemeteries since the Dunning site in northwest Chicago closed. I'll print out what I have. The police report number is in the upper right hand corner."

Jack listened to the printer cycle and spit out the sheet of paper. Finch grabbed it and handed it to Patrick, and they scanned it together.

"The three most important pieces of information are the police report number, date of birth, and date of death," Finch said. "I suggest you head to the Cook County Clerk's Office, Bureau of Vital Records in the Daley Center before they close and ask for Lillian Richards to pull the death certificate. There isn't anything Lillian doesn't know about where the dearly departed are buried."

Patrick offered his hand to Finch. "Once again I find myself in your debt."

"This wouldn't have something to do with the death of the mayor's sister, would it?" Finch asked.

Jack laughed. "If we don't answer your question, would that be a good enough answer?"

"I'll add it to a long line of secrets I'll be taking to my grave. Say hi to Lillian for me."

Finch's phone rang and he waved Jack and Patrick goodbye.

"I'm guessing Lillian is about to have a visit from two of Chicago's finest detectives," Jack said as they left the building and headed for his car.

"It's her lucky day," Patrick replied.

# Chapter 12

Parking was usually a pain around the Daley Center, but the parking gods must have been shining on them, Patrick thought as Jack zipped into an open space before the next car came by. "Now I know this is our lucky day. If we beat the rain into the Daley Center, it'll feel like we won the lottery."

They made a quick dash into the building as large droplets pounded the pavement behind them. The Bureau of Vital Records was located on the east concourse level. They flashed their badges at the counter and asked for Lillian Richards. Patrick checked his watch. They had ten minutes before the place shut down.

A middle-aged, dark-skinned woman with a multitude of thin braids tied back with a colorful scarf stuck her head around a cubicle wall. "I'm Miss Lillian. Can I help you?"

"A mutual friend of ours named Finch sent us. He raves about you all the time," Jack said.

"Does he now?" she replied as she approached the counter. "If he thinks I need more work, he's sadly mistaken." She waved her hand dismissively. "So, detectives, what can I do for you?"

After introducing himself and his partner, Patrick pulled out the sheet of paper. "We're looking for the death certificate for George Ryder. Here are the dates of birth and death."

"Well, this is a rare request. Usually, it's the lawyers looking for this kind of paperwork. Give me a moment to rev up the old, and I'm not joking about old, computer and I'll see what I can find for you."

Patrick checked his cell phone while they waited. "There's a text from Sylvia wanting to know when I'll be home for dinner. You're invited, of course. The menu includes green salad, baked potatoes and steak, but no buttery garlic bread. Boo!"

"Hey, don't complain. Knowing Sylvia, it'll taste better than any high-class restaurant in Chicago. I graciously accept, green salad and all. We should pick up flowers for her on the way to your house."

Patrick sent a text back to Sylvia. "Texting my wife seems weird."

"I bet your daughters would be proud of dear old Dad."

Before Patrick could comment on the dear old Dad reference, Miss Lillian returned with a death certificate in hand.

"Before I provide you with the answer to your prayers, I need a reason why you asked me to pull this particular death certificate."

"This is in regards to an ongoing case that I can't address," Patrick replied politely.

"Well, Mr. Detective, I have to fill out this here form and charge for it. How about you pick one of the offered reasons and make a donation to the Greater Chicago Food Depository collection container, and we'll call it even." Miss Lillian pointed to the container on the counter. "Our office is trying really hard to beat the other departments. We collected the most last year for Thanksgiving, so you can imagine how we would hate to lose this year."

"Jack, do you think we can spare some loose change for this lovely lady's good cause?"

They both pulled out their wallets and each deposited a twenty. "Would this cover it?" Patrick asked Miss Lillian.

"My gracious, yes! I'll check off the box for genealogical research. And now for the death certificate. I made each of you a copy. And don't worry, we lock the container up in a safe every night."

Jack and Patrick pored over the information on the certificate.

"Wait a minute, wasn't Homewood Memorial Gardens the cemetery back in 2010, where the Cook County sheriff's office found bodies stacked eight deep in a single grave?" Patrick asked.

"You're right about the eight pine boxes being stacked per grave, but wrong date," Miss Lillian said. "This hit the news in February 2011. It definitely was a disgrace. Now, can I do anything else for you, detectives before we close?" She pointed to the clock.

Patrick looked up. "Sorry we kept you late. We really appreciate your assistance. Here's my card in case you think of anything or if we can return the favor. If your supervisor questions why you ran late, just have him give me a call. Thank you, Miss Lillian."

Back in their car Patrick reread the death certificate. "Jack, there isn't a family contact or address listed."

"What about the wife and son?" Jack asked.

"All the information appears to come from the police report. Ryder's date of birth probably came off an Illinois driver's license or state ID. According to the police report he lived up in the Humboldt Park area. Do you feel like a drive before dinner?"

"Patrick, it's nearly six. Sylvia has dinner ready for us. How about we canvass the area early tomorrow morning before the wake? Besides, we might get a better feel in the daylight."

Patrick's face brightened. "I like your line of thinking. One more day won't make a difference, especially since Ryder's been dead for years."

# Chapter 43

"Ian, could you go ahead and close our gentleman while I wrap up recording the organ weights? We still have two more cases before I have to leave," said Claire.

"No problem, Dr. O'Shaunessy. What time is Mr. Biaggi picking you up?"

Claire laughed at hearing Frankie referred to as 'Mr. Biaggi'. He'd been 'Frankie' since she was a young girl. In her early twenties she had lost her . . . *not going there*, she reprimanded herself. Thank heavens Patrick never found out. She crossed her fingers that Jack would never learn the truth, either. "In about an hour," she answered, steadying her voice.

"Then we better get a move on or you'll be wearing your scrubs and smelling like the morgue," Ian replied.

"Hey, I thought I was the supervisor and should be the one pushing you!" Claire said.

Ian chuckled. "Sorry, but as the saying goes, I didn't get the memo."

"Thanks for the distraction. You really are the best." Ian had no idea how much she appreciated his banter, especially this morning. Not only was the morgue knee deep in autopsies, but her lunch break would be spent at Elizabeth's wake. Autopsies never affected her appetite unless they were children or someone she knew. But having to see someone she cared about in a casket took food off her lunch menu. This just shouldn't be.

*Focus,* she told herself. What paperwork she didn't complete this morning would be waiting for her when she returned later in the afternoon. Tomorrow, she would be off the entire day because of the funeral, reception and cemetery service, so today's work couldn't wait. The morgue was running at peak capacity. As she'd often heard Thomas say, "We're having a dead body pile-up," or, "There's standing room only in the autopsy suite." The morgue humor brought a slight smile to her face. The temperature had dropped outside for the last couple of weeks. One would think the criminals would want to stay inside.

Of course, not everyone passing under her knife died as a result of a violent crime. In her last case, the man died in a vehicle accident. He'd driven head-on into another car. Thankfully, the passengers in the other vehicle survived with no life-threatening injuries because they all had their seat belts on. She and the team had to determine why he crashed. Was he drunk? Did he fall asleep at the wheel? Or was he incapacitated as a result of a stroke or a heart attack? The police, lawyers, insurance companies and family were all waiting breathlessly for her answer.

Claire completed recording the weight of the organs as Ian pulled the drape over the body and moved it to the cooler. Thomas already had their next case set up in the bay across the room so this one could be cleaned. A few minutes later, she and Ian began the next autopsy.

They had completed the three assigned cases before Claire left to change. Ian would take a lunch break and help other pathologists until she returned. A wave of sadness rolled over her as she thought of Elizabeth, vibrant and alive one day and dead the next. It wasn't *right*. None of this was.

Quickly she freshened up in the locker room, then went to grab a snack in her office. She'd never felt less like eating, but made herself chow down an apple. Security would have enough to do at the wake without her toppling over. She'd just finished when Frankie arrived.

"Ready?" he asked. "Sol's waiting in the car."

She put on her jacket and grabbed her purse out of the bottom desk drawer. "You look nice," she said. She couldn't remember the last time she saw Frankie in a suit and tie. He usually wore jeans, a knit shirt and his black leather motorcycle jacket. He even had a fresh haircut.

"Thanks. I may not have known Elizabeth O'Connor personally, but this is a tragic loss for her family and the community. I hope they hang the person responsible for taking her life."

"Patrick will find him," she said with complete confidence. "Let's go."

A few minutes later, Sol dropped Frankie and Claire off at the assigned rear entrance to McDuffy's Funeral Home. They presented their IDs to the police and were waved inside. The funeral home staff guided them to the guest register and then into the chapel.

In spite of the request to give donations to Elizabeth's programs instead of flowers, the place overflowed with every conceivable fresh bloom and arrangement. The scent was pure heaven to Claire's nostrils, a far cry from the daily odors of her job. The public, of course, wouldn't know that all these gorgeous pieces had been individually checked upon arrival by personnel from the bomb and arson squad. Too many mass casualties from various explosive devices had occurred across the county and Chicago refused to make the list, if at all possible.

Besides checking the floral arrangements, the police department had set up two metal detectors at the entrance to the funeral home. With Elizabeth's death a possible murder, and concern for the mayor as the ultimate target, all units were on high alert. This would slow the line down, but everyone's safety was the concern of the Chicago police and fire departments. Security would be tight at the funeral tomorrow, but no metal detectors would be present at the church. Apparently Father Murray believed no one would consider attacking in the house of our Lord. Claire figured Father Murray must not watch the television news or have access to the Internet.

As they entered the chapel, Claire saw Patrick speaking with Michael and his brother Stephen at the end of the receiving line. Several of Elizabeth's children stood next to their father while the others were nestled on the couches in the arms of family. She didn't see Jack.

When their turn came to go up to the casket, Claire let Frankie take her elbow for support. For a brief moment, she forced herself to look at Elizabeth. In a sense it was more difficult to see her laid out in the creamy satin casket than on the autopsy table. At the morgue, Claire focused on the task at hand, not the person. Here, she didn't have that option. Elizabeth wore a rich blue dress with a pearl rosary draped around her fingers. McDuffy's had done a beautiful job.

Together she and Frankie knelt and privately said their own prayers before joining the reception line to speak with family members. Elizabeth's oldest daughter took Claire's hands and spoke of the wonderful times they had when Claire babysat. It ripped Claire's heart out to see this good family suffer. Her family had its share of losses. She knew the pain and feeling of emptiness never quite left you.

Stephen stood tall at the end of the reception line. His face looked so strained that if it were glass Claire was sure it would shatter. Michael was next to his brother-in-law, in no better shape. She knew he felt the weight of his sister's death on his shoulders.

Patrick stood behind both men, not as a cop, but an old friend. "Hi, Sis," he quietly addressed her, and gave her a big brotherly hug. She spoke with Michael and Stephen only for a brief moment since there were so many family members and close friends who wanted to pay their respects before the public viewing.

"Thanks for your assistance, Frankie." Patrick shook his hand.

Claire motioned Patrick aside. "Any news?" she whispered.

"We're working on a lead. It's a long shot, but we've worked with less."

"Where's Jack?"

"He left just before you arrived. He drove Father Murray back to St. Pat's so Father wouldn't have to deal with parking. McDuffy's held the south lot for the private wake, which they'll open after we leave. I understand the north lot is full and people are already in line. Jack will be back and we'll stay until the end. Why don't you go before traffic gets heavy? Frankie, is Sol waiting for you?"

"Yes, he's out back," Frankie answered.

"Call me when you leave," Claire told her brother. She gave him a sisterly kiss on the cheek.

Patrick nodded. "I'll call later. Now go."

# Chapter 44

For the first time, Jack felt grateful he hadn't been raised in Patrick's old neighborhood. It wasn't hard to read the pain on the faces of family and friends. At least he was one step removed. He needed a clear head to do his job at a hundred percent. The look on Patrick's face told him of his partner's fight to be the detective and not slide across the aisle to being a very close friend.

Both of them moved separately through the crowds during the public wake. Not one person had triggered his sixth sense that something possibly wasn't right. They caught up briefly in the private family room for a quick sandwich.

"What do you think?" Jack asked his partner as he spread mustard on the ham sandwich and added a few chips to his plate. "Want me to fix a sandwich for you?"

Patrick nodded as he opened two cans of pop. "So far, nothing. This nut job, he must have heard the nightly news and is lying low. My gut tells me he'll try something, but whether he'll make a straight out attempt at Michael or do something else, I just don't know."

"I'm sure Michael is praying the idiot holds off and doesn't try anything today or tomorrow, for the sake of his family," Jack said. He handed Patrick a sandwich. "I can't imagine how much pressure Michael is under."

"I had my hopes up this morning there'd be someone at the old address who remembered George Ryder. Too bad about the vacant lot. I wonder when they tore the building down."

Jack finished a bite before answering. "From the age of the other buildings in the neighborhood, neglect probably did it in. Someone with a few bucks to blow will probably come in and renovate the area. In less than ten years everything will be new." He had lived in Chicago since he was a kid, and had seen these two scenarios play out repeatedly.

Patrick wiped his mouth and dumped the paper plate in the trash. "I'm heading back out."

Jack checked his watch. "In about fifteen minutes they should be closing the doors and asking the people inside to finish."

"Tomorrow's going to be a long day. I'm ready to head home. Let's go help the uniforms wind down the show."

Jack followed his partner out of the family room. He'd missed seeing Claire earlier and wondered how she was doing. For Patrick and Claire, losing someone from the old neighborhood was like losing family. He made a silent prayer that the stress didn't take a physical toll on Patrick, since their last case put him in the hospital.

\* \* \*

Derek drove past McDuffy's Funeral Home as a patrolman directed the remaining cars out into traffic. Between the outside lights and the police car beams, the place shone like Christmas. Anticipation filled his veins. Tomorrow . . . tomorrow would be his day of fulfillment.

No one could stop him now. He had waited for this day for years and no one could take it away from him. To add to his joy, Mr. Floyd had gone to the state funeral directors' meeting in Springfield. This couldn't be more perfect! Even that morgue doctor couldn't get in his way.

# Chapter 45

Claire sat impatiently in the back seat and Frankie in the front passenger seat of Sol's SUV waiting for the funeral procession to start. Only Elizabeth's family had been allowed in McDuffy's chapel prior to her casket being placed in the hearse. The police directed everyone else to remain in their cars in the procession line. Orange "Funeral" signs were placed on the dashboards and the drivers were asked to turn their dim lights on. She couldn't see Patrick or Jack, but knew from her brother's earlier call they were inside and would be the second lead car in the funeral procession. Sol's vehicle was near the rear.

Elizabeth's family, the Keeleys, and her husband's family, the O'Connors, were large Irish families. From the looks of things, they must have rented every black limousine in Cook County. She didn't know if Michael would ride with his family or with Patrick since he believed he was a target. He wouldn't want to put his family at risk. Jack had mentioned they would be driving in a secure vehicle. Did he mean the car had bulletproof windows?

From where she sat, she could see more than a dozen squad cars. The murderer would certainly be a fool to try anything at McDuffy's or on the way to St. Pat's. The police had blocked off the route at every intersection and alley. From what Patrick had told her, Keeley Liquor Distributors had made a sizeable donation to the Chicago Police Department to help offset the cost for their assistance.

A few minutes later mournful notes could be heard from the bagpipes as six of the O'Connor and Keeley men escorted Elizabeth's casket to the hearse. One by one, each man released his hold, stepped back and saluted the casket of the woman who'd meant so much to them. Michael and Stephen brought up the rear. The musicians continued to play until everyone took his or her seat in their assigned vehicles. Finally, the patrolmen escorted the immediate family members to the limos. For a brief moment,

Claire caught a glimpse of Patrick and Jack on either side of Michael before they entered their car.

Suddenly, flashing blue and red lights flooded the street from all sides as the lead car inched away from the curb and drove slowly down the center of the street. The sun broke free from a thick cloud cover. Claire felt like the heavens were welcoming Elizabeth. The procession followed with squad cars on both sides of the line of private cars and limousines. All along the route people filled the streets. Many made the sign of the cross as the hearse passed. Claire noticed Sol had put a box of tissues in the back seat. She'd need them before the day was over.

After what seemed like forever, they arrived at St. Patrick's Catholic Church. The police directed Sol's vehicle out of the line of cars to the rear of the church while other vehicles, with the exception of the hearse and family cars, were directed to the parking lots. Spectators and television crews filled the park across the street from the church. Sol dropped Claire and Frankie off at the guarded rear entrance. After showing identification, they were escorted to their pew by an usher and handed a program.

Very shortly after they were seated, the church filled with sound from the organ announcing Elizabeth's entrance. Everyone stood as the pallbearers escorted her casket down the aisle. The aroma of burning incense filled the air as Father Murray swung the censer back and forth.

The mass, words spoken by a few family members, and communion lasted well over an hour. Afterwards, the congregation left for brief refreshments at the attached school. Michael, Stephen and Paul formed a short reception line to thank everyone for their support while two policemen remained in the church with Elizabeth's casket.

The caterer had set a lovely table with coffee, tea and juice along with mouthwatering pastries. Claire hadn't realized how hungry she'd become until she saw the mound of cranberry and blueberry scones, not to mention the buttery sweet rolls. It was hard not to take one of everything. She joined Frankie, whose plate was overflowing, at one of the tables.

"I hope you're saving some of those for Sol?" she said.

"Gotta feed our chauffeur. I need to get Sol a cup of coffee before we leave. My guess is lunch is a long way off," he answered.

"You're probably right. Maybe I should get something for Patrick and Jack?"

"I saw them at the head of the line. Most likely they had to go back outside right away since they're on duty." Frankie devoured an almond pastry in a couple of bites.

Claire finished her cherry-filled pastry before wrapping the cranberry scone in a paper napkin and sticking it in her purse. "We should get back to the car, plus I'd like to talk with Patrick, if I can. I want to make sure he's doing okay. I'll watch Sol's treats while you grab him a cup of coffee."

A few minutes later they dropped off Sol's snack and then joined Patrick outside. The morning sunshine had vanished behind dark clouds, which only dampened Claire's mood.

"Patrick, how are you holding up?" Claire could see he looked tired and strained. His forehead lines seemed deeper and his eyebrows practically rested on his eyelids. She noticed Jack hovering like a mother cat.

Her brother gave her a big bear hug. "I'm all right. How about you?"

"I've had better days. Say, where are the girls?"

"Our sisters headed over to Paul's house with all the young ones. Paul thinks they've had enough for one day. They aren't going to sit still much longer. We've assigned several cadets from the academy to give a hand."

"That's unusual," Claire said.

"Actually, they volunteered. Several had earned community service hours for National Honor Society, confirmation, and scouting through Elizabeth's programs. They felt they wouldn't have made it into the police academy if it hadn't been for her direction," Jack said.

"Hey, Claire," said Frankie. "I think they're getting ready to leave. I can see the ushers bringing the casket out of the church."

"Okay," she said. "What about you two?"

"After the chapel service at Queen of Heaven, Captain Ramos wants Patrick to go home and rest," Jack said. "We'll see you out there."

Claire hopped into Sol's SUV as Elizabeth's casket entered the hearse. The sidewalks were packed with extended family and friends. At last, the procession began its final journey. She felt exhausted, mostly from the emotions. She closed her eyes as Sol pulled away from the curb.

"Are you okay?" Frankie asked.

"Yes, just tired."

"They're picking up speed so the trip shouldn't take too long. I listened to a couple of the cops talking. Apparently, Chicago will get the entourage to the cemetery and the Hillside police will take over there," Sol said as he followed the funeral line.

"I forgot to ask Patrick if they spotted anything suspicious," Claire said.

"I didn't hear anything. I bet if anyone showed up, he left once he saw all the security in place."

"I pray for Patrick's sake, and for Michael's family, that nothing happens. Today has been long and hard enough without some maniac pulling something horrendous. Patrick told me SWAT will be at the cemetery chapel until everyone leaves. Michael and his family will be escorted back to Paul's."

Claire took advantage of the ride to think and rest. The stress of the past few days had worn her out. Thankfully, the final service would be short. With the threatening late afternoon weather, people could get home before the downpour. She looked forward to tomorrow, when she planned to take back her life, no matter what Patrick, Jack or Frankie wanted. She might miss Frankie's daily thermos of cappuccino, but normalcy would taste even better.

# Chapter 46

Derek left the line on the church steps the moment he realized he'd forgotten he'd need an invitation to get in. He excused himself, mumbling that he'd left something in his car. Someone said they would hold his place in line. He waved thanks, knowing it wouldn't be necessary.

He returned to Floyd's Funeral Home before the church service concluded. Not only was Mr. Floyd out of town, but nothing was scheduled for today. Quickly he changed into black pants, white shirt with black tie, and a long black coat. Funny how his funeral attire made him feel more important than his hospital job. In reality, Chicago General Hospital paid a lot more and the level of responsibility far outweighed his job at Floyd's.

Earlier that morning he'd loaded an empty casket in the back of the funeral home's hearse and covered the sign on the side with a fake name. He'd parked his car out of sight in the garage before leaving in the hearse. In the back he'd thrown flowers he'd pulled from old arrangements in case he needed a prop. You never knew when you might have to visit a grave site as a mourning family member. He could play a grieving relative if necessary.

Thoughts of his parents came to mind. He had no idea whether his mother was still alive. His dad had been buried somewhere on the South Side in a mass grave, and he'd never visited.

Derek took an indirect route to Queen of Heaven Cemetery, figuring the Hillside police would be monitoring the area. The main entrance was off South Wolf Road, on the east side of the property. He entered on the southwest side of the cemetery just off Hamilton Avenue, several blocks south of Roosevelt Road. Once inside the cemetery he circled north on an inner road. He'd planned to arrive before the funeral procession. The 'graveside' service would be held in the chapel. Today, the families wanted comfort-controlled inside temperatures, comfortable chairs, and none of the harsh realities of the casket being lowered six feet down into a cement vault with a backhoe dumping dirt on top of their loved one. *Get real, people!* he wanted to yell at them.

Even Mother Nature seemed to be on his side. She'd covered the earlier blue sky with dark, threatening clouds and sent a wet mist. This would encourage people to move to their vehicles quickly after the service ended, rather than linger.

From his hearse, Derek viewed the activity across the west side of the cemetery. Hillside police surrounded the chapel area. He planned to place flowers on a random grave as a ruse to get closer. Two of the chapels appeared to be in use. One let out as he arrived. That group was very small and didn't command the attention of the police. They left quickly. The other group drove a variety of cars, which didn't impress him as Elizabeth's family.

While he waited for the mayor's entourage to arrive, he checked his equipment: silver duct tape, a 53-million voltage stun gun he'd purchased online, and his trusty pipe. He'd read that the stun gun would disrupt messages sent from the brain to the voluntary muscles. The victim would become confused, disoriented, lose muscle control and balance, making him incapable of aggressively reacting to the situation. *All this online for less than sixty bucks. Such a deal,* he thought. Because of shipping restrictions for Illinois, Derek had it shipped to the Little Rock address while he was on vacation. *Problem solved!*

The glare of flashing lights in the distance by the main entrance to Queen of Heaven Cemetery caught his attention. The mist only accentuated the continuous band of light that seemed to go on forever as it approached the chapel. Elizabeth's funeral procession had arrived. Time to go to work.

The mid-afternoon sky gave the appearance of dusk invading the daylight. Derek watched the casket being unloaded. Once everyone entered the cemetery, most of the Chicago police contingent left, except for the vehicles providing the Keeley family an escort home. This left a couple of Hillside police cars. The mayor would probably have an escort home, Derek realized with a sinking feeling. His hopes of getting close to Michael Keeley were all but dashed.

He noticed several reporters and accompanying cameramen coming around from the north side of the chapel. The news service trucks must be parked in the back. While they all wanted in on the story that had been unfolding since this morning, they seemed to respect the family's space. He scanned the group of reporters and his eyes locked on Jillian Garcia. He still had a bone to pick with her. She owed him for her cameraman capturing him on film at the morgue. If she wasn't careful, she'd get her due.

Two of the cameramen walked out toward the graves for better shots of the chapel. One even shot footage of some of the graves. *Damn!* Derek turned and walked to his vehicle. He wanted to run screaming for the hearse, swearing at the cameramen for interfering with his plan to make Michael or some other Keeley pay for what the Keeleys had done to his family, but he knew better than to draw attention to himself. Instead, he picked the next headstone and knelt down to place the flowers at the base. He bowed his head for a brief moment, made the sign of the cross, rose and walked slowly to the hearse.

Once safely in the driver's seat, he drove north out of the cemetery. He turned east on Roosevelt Road and at the light went south on Wolf Road to the main entrance. Back inside Queen of Heaven, he continued north on the east side until he arrived at the parking lot for the Queen of All Saints Mausoleum in the northeast section of the cemetery. From his position, he could see the north entrance of Queen of Heaven on Roosevelt Road, which lined up with Mt. Carmel Cemetery, directly across the street. He gripped the steering wheel hard, fighting to control his frustration. For now, all he could do was wait and see how the afternoon played out.

# Chapter 47

Jillian Garcia signaled to Jim, her cameraman, that she was ready to shoot the next segment for the nightly news. Positioning herself in front of the Queen of Heaven Chapel, she tested her microphone and made sure she wasn't blocking another news reporter. "Are you ready?" she asked.

"Take one step to your right."

She did as he asked. "How's this?"

"Perfect. Okay, three, two, one. Recording."

"Good evening, this is Jillian Garcia reporting to you from the Queen of Heaven Cemetery in Hillside, Illinois. Behind me is the chapel where the final service is being held for our mayor's sister, Elizabeth O'Connor. Because of the hour of the day, and the impending thunderstorm, Elizabeth will be buried tomorrow in the family plot across Roosevelt Road, in Mt. Carmel Cemetery.

"This has been a long day for the O'Connors and the Keeleys. Both families have asked not to be interviewed and all the news stations have honored their request. Our station will do a final wrap-up after the tomorrow's burial. The Hillside police, along with both families, have asked the public to respect their privacy and not visit Mrs. O'Connor's grave until spring when the headstone will be placed.

"As of today, the official cause of death has not been released by the Office of the Medical Examiner for Cook County. We're told the final laboratory tests can often take up to six weeks or more. WTLV will keep you updated as information is released. This is Jillian Garcia signing off for WTLV Chicago. Have a nice evening."

She eyed Jim as the little red light on the camera winked out. "What do you think?"

"You did great. It's a wrap. Do you need a ride back to the station?" Jim asked.

"Thanks, but I drove. I want to drive through Mt. Carmel to see if there's anything I need to research before I do the final segment after the burial. Then I'll head over to the station."

"Okay. See you later." Jim grabbed his camera bag next to his feet and headed to the truck.

Jillian used the next chapel entrance over to enter and use the facilities. When she left, most of the attendees were exiting the chapel. She saw the mayor enter a squad car and leave. Several other family members were assisted into waiting limos. After the last car had left with the Chicago police escort, the Hillside police cars dispersed.

*Perfect timing*, Jillian thought. Now she could make a quick drive through Mt. Carmel Cemetery to check the location of Mrs. O'Connor's grave. She also had two other items on her agenda. The front office for Queen of Heaven wouldn't release the location of Al Capone's grave, but a friend had mentioned the general area of the Capone family monument. His flat headstone was supposed to be in front of the monument. The other grave that piqued her interest was the Italian Bride, Julia Buccola Petta, near the north entrance to Mt. Carmel on Harrison Street.

Her friend's directions were right on target; Jillian found Al Capone's grave without any trouble. She remembered hearing rumors that Capone had been buried in McHenry County and not Mt. Carmel because the Catholic Church didn't approve of his line of work. He'd allegedly given the order for the St. Valentine's Day Massacre to stop George "Bugs" Moran, head of a rival gang. After shooting a couple pictures with her cell phone, Jillian headed for her next stop, Elizabeth O'Connor's final resting place.

Thankful the cemetery sections were well marked, she easily located Section V, in an Irish section west of the Bishop's Mausoleum. Even in the fading daylight Jillian could make out a tarp covering what she assumed would be Mrs. O'Connor's grave, according to the names on the headstones in the immediate area. This wasn't a site she wanted recorded on her cell phone. Chicago's loss of a wonderful lady still hurt.

Moments later, Jillian arrived at the Italian Bride's monument. The only light left now shone from streetlights and rush hour traffic on Harrison. Perhaps tomorrow she'd spend more time at the burial place of this well-known Chicago apparition, but for now she couldn't resist a closer look at the life-size statue depicting Julia Buccola in her wedding dress. She remembered the story of how Julia's mother, Filomena, had been plagued by dreams that Julia was buried alive.

It took Filomena six years to convince a judge to have her daughter exhumed. When her casket was opened, everyone was shocked at Julia's perfect condition. She'd died in childbirth and her baby was tucked in her arms. According to Italian tradition, if a woman dies while giving birth, she is buried in her wedding dress. A photo taken at this time became a cameo on the front of the headstone.

As Jillian bent over to see it, something pierced her neck and she collapsed to the ground. She heard someone say, "Stupid fool," before she lost consciousness.

# Chapter 48

"What do you mean, you can't find her?" Scott Christie yelled. "Jillian and I are on the air in twenty minutes. Who saw her last?" Panic rushed through his veins. It wasn't like Jillian not to be on the set and ready to go at least an hour ahead of their nightly broadcast.

"She was scheduled to shoot the final service for the O'Connor funeral and return to the station," answered Mark, the production manager. "Where's Jim, he shot the footage today."

"Hey, what's the problem? You can hear Christie yelling all the way down the hall," Jim said as he walked into the break room and set down his camera equipment.

"No one can find Jillian. She's not here and she didn't answer her cell phone." Scott paced back and forth while his heart felt like it wanted to jump out of his chest. "Did you and Jillian have any problems with your assignment today?"

"Actually, I was amazed everything ran as smooth as it did considering the volume of people everywhere."

"When and where did you last see her?" Scott could barely control himself. Sure, he could do the broadcast solo, but that didn't tell him what had happened to his co-anchor—and hopefully his future wife and mother of his children.

"I last saw her at the Queen of Heaven Chapel. She planned to visit Mt. Carmel Cemetery before coming back here, to see if she needed to research anything for her wrap-up piece tomorrow."

"You left her alone in the cemetery?" Scott got right into Jim's face. "What were you *thinking*?"

"She said she was just going to drive through. I thought she'd be back here just a few minutes after me. I'm not her guardian!" Jim yelled back at Scott.

Mark pushed his way between them. "This isn't getting us anywhere. Jim, you check with front door security and see if she's come in. Lou, get the weather team to extend their forecast and stay on the air. I don't care what part of the country they talk about. Meanwhile, Diane, I want you to try Jillian's cell and home numbers. Call the Hillside and Chicago police for any car accidents. Jeff, get the tech guys to go on the Web for Find My Phone and see if they can track down a GPS reading on her location. If she doesn't appear to be driving into the parking lot right now, call the police and give them the location of her phone."

"What about me?" Scott demanded.

"You're going to calm down because you might have to go on the air and ask the viewers for help in locating Jillian. Okay, let's give everyone a few minutes to complete their assignments and we'll go from there."

Jeff, one of the production assistants, spoke up. "Mark, the tech guys said it looks like her cell phone is in the cemetery. I called the Hillside police 9-1-1 dispatch."

"Thanks, Jeff. Can you stay with Scott for a moment while I check with the guys upstairs? I needed to find out how they want us to handle this," Mark said.

"No problem," he answered.

Scott wanted to run his hands through his hair, but too many years of training kept him from doing it. *Jillian, where are you*, he silently called out. His gut told him something was very wrong, but he couldn't imagine what had happened. He started to pace, but Jeff stopped him.

"Here." Jeff tossed him a bottle of water. "Pretend it's something stronger and sit down."

"Thanks." Right now he needed Jeff to tell him what to do. He couldn't think straight.

Jeff sat down next to him and spoke in a low tone. "Look, Scott, I know you don't think any of us have any idea how you and Jillian feel for each other, but the cat's been out of the bag for some time now. At work you both play it really cool and that's why most of us figured it out. So I know there's more riding on finding Jillian than needing her to co-anchor the show. Those of us who know aren't going to say anything, so you can stop worrying about that. But you need to pull yourself together and be ready to go with whatever the guys upstairs say. Do you think you can do that?"

Scott got up and tossed his empty water bottle into the recycling bin. "Let me hit the head and I'll be ready to go. By the way, thanks." Once inside the men's room, he pounded his fist on the stall wall. *This can't be happening.* Their job was to report the news, not be the news. A few minutes later he calmly returned to the break room. Mark and the crew were waiting for him.

Mark handed Scott a sheet of paper. "This is the copy being put on the teleprompters right now. Rachael will stand in for Jillian, who is off tonight. The police want to keep this quiet for the moment. Because we had the weather team give an extended forecast on the floods in California, your show will be cut by ten minutes. Since the O'Connor funeral dominated the news today, there wasn't much else going on. Rachael will give a brief overview of the funeral with a few short clips of Jillian reporting from the scene. Let Rachael take the lead. Do you think you can go with this, Scott?"

"Yes. With ten minutes less air time to fill, I'll be fine." Scott pasted a slight smile on his face while clenching his teeth. It would be damn hard, but he would do it because he was a professional and he knew Jillian would expect him to pull it off.

"Okay, everyone. Let's go." Mark led them out to the area behind the cameras. Once they went to commercial break, Scott and Rachael took their places at the news desk on the set. A few minutes later they were on the air.

# Chapter 49

"Detective Miller, I think we found Garcia's cell phone stuck in the grass in front of the Italian Bride's monument," Sergeant Perchowski called out as he approached Jack. He handed Jack a paper bag containing a phone. "The evidence tech took photographs before they bagged it. Her purse and a notebook are on the floor behind the driver's seat of her car. I ran the plates to verify ownership. The car doesn't look like it was tampered with, but the grass in front of the monument is matted with wet soil, possibly from a struggle."

"Thanks, Sarge." Jack wished he could see who Jillian Garcia spoke with last, but he couldn't risk destroying any evidence. Using his own phone, he called the television station to see if anyone remembered Jillian calling in recently. The operator didn't sound too positive, but promised to check.

"Hey, Sarge, did your guys find anything else?" Jack asked.

"Not yet. We have the police academy cadets helping us search the Mt. Carmel Cemetery, and the Hillside police are working the Queen of Heaven Cemetery. By the way, those guys from Hillside are really grateful we consented to come back and assist. They just don't have the manpower. Bottom line, unless we find the reporter soon, we'll have to come back in daylight to search for more clues. This may not have a good outcome." The sergeant's phone rang. "Let me take this."

Jack stood by, hoping the call brought some news, but from the look on Perchowski's face, he'd already known the information wouldn't be promising. "Any luck?" he asked as the sergeant hung up.

"None. No sign of her anywhere on Mt. Carmel's grounds," Perchowski answered. "I'm still waiting to hear from the Hillside police. I sent the cadets over there to help. Queen of Heaven has more trees and bushes, especially along the south fence that backs up to the Fresh Meadow Golf Course. By the way, who has jurisdiction over the phone and her car?"

"I'm sure it's Hillside, but I'll call Captain Ramos and see what he can arrange since we're all in Cook County."

"Sure, go ahead. I'm going to check with my guys one more time, then head over to Queen of Heaven." Sergeant Perchowski radioed his team as he walked away.

Jack hit the captain's number on speed dial.

Ramos answered immediately. "Any news?"

"Perchowski's men found a cell phone at the base of the Buccola monument, which is close to the north entrance off Harrison Street. I called the television station to see if anyone remembers Garcia calling in. The operator said she'd check, but I have my doubts. They probably get tons of calls daily."

"Buccola . . . Isn't that the Italian Bride's monument?"

"Yes sir, it is."

"I haven't been there since middle school. Any chance Julia's apparition is available to help us out?"

Jack heard the captain's little chuckle. He shook his head. He never would have guessed Captain Ramos followed any of Chicago's well known ghosts. "I don't believe so, Captain. The reason I'm calling is, evidence found should be in Hillside's jurisdiction. Also, Garcia's car and purse appeared not to have been touched. Do you want me to hand the car and phone over to Hillside, or should we see if we can turn them over to our forensic guys?"

"Technically they should pass the evidence to Cook County. Give me a minute to check their workload and contact Hillside. I'll call you right back. Go ahead and fill out the chain of command forms for both the phone and the car with its contents," Captain Ramos said, and disconnected.

Before Jack could drop his phone into his jacket pocket, it rang. He saw Perchowski's name on the caller ID. "Hi, Sarge, any luck over there?"

"None on this side of Roosevelt Road. Hillside suggested we suspend the search until daylight. I tend to agree with them. In the dark we might actually damage evidence. They said it was your call."

Jack sighed. "Since we haven't found Jillian Garcia or any other major clues to her disappearance, I'm in agreement. Also, since we found the cell phone and car at Mt. Carmel, that's where we should start in the morning. I put a call in to Captain Ramos. As soon as I hear back, you can speak with Hillside's officer-in-charge. Can you wait over there for a bit longer?"

"No problem," Perchowski said.

A muffled beep sounded in Jack's ear. "I think the captain's trying to call. Be back with you in a minute." Jack hung up as the captain's number flashed across his screen. "Detective Miller speaking," he answered.

"Miller, I just spoke with Hillside and they said for you to take procession of the phone and the car plus contents since Cook County's labs are backed up. Go ahead and write them a receipt for their paperwork. What's your plan right now?"

"I'm in agreement with Hillside to suspend the search until tomorrow. We feel confident Jillian Garcia isn't in either cemetery and we're concerned we might damage any other possible evidence in the dark. Heavy fog just rolled in, so even extra floodlights wouldn't help us see any better. I recommend we start at Mt. Carmel tomorrow since that's where we found her phone and car. We'll need to speak with Queen of Heaven's office first thing in the morning to see what they have scheduled, including Elizabeth's burial."

"I'll take care of that for you. Go give Hillside the paperwork and make sure all the cemetery gates are secure."

"Thanks, Captain. I'll keep you posted on any new developments."

Jack called Perchowski back and shared the plan. He told him to secure the gates for the night while he would do the same at Mt. Carmel. With the change of custody paperwork filled out for the cell phone and car, Jack sent the evidence tech over to Hillside to sign off while he waited for Chicago's crime scene tow truck to arrive and take possession of Jillian's car. The tech returned as the driver loaded the car on to the flat bed. With the last of paperwork completed, the tech left for the forensic lab with the cell phone. Meanwhile, one of the cemetery security officers stood by ready to lock Mt. Carmel's back gate as soon as the tow truck left.

Jack didn't even have the chance to close the door on his police car before his cell phone rang again. Exhausted and hungry, he looked at the caller ID and recognized Claire's number. "Hi. Are you okay?" he asked.

"I'm fine, but Patrick is over here doing his usual pacing. Where are you?" Claire asked.

Jack didn't have the energy to explain. "Does Frankie have any leftovers?"

"Sure. Haven't you had dinner yet?"

"No, I'm leaving Mt. Carmel Cemetery now."

"What?"

He could hear Patrick yelling in the background. "I'll explain it to both of you when I get to your place. Fix me a plate and I'll be there in thirty minutes."

# Chapter 30

Claire watched Patrick patiently hold his tongue while Jack polished off a large piece of Frankie's spinach lasagna and a slice of buttery garlic bread. After a few sips of a cold beer, Jack opened up.

He explained that Jillian Garcia from the WTLV television station hadn't returned to work after reporting live from Queen of Heaven Cemetery following Elizabeth's afternoon service. Her cameraman, Jim, told the police she planned to drive through Mt. Carmel Cemetery on her way back to the station. "She wanted to see if there was anything she needed to research for her closing segment after the private family burial for Elizabeth."

"I remember," Patrick said. "The cemetery people suggested delaying it till tomorrow because of the thunderstorm forecast for this afternoon."

"Yeah. Anyway, no one's seen or heard from Garcia since." Jack sipped more beer. "Chicago assisted Hillside in the search of both cemeteries, and her cell phone's GPS led us to the north end of Mt. Carmel. The Hillside cops found the phone in the grass at the base of the Italian Bride monument. There's a history of people claiming to see the bride's apparition in the cemetery, but no one had any idea why Jillian's car was parked in front of that monument. Captain Ramos spoke with Hillside and they agreed to allow us to send the phone and car through Chicago's forensic channels. Other than that, nothing that points to where Jillian is. We suspended the search when it got too dark . . . no sense destroying potential further evidence because we can't see what we're blundering through. We'll resume in the morning."

"Why didn't you call me to help?" Patrick asked.

Jack gave him an exasperated look. "Do you remember Captain Ramos saying something to the effect that you had to go directly home and rest after the cemetery service? Wearing a path in Claire's carpet doesn't sound like rest to me."

"I did go home, but when I called Claire and she hadn't heard from you, I got concerned."

"That's a lame excuse. Why would you expect me to check in with Claire? You could have called me."

Patrick looked a bit sheepish as he responded. "Because of all the craziness going on in Claire's life, and I needed a reason to escape my daughters and their friends. I can't stand their music," He leaned back in the dining room chair.

Jack chuckled. "Okay, you got me on both accounts."

"Would you two stop for a moment and get to the meat of the situation? Why Jillian Garcia? Why this cemetery? And does it have anything to do with Elizabeth's death or is it a diversion from Michael being the target?" Claire asked.

Jack called out, "Frankie, is there any coffee left?"

From the kitchen, Frankie answered, "I'll put on a fresh pot of decaf. Something tells me we're going to be at this awhile."

"Thanks. I could certainly use a cup of something hot to drink. The dampness put a nasty chill in the air at the cemetery," Jack said. "Also, thank you for dinner. I truly appreciate your cooking."

"Not a problem. Let me know if you want more." Frankie set down some coffee mugs on a tray with cream and sugar, along with a plate of his mother's homemade cannoli.

Claire got up and gathered several pads of paper and pens from her desk drawer. She wrote Jillian's, Elizabeth's and Michael's names across the top of three different pads. "Patrick and Jack, since both of you look exhausted I'm going to conduct this meeting."

Patrick started to protest, but Jack stopped him. "Maybe a fresh set of eyes will help. I don't know about you, but I'm beat."

"Since we're all in agreement, let's start with Elizabeth." She lifted her pen to write. "I started a list about her. She has six children, championed many good causes in Chicago, was admitted for a routine total abdominal hysterectomy, died unexpectedly from gas gangrene and is scheduled for burial tomorrow."

"Don't forget to add, she's the mayor's sister," Patrick said.

"Thanks, Patrick. Okay, I know we've been over these before, but humor me. Let's take each one again."

Jack reached for one of Mrs. Biaggi's cannoli and Frankie served the coffee. "I don't believe being the mother of six or the champion of causes has anything to do with her death. I think you can cross off her burial, too. Being scheduled for this surgery seems to be the key to her death. As for being the mayor's sister, well, that may be what incited this incident when you consider all the other attacks on the family."

"Patrick, do you have anything to add?"

"No. I hate to say it, but we're stuck until we find the person responsible for Elizabeth's death."

"How about you throw out some ideas regarding Michael?" Claire poised herself to write them down.

"Let's begin with he's the mayor. As a prosecutor before that, he put away a lot of criminals. I can't believe anyone in the city council or politically connected to Chicago would use Elizabeth to get back at him. As for the guys he sent to prison, we've already ruled them out because relevant dates didn't match the incidents." Patrick went on. "Michael and I worked up a list of all the possible stalking events the entire Keeley family experienced. We believe they were aimed at hurting Michael. We just don't know the reason for it. In regards to the family business, we came across the firing of a guy named George Ryder approximately fifteen years ago. Unfortunately, he's been dead for quite a while. We've tried to find his wife and son, but found nothing so far. We even tried visiting his last known address. No luck. Could there be another unhappy ex-employee from the Keeley family business? Possibly, but we haven't found him. Paul Keeley's office continues to research other leads for us."

"We're no further ahead than we were twenty minutes ago," Jack said. "At least Jillian Garcia's kidnapping could be a fluke. At this point, it's an alleged kidnapping, but she's missing and all her things were still at the scene. She could have been mistaken for someone else or simply in the wrong place at the wrong time."

"That's it! You guys are missing the boat," Frankie said as he topped off everyone's coffee cups. "All three—no, correction, all four—including the business with Claire, are connected."

Claire almost dropped her coffee mug. "What?" she chimed in, along with the others.

"Look at it this way. Your primary incident is Elizabeth's death. Next, Jillian Garcia reported on it from the morgue, followed by Claire receiving flowers from a fake florist. Why is

Claire involved, you ask? She's a definite threat to someone because she performed the autopsy. This person knows he needs to throw Claire off her game. So he sends her a fresh human heart, hoping she'll be so upset she'll be put on medical leave. Then, to make sure Claire stays distressed, and to get rid of the only witness who can ID him, he kills Fred Drake. More guilt for Claire, giving him two threats eliminated. Now enters Michael and the Keeley family for the wake and funeral. Everyone worries about Michael's safety, but he's too hard to reach. But Jillian, who reported the first night and has been on the story the entire time, was easy pickings. He's telling us he'll take out who he wants, when he wants, and we can't stop him. The question is, how did Jillian become a threat?"

Jack grinned. "Frankie, you're a genius. Are you sure you're not a secret agent? If I heard you correctly, Jillian Garcia is a major key to solving Elizabeth's murder. But what does she know that we don't?" He sobered. "And where is she? I sure hope she's still alive."

"Tomorrow morning, we have to ask Captain Ramos to request all the film coverage from Jillian's reports on this case. See if anyone shows up in the crowd more than once. This could be our best chance at a lead," Patrick said.

Claire stood and walked toward the door. "Okay, I think it's time we all got a good night's sleep. Time to go, Patrick and Jack. I'm kicking both of you out now."

Once they were out the door, Claire turned to Frankie. "Thanks for speaking up tonight. Fresh eyes do make a difference."

"My pleasure," he said. "Now take your own advice and go to bed."

"You won't have to tell me twice. I'm exhausted." She turned and headed for the bedroom, knowing tomorrow would be another rough day.

# Chapter 51

Derek half carried, half dragged Jillian out of the hearse, through the garage and to the elevator. Once he had her in the basement, he managed to get her on top of a gurney and then swore at her. "Dumb broad, who'd have thought you'd weigh this much."

The activity must have stimulated Jillian, because she started to squirm, her eyes bulging in fear.

"Stop moving around or you'll fall off the table," he yelled. Quickly he secured several straps across Jillian's body to keep her in place. Then he removed a couple of long plastic strips from his pocket. Normally, they held computer and office cords together, but he'd found another use for them. He wrapped them around her ankles and wrists, and then connected them to the sides of the cart. Pretty clever of him to purchase them at a hardware store in Rockford, making it difficult for the cops to trace.

"Time for another sniff." He poured a generous amount of ether onto a face mask, settled it in place, and slipped the elastic cords over her ears. "This should calm you down for a while." He'd found it amazing what he could buy online. Along with the stun gun, he'd treated himself to a bottle of ether while he vacationed at his secret apartment in Little Rock.

She was out again. He checked her breathing, estimating her air flow rate by the rise and fall of her chest. *Don't kill her too soon.* He needed her alive until he could find a vendor for her tissue and bones. They all wanted fresh specimens.

He had three days left to locate a source before Mr. Floyd returned. The usual two vendors he'd used told him business was slow and they had a full inventory. Derek didn't buy their excuse, but he knew better than to push. He had a couple out-of-state companies he'd worked with that might be possibilities.

Since he'd have to stay overnight in the funeral home to keep an eye on Jillian, dinner would consist of a peanut butter and jelly sandwich. He'd sleep on a couch in the back lounge area. Jillian shouldn't wake up, but if she did and started screaming or tried to get loose, he'd hear her and take care of it. He moved in the dark because he couldn't risk anyone mentioning to Mr. Floyd that they'd seen the lights on while he was gone. However, the computer in the inner office couldn't be seen from the outside, so he could use it for his research. Mr. Floyd had purposely blocked out the windows long ago so he wouldn't be disturbed on days he didn't have a wake.

Derek smiled to himself as he made his way through the blackness. Everything was working out the way he wanted.

\* \* \*

After playing poker with her cousins during last summer's vacation, Jillian knew when to "hold them." This was that time. She'd held her breath when that lunatic put the mask over her face, dosed with some chemical—the smell had warned her. She made her upper abdomen rise and fall, giving the illusion she was breathing. Luckily, he left the area heading rightward and turned the light off. She felt as if her lungs would explode as she gripped the dry paper mask with her teeth and pried it down with her chin, using her shoulder for support. She'd seen it done on a crime drama and couldn't believe it worked. Amazing, how educational television could be.

She turned her head away from the mask and gulped in air. She could smell the chemical but at least she was inhaling less with the mask riding at chin level. She wasn't dizzy, but then no one was asking her to stand up, either.

Jillian remembered taking an elevator down so she guessed she was in the basement. From what she saw as her kidnapper dragged her to the cart, the guy had no idea she'd remained conscious through all of this. He'd bought her passing-out act. The moment he'd grabbed her, she knew she didn't have the strength to fight him off and win, so she played possum. It was her only hope.

Her eyes had adjusted to the darkness by now, and she could make out a staircase at the opposite side of the room from the elevator. Scratches in the dirt on the basement windows provided a small amount light from the outside. Just enough to give her an opportunity to visually search the room.

At the moment, escape wasn't an option. She had one strap across her abdomen, one above her knees, and a third one crossed her chest under her arms. She could feel her wrists and ankles had been secured with something thin, which prevented her from releasing the other straps.

By now, everyone at the TV station, especially Scott, must be going crazy because she'd missed her broadcast. They'd call the police. Who'd search the cemetery and find her cell phone and car, but none of that would lead them here. She was completely on her own and scared to death. Jillian had been in tight spots before, but never alone and like this. The best thing she could do was try to relax, do some gentle breathing and survey her surroundings.

The muffled sound of footsteps above her reminded Jillian the monster had not left the building and could come back at any moment. He'd expect her to be sedated with the mask over her nose and mouth. Before anything else, she had to replace the mask. She hated the thought of having to breathe whatever chemical he'd poured over it. The smell seemed alcohol-based, so perhaps it had dried.

Repositioning the mask proved much more difficult than removing it. Jillian struggled, rubbing it against her shoulder and tugging with her teeth. Luckily, the elastic straps were still in place over her ears. Finally she had it back in place. The fluid had dried, but the odor remained present. It reminded her of nail polish remover. The taste was worse. It stung her mouth. Bathtub gin would have been better. What she wouldn't give for a piece of gum to kill the flavor it left on her tongue and lips. For a brief moment she lay still, trying to collect her thoughts. The smell from the chemical gave her a headache and upset her stomach. At least she was conscious and could think reasonably clearly for now, but for how much longer would she last?

What did this guy want with her? If he was into killing, she should be dead right now. He wanted something, but what? Money? If he thought she made the big bucks, he'd be very disappointed. Perhaps he envisioned a hefty ransom payment from the station. How much would he want and would they pay? Jillian had no idea what their policy was for this situation, or if they had one.

Somewhere a phone rang and her kidnapper answered it. She tried to listen, but couldn't hear what he said. After the brief call, Jillian heard him swear, then pound his fists on something. Whoever called had made the guy angry. Would he take it out on her? All she could do was wait and pray. If something happened to her, who would take care of her elderly grandmother? Her parents had passed, her younger brother was stationed overseas with the Army, and the rest of her family was scattered between Texas and Mexico. *Jillian, pull yourself together. You have to make it. You didn't become an investigative reporter by being a wimp!*

Although she'd started to get a bit foggy, she desperately tried to listen to what went on above her. A toilet flushed, and then a door slammed. The next sound came from outside. Did he decide to leave? An engine started and the vehicle noise seemed to fade within minutes. He did leave! The silence was eerie. She had no way to gauge what time it was, but thought it might be mid-evening by the faint light coming through the scratches on the windows. How long did she have before he returned? What could she do to help herself?

Jillian knew she had to be in the best possible shape, both physically and mentally, to have any chance of getting out of here alive. First, she had to stop panicking. *Okay*, she thought, *I have a right to panic*. Who wouldn't under the circumstances, but it was a luxury she couldn't afford. She had to keep a clear head. Also, she didn't know what chemical he'd used on the face mask, but it couldn't be healthy for her. She'd removed the mask once before and could do it again. This time she decided to push the mask above her upper lip, but below her nose. This meant she could breathe only through her mouth with her upper lip extended over her lower lip. After a few attempts, she got the action down pat for uncovering her mouth and chin quickly. With the mask resting on her upper lip, she let the cleaner air fill her lungs and the fog in her head started to lift.

The light shining through the scratch marks on the window wasn't great, but at least she could scan the room. She noticed one more table next to her and boxes piled up everywhere. An old basement utility sink sat under the window. She had no idea of the building's use. Darkness made it impossible to read the labels on the boxes. Jillian had almost forgotten about the elevator. She wondered what sort of old building would require one.

Even though she'd played possum for her captor, her reporter's training for noticing detail had finally kicked in. She was about five feet six inches tall, and the man had been only a couple inches taller than her. He had a weird chemical smell about him, but not the same odor as the chemical he'd used on her face mask. Thinking back, he'd come prepared to kidnap her. Who travels through a cemetery with a stun gun and a roll of duct tape? At least he'd removed the tape from her mouth, for which she was grateful. What was he doing in Mt. Carmel Cemetery at that time of day? How did he know she would be there, or had he expected someone else?

Mt. Carmel Cemetery had been closed during Elizabeth O'Connor's chapel service, but Jillian assumed it had reopened to the public after the mayor and his family left. So who had this guy expected? The only answer that made sense was someone from the mayor's family. They might go visit the graves of other family members while they were out there. Had he targeted someone specific or planned just to take whoever was handy?

Fresh fear made her shiver, and she closed her eyes to keep back tears. So much for this weirdo having grabbed her for ransom money. Like so many crimes, she'd simply been in the wrong place at the wrong time.

# Chapter 52

"Where in the world do you think you're going," Frankie asked as he put the last of the coffee cups away.

"Out, that should cover it," Claire answered. She stuck her IDs in her back jeans pocket and zipped up her jacket.

"Whoa, not without me. Patrick will have my head if I let you leave by yourself."

"Frankie, I'm only going over to Chicago General Hospital. I just have to check on something, then I'll be right back. I'll use valet parking, and I have to check in with the evening nursing supervisor and security. I'll be perfectly safe." Claire knew Frankie felt committed to her safety, but she wanted her independence back. For the second time in two months, something had happened to place her under virtual house arrest. She was at the end of her rope.

Frankie blocked the front door to her apartment. "Why do you have to go tonight? And what do you think you'll accomplish?"

In frustration, Claire sat down on the armrest of her living room couch. "I have this gut feeling the answer to all of this lies at Chicago General. I don't know why this nags at me, it just does."

"All right. I'll take you." Frankie grabbed his jacket out of the closet and turned the coffee pot off. "Do you have your cell phone with you?"

She saw him check for his. "Of course," she responded.

Several minutes later, Frankie exited Claire's indoor parking garage and turned toward Harrison Street. "What's your plan?"

"After I'm cleared by the evening nursing supervisor, I want to return to the surgery. Something about the handling of the donor tissue in Elizabeth's case bothers me. I wish I could put my finger on it, but if I see the unit set up again, maybe it'll come to me."

Frankie turned on Harrison Street and headed west. "How much time will you need in surgery?"

"Maybe fifteen or twenty minutes, plus a few more minutes to get suited up before going in and take things off when I leave the unit."

"So we're talking twenty five plus minutes at the most?" Frankie asked.

"That's all the time I need. If I find something and want to investigate more, I'll use the in-house phone to call security to let you know, in case my cell phone won't work upstairs."

"If you aren't back in twenty-five minutes, I'm checking with security and calling your brother and Jack. Do you understand?"

"Okay." Claire knew Frankie meant it, but she had to do this even if she risked the wrath of the men in her life. She had this deep feeling that the answer lay right in front of them somewhere in this hospital. Her greatest fear was not being able to figure it out. Elizabeth and Fred had both died. Jillian Garcia was missing, and Claire prayed the reporter wouldn't be his next victim.

They were nearing the hospital, and Claire rooted in her pocket for her ID. Her index fingernail snagged on the edge of it. "Shoot," she said.

"What's wrong?" Frankie asked.

"Nothing major." She pulled out her ID and waved it at him. "I broke my fingernail earlier, and I left my clippers in my purse back at the condo."

"There's a pair in the front tray of the console."

"Thanks." Claire spotted them, clipped her broken fingernail, and reached over to return them. "Hey, this is pretty cool. They have Biaggi's Garage on them."

"Dad gives them out to all our customers. Keep the clippers. He has several boxes back at the shop."

"Tell your dad I like these. They're nice and heavy." She slipped them in the front pocket of her jeans. "You never know when you're going to need fingernail clippers."

Frankie pulled into Chicago General's main driveway circle. "We're using valet parking so I can keep my eyes on you."

Claire thought about arguing, but changed her mind and left the car. At the front desk, she requested the evening nursing supervisor. About ten minutes later, the supervisor and security had the logistics worked out. "Frankie, you'll have to remain down here in the lobby while I'm upstairs."

"Remember, if I don't hear from you within twenty-five minutes, I'm calling security, Jack, and Patrick."

"Okay, you'll hear from me," Claire answered as she clipped the temporary ID to her jacket and left with security. On the seventh floor, the security guard offered to wait just outside the surgical suite doors.

The guard entered the code on the key pad. "I think they've finished the appendectomy. They sent the patient to recover in ICU because of the late hour, but you might run into the cleaning staff. If they have any questions, just send them out to me."

"Thanks for your help. This shouldn't take too long," Claire said as she left for the locker room. Quickly she pulled on the required disposable cover-up, shoe covers and hat over her clothes and entered the surgical suite. She inspected the storage area for donor tissue and bone. Protocols were posted on the doors for the refrigerated specimens. Nothing caught her eye, so she crossed the hall to the sterile area where techs set up the surgical carts for morning cases. She could hear voices in the next room over. Must be the housekeeping crew finishing up. Again nothing caught her attention. Discouragement made her shoulders sag. She must have been a fool to think the answer would simply jump right out at her. It had been a long hard day. She should have waited until she'd had a good night's sleep.

She heard someone say goodnight as she entered the dirty utility room where the used case carts waited to be loaded onto the elevator and sent down to the basement for sterile processing. Her heart sank further as she looked around. Everything looked in order. What had she expected to find? The whole trip had been for nothing.

She was turning to leave the area when someone yelled, "You bitch!" It was the last thing she heard before sudden pain erupted on the right side of her head and the utility room faded to black.

# Chapter 53

Derek swore. Why couldn't Dr. O'Shaunessy leave well enough alone? From the day he met her, he knew she would be a thorn in his side. He had to think quickly before anyone came into the area. Housekeeping had left, but someone might have forgotten something and returned for it. He removed the instrument tray and shelves from the appendectomy cart and locked the wheels. His only choice—get the doctor out of the area before anyone spotted her.

He dragged her unconscious body over to the cart and pushed her into the compartment. He struggled bending her knees because of her tight jeans. This made him want to hate her even more. Finally he had her secured, and he checked to make sure she was still breathing. Next, he raced back to the men's locker room and retrieved his personal belongings. Upon returning to the dirty utility room, he stuffed the hearse keys in his pocket and everything else in the case cart along with the doctor and unlocked the wheels. He put the dirty instrument tray and shelves into another case cart and pushed both of them over to the elevator. Once he and the carts entered the elevator, he hit the button for the basement. Thank heavens sterile processing was closed at this hour.

The elevator clunked to a halt. He pulled the case carts out and pushed the one with the doctor into the morgue. Removing her from the case cart took even more effort than putting her in. Placing her on the gurney used up yet more effort and time, making him sweaty and nervous. He covered the gurney with the fitted dark green velvet transport blanket. Next, he ran outside and backed the hearse to the rear doors where funeral homes parked. Once he had her loaded, he cautiously drove into the alley and made his way south. He panicked for a moment when he remembered the security cameras outside the back doors, but then he smiled. He'd forgotten to remove the sign for the fake funeral home after his excursion to the Hillside cemeteries. Once again, luck was on his side.

* * *

Frankie held his cell phone in his hands. The second the twenty-five minutes passed, he called Claire. After four rings, her phone went to voice mail. He immediately asked the receptionist at the front desk to page security. When an officer answered, he explained his situation and asked to be connected to the guard who took Claire up to surgery.

"Officer Nolan, how may I help you?"

"Hi, I came with Dr. O'Shaunessy and I'm waiting for her down in the lobby. She hasn't returned in the timeframe we'd agreed on. I think there may be a problem. Where are you now?"

"I'm right outside the surgical suite. She hasn't come out yet."

"Could you please check on her? She's been stalked several times recently and I'm concerned for her safety."

"Well, no one has entered the unit since I let her in. Housekeeping left about twenty minutes ago. She should be right inside, but I'll check for you."

"Thank you. What floor are you on?" Frankie asked.

"Seven. I'm entering the unit now. I'll call you right back."

Frankie hung up and called Claire's cell phone repeatedly. When he heard Officer Nolan calling back, he switched over to take the incoming call.

"She's not in the surgical suite, but I hear a cell phone ringing in the women's locker room," Nolan said.

"That's me calling. Okay, I'm calling the police. Please keep looking." Frankie didn't even wait for Officer Nolan's response. He called the hospital operator to report a code pink, meaning a baby was missing, because he knew the entire hospital would go on automatic lockdown mode before the police could arrive. Then he dialed 9-1-1 to report a kidnapping. Jack and Patrick could yell at him later, but the lockdown might save Claire. If he waited for the police, that window of opportunity would be lost. The evening supervisor was next on his list and he explained what had happened as the sound of sirens filled the area surrounding

Chicago General. He apologized for faking a code pink, and told her why he'd used the ruse.

Finally, he called Jack. Instead of the cussing-out he'd half expected, Jack's response was swift and terse: a single muttered swear word, and then, "I'm on my way."

Within minutes, police swarmed the lobby and all entrances and exits. Frankie demanded to get in touch with whoever worked up in housekeeping that evening. When Officer Nolan mentioned the finished appendectomy case, the nursing supervisor ordered the operating room report pulled to see who'd been on call for emergency surgeries. She murmured half to herself as she scanned the report. "The circulating nurse went to the ICU to recover the patient. The surgeon left, and the resident returned to the ER assess other patients. The operating tech . . ."

She frowned. "That's weird." She looked up at Frankie and the security guard. "Derek Ruger was the operating tech for the appendectomy case and he never punched out. I'm going to ICU to speak with the circulating nurse."

Jack arrived as Officer Nolan reported to the police. "Get me Ruger's home address and phone. Frankie, what happened? What was Claire doing over here?"

Frankie gave Jack a rundown on the evening since he and Patrick had left. "I thought I could keep her safe if I went with her, but . . ." He shrugged, looking miserable.

"Let's hope she's somewhere in the hospital and forgot to watch the clock," Jack said.

About fifteen minutes later, hospital security notified Jack they had located a surgical case cart in the morgue, where it didn't belong. The shelves and instruments weren't inside. Also, one of the hospital gurneys was missing from the morgue. Jack had security pull the video feed for the back entrances. A few minutes later he and the head of security watched the tape. The driver loading a gurney into a hearse was short and stocky, otherwise unremarkable . . . though Jack couldn't shake a feeling he'd seen the guy before.

"Can you pull up a record of who's being removed from the hospital?" Jack asked.

The head of security checked with the nursing supervisor, then turned to Jack with a grim look. "I hate to tell you this, but no funeral homes were scheduled to make a pickup and no one has died in the last thirty-three hours. Also, they've identified the driver as the operating tech for tonight's appendectomy case, Derek Ruger."

Officer Nolan entered and gave Ruger's information to Jack, who immediately called Captain Ramos and requested a team be sent to Ruger's apartment. "I better go tell Patrick before he hears it from another source."

As he and Frankie left the security office, the evening nursing supervisor stopped them. "I spoke with the circulating nurse and she said Derek Ruger was unusually agitated. He isn't the most pleasant guy in general, but tonight he seemed very distracted."

Jack thanked her for the information. Every muscle felt tense with adrenaline, and his heart was pounding like it did after a hard run. "Let's go, Frankie. Do you want to follow me?"

"No, go ahead. My SUV is in valet parking. I'll meet you at Derek Ruger's place."

# Chapter 54

"Patrick, calm down. We're going to find Claire. You having another heart attack won't help." Breaking the news to his partner that his sister was missing made Jack's top ten list of the hardest things he'd ever had to do. Especially since, during their last case, Claire had willingly gotten into the perpetrator's car.

"What was she thinking? Frankie should have stopped her." Patrick rubbed his forehead with both hands as Jack raced down the street with lights glaring and sirens going full blast.

"You know how Claire is when she gets something into her head, there's no stopping her. At least Frankie went with her and sounded the alarm when she didn't return at the promised time." Jack cut the lights and sirens as he turned down the street where Ruger lived. The night sky was a mass of swirling blue and red. Patrick jumped out of their car before Jack had it in park. Jack ran to catch up with his partner and grabbed his upper arm to stop him from racing up to the building.

Frankie joined them as they reached the crime scene tape. "You said you'd stick to Claire like glue!" Patrick yelled.

"Patrick, I'm so sorry, but they wouldn't let me go up to surgery with her. Hospital security waited for Claire at the door to the unit. How could any of us know the person responsible for Elizabeth's death might be there tonight?"

Jack nodded an okay to Frankie as he watched the worry lines deepen on Patrick's forehead. "I see Captain Ramos ahead. He must be directing the operation. Frankie, you'll have to wait on this side of the crime scene tape."

"Not a problem," Frankie replied.

Jack and his partner headed toward Ramos. "I thought I told you to go home and rest," the captain called out to Patrick.

"That's before my sister went missing," Patrick responded.

"Sir, can you give us an update on the situation here?" Jack asked.

"SWAT arrived first and checked the apartment. No one's in there. The evidence techs are inside processing the place."

"I want to go inside," Patrick said.

"You should wait until the team in finished," the captain answered.

Patrick ignored him and headed for the apartment.

"Jack, stay with him," Ramos said. "I haven't seen the inside, but I understand there's some pretty disturbing stuff in there."

"Okay, Captain." Jack came up on Patrick's tail. "Are you sure you want to do this?"

"No, but I have to," Patrick said.

"All right, but I go first and you follow. No argument. The minute you don't feel okay, you're going to tell me, understood? Frankie can wait with you or take you home."

Patrick didn't answer as he followed his partner up the stairs to the second floor. They signed in at the apartment door with the evidence tech and put shoe covers on, so as not to track anything in to the potential crime scene. They also got instructions to not touch anything. If they wanted anything moved, they needed to call a tech first.

The apartment was lit up like the Water Tower Shopping Center for the Christmas rush. Jack spotted the wall first. The markings covered its entire surface. Patrick came up right beside him.

"Oh my God!" Patrick exclaimed. "Do you believe this?"

All Jack could do initially was gawk. "Ruger must have written the entire Keeley family tree on this wall. Does it look accurate?"

Slowly, without actually touching the wall, Patrick ran his finger from Timothy, the father, down to each Keeley son and daughter, then their spouses and children. Ruger had even annotated their pets. Some of the family members had photos posted by their names. Off to the right side of the tree hung a picture of Claire and Jack behind the morgue the night of Elizabeth's death. Ruger had used a red marker to cross out Elizabeth's name and picture.

"This is mind-boggling. He has all the information correct. This guy must be Claire's stalker, just like Frankie said. He couldn't have acquired all this information overnight. This took years of research on the family, and he wrote everything on the wall with a calligraphy pen. That takes a lot of skill."

For several minutes their eyes were glued to the wall. Only Patrick spoke as he went from name to name mentioning an event from the list he and Michael had worked on. He filled Jack in on the details of earlier attacks that happened before Jack became his partner.

Finally, they reached the far right end of the wall. Jack yelled, "That's it! We have to see the captain right away."

"What are you talking about?" Patrick asked.

"See the picture of Claire and me? It was taken behind the morgue the night the transport van brought Elizabeth in to be autopsied. He had to be standing right there. He knew what was going to happen and he made it a point to document his achievement. I'm sure he's the one who killed Elizabeth and I'm sure we can prove it because he had access. We have to get the captain to request Jillian Garcia's film footage. She did her reporting from this same area. That's why he saw her as a threat and kidnapped her."

Jack stepped out of the apartment into the building's hallway and called the captain. "Sir, my guess is Derek Ruger is responsible for the mayor's sister's death. I think we'll find his face in the footage shot by Jillian Garcia's cameraman for the news report the night Mrs. O'Connor was brought to the morgue. Ruger not only kidnapped Claire, but Jillian Garcia as well. I just don't know where he has them stashed. Maybe it's time to put this out on the air and see if the public can help us. We can use Ruger's picture from his hospital ID."

"I'm on it. How's Patrick holding up?" Captain Ramos asked.

"He's okay. I'm sure finding the Keeley family tree written on the wall, including Claire's photo, caught him short. Okay, I'm going back in to see what else the evidence techs found. We'll keep you posted."

Jack turned around as he disconnected and found Patrick in the hallway. "Are you all right?"

"I'm stepping out for some fresh air. It's hot inside with all the floodlights on. I just sent pictures of the wall to Michael. He should be kept abreast of the situation."

Ten minutes later, Jack and Patrick re-entered the apartment after putting on new shoe covers. One of the techs called them over. "Check this out," the man said, gesturing toward a collection of photos. "Guy's got a darkroom. I found them drying in there."

Jack concentrated on each photo. "Some of these were taken across the street from Claire's condo building. Here's a late afternoon shot from the corner of West Harrison Street and South Leavitt, near the back entrance of the morgue. This one shows Claire leaving the building during a light rain."

The evidence tech took the photos from Jack and placed them in a brown paper envelope in a large plastic container. "All of the photos are dry, so I'm packaging them up. We took a number of shots of the wall in the living room and the rest of the apartment. So far we haven't found anything to tell us where Ruger's gone. Sorry we couldn't help more."

"This guy only owns one DVD, *Silence of the Lambs*. Don't you find that weird?" another tech called out.

Jack just shook his head. "This guy is a weirdo, that makes him even scarier," he said to himself so Patrick wouldn't hear his comment. The last thing he wanted to do was pile on more worry for his partner.

"Let's make a complete walk through of every room before the captain closes the investigation.

Patrick entered the bedroom first. "What's with all the boxes?"

Jack called for the crime scene tech. As soon as the tech gave him the okay, Jack put on disposable gloves and opened one of the boxes. "I think he's planning on moving. This one appears to be photography equipment." A second box held clothing and personal items.

At a little after two in the morning, the captain shut the investigation down. The techs hadn't uncovered any more leads and everyone was exhausted. "All the news stations, both radio and television, have the information about Ruger and his kidnap victims. His picture will be on the front page of the morning papers. We have the make and license plate number for his vehicle from the Department of Motor Vehicles. He's not going to get very far. He knows he can't return here or go to work. We'll check Chicago General to see where his paychecks are deposited and if he has a debit card. I'll check protocol to have an alert put out in case he tries to use it.

"The team found a second car with Arkansas plates in the garage. From the contents inside the car, it looks like he was planning to split soon. The car and plates are registered to a George Ryder in Little Rock. I've notified the police in case Ruger shows up and we'll check the local banks down there also."

Jack looked at Patrick. "Where have we heard that name before?"

"That's the guy who was fired by Keeley Liquor Distributors some fifteen to twenty years ago. He's dead. We have his death certificate." Patrick paced back and forth. "This is unbelievable, and I don't believe in coincidences."

"Wait a minute. Think about these two last names, Ryder and Ruger. Could Derek Ruger be George Ryder's son and have used his father's identification to provide a cover in Arkansas? Could his real name be Ryder, not Ruger? Captain, you have to put both names out there so he can't hide under his father's name," Jack said. "Maybe Finch can research a birth certificate for a Derek Ryder. We can get his date of birth from his employment records and off his driver's license, unless he lied about that too."

Ramos nodded. "Okay, we have our work cut out for us, but right now I'm ordering you to take Patrick home. He won't be any help to Claire if he lands back in the hospital."

"Yes, sir," Jack answered.

Patrick clenched his fists. "No! I'm not leaving. I'll bet anything the answer is right here. Claire's my sister. You can't stop me!"

"Detective O'Shaunessy, if I have to take my order to the level of requiring disciplinary action because you're being so bullheaded, I will to protect your health. You can come back in the morning. I'm standing firm on this." Captain Ramos pointed toward their car. "Now, go."

"But Jack," Patrick pleaded.

"I agree with the captain. Claire's been in tight spots before. We have to have faith in her. We're going to find her." Jack opened the passenger door for his partner, and after Patrick reluctantly got in, proceeded to the driver's side. He glanced over and thought he saw a tear roll down Patrick's cheek.

"We're going to find her," he said again, quietly, as he started the engine. He sent up a silent prayer that both Patrick and Claire would survive this nightmare unharmed.

# Chapter 55

Derek shoved the gurney into the elevator, grabbed the blanket off Dr. O'Shaunessy's face and removed the duct tape that covered her mouth, but not from around her wrists. He needed her alive until he found a buyer for her organs. He couldn't risk her throwing up and aspirating her stomach contents into her lungs. If he didn't find a buyer for her and the reporter soon, he could dispose of them in the crematory out back, or in any number of corn fields on his way to Little Rock. They had to be out of here before Mr. Floyd returned.

When the elevator doors opened, he pulled the gurney out and looked over at the table where he'd left Jillian Garcia. The reporter's limp form was barely visible in the darkness. "Good. She's asleep," he said, out loud to reassure himself. Working carefully, he lined the gurney up with the second table, then used the sheet under O'Shaunessy's body to transfer her from the gurney. He checked her breathing. It was slow but within a reasonable range. He strapped her to the table above her knees, across her abdomen and shoulders. He decided to leave the tape on her hands, rather than risk waking her up by pulling it off. She wasn't going anywhere. The doctor was out cold.

It had been a long day, and he needed some sleep. He returned to the elevator, went up to the back lounge, and slung himself down on the nearest couch. Exhaustion took over quickly and he fell into a deep sleep.

* * *

The minute the elevator doors shut, Claire opened her eyes. The right side of her head ached. Actually, her whole head throbbed. What had he used to knock her out with? She tried to reposition her head, so she wasn't lying on the injured side. Something was pinning her down . . . something thin and strong, crossing her body from shoulder to hip and also across her knees. Restraints. Her captor had strapped her down. Fear jolted through her. Who was this creep, and what did he want with her?

She made herself breathe deeply until she felt calmer. Slowly, her eyes adjusted to the darkness, which wasn't quite total. After a few minutes, she noticed someone else in the room on a table next to her. A woman, apparently restrained, just like she was. When her kidnapper said, "She's asleep," she'd thought he meant her. Who was this other woman? And where were they?

"Hello, are you awake? I'm Claire O'Shaunessy," Claire whispered to the woman. In the faint light from scratches in the painted-over windows, she watched the woman push a face mask above her lips using her teeth and shoulder.

"Hi," the woman said quietly, in a drained voice. "I'm Jillian Garcia."

"You're the reporter!"

"Yes."

"How did you end up here?"

"I was kidnapped at Mt. Carmel Cemetery. What about you?"

"I'm a forensic pathologist from the morgue. I went over to check something out at Chicago General Hospital regarding a case I'm working on and was attacked in the surgical unit," Claire replied.

Jillian kept her voice as quiet as she could. "I don't know why he has us, but I don't think the outcome is going to be good. We have to get out of here before he comes back."

"He'll hear us if we use the elevator."

"There's a set of stairs over my right shoulder. He has me secured to this cart. I can barely move. There are three straps across my body, plus he used some sort of plastic handcuffs to tie my hands and feet down. What about you?"

Claire relaxed her body to see if she had any wiggle room. "I have one strap across my shoulders, but he didn't put my arms under the middle strap. There's one above my knees."

"What about your hands?" Jillian asked.

"Tied together with duct tape. Let me see if I can find an end and pull the tape loose with my teeth."

"Please hurry." A sharper note of panic entered Jillian's voice. "How are we going to cut the plastic straps?"

"We'll think of something." Claire had no idea what, but showing her own fear would only make Jillian's worse. Then the answer hit her, and she gave a breathy laugh. "Would you believe a friend gave me fingernail clippers this evening, and they're in my jeans pocket? Let me get my hands free. Can you look around and see if there's anything we can use as a weapon if we have to?"

"Okay, but hurry."

By pressing her left shoulder down, Claire discovered she could move it under the strap. She could only move one shoulder because it made the strap push against her throat, but she managed to move her hands up to her mouth. She searched for the end of the tape with her tongue and tried not to gag. The dirtball's hands had touched the tape. "Give me a minute. I think I've got it."

Claire was convinced her tongue would never be the same as she used it to separate the edge and push back the top layer of tape. Because her captor had crossed her hands, she could use her fingernails to separate the top edge more from the next layer. Once she had a couple of inches to work with, she gripped the end piece with her teeth and pulled. Next she reversed the process with the fingers on the other hand. Thanking her lucky stars that she'd taken good care of her teeth, she gave one final yank. The last couple of inches gave way, peeling up from the bottom layer. "Ouch!"

"What's wrong?" Jillian asked.

Claire could hear the panic in Jillian's voice. "I'm okay. The tape was stuck to some of the hair on the back of my hands. It smarted when I pulled it off. Hang in there, I'm making progress." She continued to pull with her teeth and fingernails until her hands were free. One piece of duct tape dangled from her right wrist, but getting rid of it wouldn't take—

Claire heard movement above them. She froze. A toilet flushed.

"Try to make it look like your wrists are still taped in case he checks on us." Jillian spoke in a fierce whisper. "Then pretend you're still asleep. He might kill us if he thinks we're trying to escape."

Claire pulled the strap down over her left shoulder, crossed her hands, draped the tape back over them and tucked the loose end underneath her wrists. She could see Jillian had pulled the face mask back into place. She heard the elevator rattle and stop at the basement level. The door slid open. With her head turned slightly, she peeked through her eyelashes. The spill of light from inside the elevator gave her a good look at her kidnapper. Derek Ruger, the surgical tech she'd interviewed at Chicago General.

The elevator door banged as Ruger held it open. He stared over at them for what felt like forever. Finally, apparently satisfied they were asleep, he released the door. It eased shut, and Claire heard him return to the floor above. A few minutes later, no more sounds came from upstairs.

# Chapter 56

Even though Patrick wasn't happy with the captain's directive, he understood Ramos's command. As much as he didn't want to admit it to Jack, he was exhausted both physically and mentally. So why couldn't he fall asleep? Jack snored on the family room couch while Patrick tossed and turned on the one in the living room, his mind still operating in high gear.

They had missed something important, but what? All his years as a homicide detective had fine-tuned his sixth sense. With his eyes closed, he played back the scene at Derek Ruger's apartment. He and Jack had spoken with the captain before ducking under the crime scene tape and entering the three-flat. At the top of the second-floor stairs, a patrolman logged them in and issued shoe covers. Then there was the unbelievable shock of the Keeley family tree written on the living room wall, with a red X through Elizabeth O'Connor's name and picture.

After pointing out to Jack which family members and pets had been victimized, Jack had realized the importance of the photo of him and Claire at the morgue. Patrick turned on his side and adjusted the pillow under his head. His mind wandered back to Jack telling the captain about the photo.

He remembered being shown some photographs the evidence techs had found in Ruger's darkroom. He'd almost forgotten he'd sent snapshots of the wall to Michael's cell phone. He and Jack had wandered around the small one-bedroom apartment before leaving, grudgingly impressed with how Ruger had kept everything in order. He had simple and cheap furniture, except for the antique desk. That piece must have cost Ruger a few bucks. Patrick's grandmother had one just like it. He'd proven to her at a young age that he took care of his toys, so she'd shown him a secret panel. First, she'd removed a small drawer, and then pushed on the side panel. A spring released it and exposed the secret compartment.

Patrick's eyes flew open. What if Ruger's desk had the same secret compartment? What if it held something that would lead them to Claire? He sat up. "Jack," he yelled. "We have to go back to Ruger's apartment, *now*. I know what we missed!"

Jack snorted awake, and Patrick heard him muttering groggily as he dragged himself into the living room. "Stop yelling. You're going to wake up Sylvia and the girls."

Patrick sat on the edge of the couch. "I know this sounds crazy, but I've had a feeling we missed something really important, and I couldn't sleep."

"The evidence techs searched all over the place and they didn't find anything else. You need to go back to sleep. Start fresh in the morning."

"No, you don't understand. Do you remember the desk in the living room?" Patrick stood, picked up his wallet and keys from the coffee table, and stuffed them into his pockets. He snatched up his jacket he'd thrown over the chair only hours ago.

"Vaguely, but that could be because we've only a few hours of sleep under our belts. What's so important about that old desk?"

Patrick slipped his feet into his shoes. "My grandmother had the same desk. There's a secret compartment. It opens by a spring mechanism once you remove one of the drawers. My gut says that's where it's at."

Jack sank into the recliner. "Where *what's* at?"

"The key to where he's holding Claire."

"There's a key? Do you know how crazy you sound? Did you read this in a Hardy Boys book when you were a kid?" Jack found the lever and elevated the foot rest, then propped his feet on it.

"Not a real key. A clue. Humor me. I'll make some leaded coffee and then we're going back. If I'm right, you can sleep all you want after we find Claire, okay?" Patrick headed to the kitchen, only to discover Sylvia had gotten there first. She'd started the coffee brewing and was cutting some generous slices of her homemade pecan coffee cake. "Did I wake you, honey? I'm sorry. I didn't mean to."

She smiled. "I'm a cop's wife. It comes with the 'I do'."

He gave her a big hug. "You're the best! I love you!"

She gave him a quick kiss on his cheek. "I'll have this ready for you and Jack in a moment. Now scoot while I pack your snack."

Ten minutes later, after watching Jack drain his first cup of coffee and devour a slice of Sylvia's coffee cake, Patrick called Captain Ramos to gain permission to re-enter the apartment. The captain sounded tired, but intrigued. "You could be right, Detective. This sounds far-fetched, but I know you won't rest until you search that desk. Good luck. You'll need it if you're wrong."

"Okay. I got it. Thanks, Captain. Sorry I woke you." He almost apologized for disturbing the captain's dog, barking in the background, but decided he'd said enough.

"What did he say?" Jack asked as Patrick ended the call.

"He said something to the effect that if I'm wrong, I'll be directing traffic on the corner of State and Madison the rest of my career. Actually, he did wish us luck."

With the beginning of morning rush hour traffic an hour away, Jack breezed down the streets to Ruger's apartment.

"Do you believe this? There are two squad cars and the evidence van parked out front," Patrick said. "I assumed the captain would send one car, but not all this." A patrolman greeted them and unsecured the door. At the top of the stairs, they went through the same ritual of signing in and putting on shoe covers before entering the apartment. A gloved evidence tech stood in front of the desk with his arms crossed.

"Good morning, detectives. I hear you're looking for a secret compartment. I've already photographed the desk from several angles. If you could direct me to the area in question along with some instructions, I'll open it for you."

Patrick wanted to do it himself, but understood the importance of following protocol, especially with two lives on the line, and a third if you counted the mayor. "If this works the same as my grandmother's desk, you need to remove the small top drawer in the center first." Patrick clenched his hands as if in prayer.

The evidence tech took a photograph of the drawer, and proceeded to pull it out of the desk.

"Using your right hand, gently press against the left interior wall and let go," Patrick said, his eyes riveted to the spot.

After a couple of close-up shots of the area at different angles, the tech did as Patrick directed. The panel sprung open, revealing the secret compartment.

"Whoa," Jack said softly. The tech trained his flashlight into the dark space.

"What's in there?" Patrick asked.

"Patience, Detective O'Shaunessy." The tech peered closer. "I see a card. A business card, from the size. I have to take a photo before I remove it. That'll matter to a jury." He snapped a picture with his cell phone, then pulled the card out and placed it on the desk, reminding Patrick to not touch it. "You can take a picture with your cell phone." The tech stepped aside and the detectives moved in for a closer look.

After Patrick snapped the photo, Jack read the business card out loud. "Floyd's Funeral Home and Crematorium. I bet this is where the hearse came from, that I saw on the security tape back at Chicago General Hospital. Because of the camera angle we couldn't read the sign on the side door. Patrick, make sure you got a clear shot of the address. I think the place is located in Englewood." Jack stepped aside and called the captain with a quick update.

Patrick checked the photo. "Clear as day. See Jack, I wasn't crazy. I can't believe this!"

Jack lowered the phone from his ear. "Okay, partner, the captain said we're to meet SWAT at the funeral home, but let the team do their job. Got it?" He turned to the evidence tech. "Thanks."

"No problem, detectives. I hope you get this guy."

It was all Patrick could do not to run to the squad car, never mind that he hadn't been cleared to return to full duty. All he cared about right now was finding Claire, and Jillian Garcia, alive and in one piece.

Once inside the car, Jack flipped on the lights and sirens, then pulled away from the curb. "I'm going to cut them when we're within six blocks of the funeral home. There's a fire station two blocks north of the building, but we don't want this guy to panic and flee. He might have Claire and the reporter at another location."

"Just drive faster," Patrick said through gritted teeth. Storm clouds were gathering outside, which felt like a bad omen. Claire had to be at the funeral home. She *had* to, or they were back to square one.

The wind picked up as they drove, and thunder rumbled in the distance. The city was in for a hell of a storm. About three blocks from the address, the SWAT team had set up their first perimeter and begun evacuating neighbors who lived next to the funeral home. Patrols were diverting drivers to other streets, given the excuse of downed electrical lines. Patrick and Jack sat tight, waiting for instructions on when the team intended to advance closer.

# Chapter 57

Claire heard Jillian's sigh of relief when the elevator door closed. For a brief moment she recalled lying on the gurney in the elevator under a heavy blanket as her head started to clear. The terror she'd felt must have been nothing compared to what Jillian had experienced during her hours trapped in this basement. She realized she was Jillian's best chance of escape.

"Claire, we have to get out now. We're running out of time. What if he comes back with a gun or a knife?"

"Be quiet. I'm almost out from under these straps." Slowly, she slid under the shoulder strap and freed her head. She felt on both sides of the table for the waist strap's release. Once she found it, she fingered the clamp. If she wasn't careful, the sound of the clamp hitting the floor would draw Ruger's attention.

Jillian's anxiousness put Claire on edge. "Can't you hurry?"

"Don't talk," Claire warned her. "I can hear the television on upstairs but I don't want to cause any noise to attract that monster. Try to relax. Do some deep breathing." With her hands on both pieces of the clamp, Claire released it. So far, so good. She gently grasped the strap and brought it up on her abdomen. Clutching it tightly, she gathered it in a ball and held it against her as she turned onto her left side. She eased her right leg free and then her left, keeping a grip on the clamp so it didn't bang against the table. She took a deep breath and thanked God for her good fortune even though they weren't out of the woods.

"Jillian, I'm free but I have to get off this table without making a sound, okay?" Claire eased the strap to the floor. Next she rolled onto her stomach and grasped both sides of the table. She draped her right leg over the edge and lowered it to the floor, then did the same with her left leg. Once she had both feet on solid ground, she stood up but held on to the table so it wouldn't shift, and to make sure she could move without getting dizzy.

She removed the fingernail clippers from her pocket and went over to Jillian. "We can't rush this, do you understand?" She understood Jillian's fear, but they might only have this one chance. Claire didn't want to think what would happen if Derek Ruger came down before she released her fellow captive.

"I'll wait for you to tell me when I can move."

Claire cut through the plastic cuffs securing Jillian's hands and feet. The process went slower than she would have liked. The clippers were small and the plastic tough, and it took several minutes for the clippers to chew through each. Next, she removed the final three straps, again being careful not to bang the metal clamps against the table or let them hit the floor. She directed Jillian to roll on her right side and catch her breath. She guessed Jillian had been strapped to this table since late yesterday afternoon, which meant she might not be to stable on her feet.

She helped Jillian finish turning onto her stomach and assisted her off the table. "Hold on to the edge until we're sure you won't pass out. I'm going to look for anything we can use for a weapon."

"How can I ever thank you? I think there's a shovel or something in that back corner," Jillian said. She continued to clutch the table while Claire walked over to the corner.

"You can thank me after we're out of here." Claire found the shovel and continued to search the basement. Daylight was breaking, which lightened the darkness to mere gloom. Muffled thunder muttered as she returned to Jillian's side with her weapon.

Jillian stood up straight and took a short step, then another. "I think I'm good to go now. Let's try the stairs."

They were halfway across the basement room when they heard their captor scream, "*No!*" Something heavy, like a piece of furniture, hit the floor as he yelled out a stream of four letter words. They heard glass shatter. *There goes the television*, Claire thought.

"Get to the stairs," she said, with an edge of panic.

Jillian bit her lip. "My legs are a little stiff. I don't know how fast I can move."

"Stay close to me and go up the stairs first. I'll be right behind you." At that moment Claire heard the gears on the elevator move. "Shoot. Keep going."

They were halfway up the stairs when the elevator door opened. They kept climbing as they watched Ruger step out. He took in the empty tables where they'd lain and swore, then looked up and spotted them.

With another curse, he charged after them. Ready to practice her famous hockey slap shot from her high school days, which had won them the state title, Claire raised the shovel. Ruger kept coming, too fast or too furious to dodge. She whacked his head and sent him tumbling down the steps.

"I've got the door open," Jillian called.

Claire scrambled after her, but heard Ruger coming up behind. The force of her swing should have knocked him out cold. "Keep going!" she shouted, as his grip closed on her ankle.

# Chapter 38

Jack held his police radio up to his ear, waiting for SWAT's command to move in. He hoped both Claire and Jillian were inside the building and safe, but his gut warned him this might not be the case. Thank heavens protocol called for paramedics to be waiting to transport anyone to the hospital if needed. He stepped over to the ambulance and quietly mentioned his partner was recovering from a recent heart attack, and his sister might be a hostage inside.

As he moved back toward the squad car, the radio crackled. "Is everyone in position?" The affirmative answers came quickly. "We're moving in. Remember, we might have two kidnap victims inside. Who knows what this Derek Ruger might try."

"Come on, Patrick we can move closer," Jack said with his heart in his throat. They stopped and took cover behind a police car several doors down from the funeral home. From this position they watched the SWAT guys batter their way through every possible entrance on this side of the funeral home, shouting out their arrival.

Without warning the sky opened up, sending a blinding downpour. Patrick moved around the car and headed toward the building. Jack sprinted after him. "What are you doing?" he yelled above the thunder.

"I'm going after Claire!"

"No, you're not. The SWAT team will get her." Jack grabbed him and pulled him over to the nearest shelter from the sheeting rain, behind a large tree on the parkway that offered them little protection. A bad place to be during a thunderstorm, but he knew they were out of options.

\* \* \*

Claire's free hand caught the railing just as Ruger tried to pull her down. She attempted to kick him in the face with her other foot, but couldn't reach him. He held on to her ankle with both hands like a vise. She jammed her boot against his fingers. The move made her drop the shovel, but he let go, cursing in pain as he stumbled back down a couple of stairs. The shovel slid past him to the basement floor.

"You'll pay for this," he screamed at her.

"Claire, what should I do?" Jillian called from the top of the stairs.

"Go for help!" Claire kept climbing. Ruger went for her ankle again, but missed. He tried a third time, but she was faster. She slammed her boot down on his right wrist and heard his bones crunch. She risked a glance over her shoulder and watched as he let go of the railing and slid to the bottom of the steps, howling in obvious pain. She steadied herself and ran up the stairs. Jillian had waited at the top. "I told you to go for help!"

"There was no way I'd leave you alone with that monster."

"Let's get out of here."

They ran into the next room, looking for an outside door. Claire recognized their surroundings just as Jillian said, breathlessly, "This is a funeral home!"

Now Claire knew where to go. "Lobby," she said. They passed through the room and reached the front foyer just as half a dozen SWAT officers burst through the door. Claire stifled a scream, then felt faint with relief.

"Are you okay?" the first officer asked them.

Claire could barely get the word "Yes" out. She pointed the way she and Jillian had come. "He's in the basement."

"Stay put. We're getting you help."

*No way.* "I need fresh air," Claire said and bolted through the front door with Jillian beside her. Rain soaked her in seconds, but she scarcely noticed. All her attention was on two figures, heading down the sidewalk just a few yards away.

"Patrick, they're safe," Jack called out. He ran across the front yard, ignoring the rain. He threw his arms around Claire and gave her a kiss on her forehead. "Are both of you okay?"

"We are now," Jillian said. A third figure broke through the police-tape perimeter and ran up to Jillian. He was holding a video camera and a microphone. Her eyes widened. "Jim," she said, then squared her shoulders. "Give me that mic."

Patrick reached them then and swept Claire up in a bear hug. She clung to him, feeling shaky as the aftermath of the ordeal hit her. "I'll be fine," she said, as much to herself as to her brother. A yard away from them, Jillian smoothed her wet hair off her face while her cameraman adjusted his equipment.

Looking professional in spite of the rain, she raised the microphone to her lips. "This is Jillian Garcia reporting to you *live* from the funeral home where Dr. Claire O'Shaunessy, of the Cook County Medical Examiner's Office, and I were held captive by the man the police are bringing out of the building this very minute. At this time, we don't know why he kidnapped us. WTLV News will report the details as soon as they become available." She handed Jim the microphone just as her knees buckled and a paramedic caught her.

# Chapter 59

Claire woke to find three pairs of eyes staring back at her. They belonged to the three men in her life: Patrick, Jack, and Frankie. "Am I in trouble?" she asked. She noticed her brother's eyes looked a little red. Plus, now she remembered Jack's expression of more than brotherly affection outside the funeral home. This was bound to bring a few remarks from the homicide department.

Frankie spoke first. "Did you have to go and get yourself kidnapped? You scared all of us to death. And don't make any funny comments about the funeral home. I'll be outside in the hallway if any of you need me." He gave her hand a squeeze and smiled as he left.

She caught Jack's eye next. He blushed and looked down. She'd have to talk with him later, once she figured out what to say. Finally, she looked at Patrick. He blinked hard a few times, then managed to say, "How're you feeling, sis? You need anything?"

Before she could answer, a nurse came in to check her vital signs and pain level. "You took quite a nasty hit to the right side of your head. Luckily, the skull film showed no damage. The ER doctor put a few stitches in, so you'll have to be careful when washing and brushing your hair for about seven to ten days. Also, you're not to get out of this bed for any reason without assistance. If you need to go to the bathroom, push the red call button on the bed railing."

Claire automatically touched the bandage. "Did they have to shave my hair?"

"Yes, but just a spot less than two inches in diameter. The rest of your hair should cover it. Get some rest and call me if you need anything."

Before Claire could ask her any questions, the nurse had gone. Captain Ramos entered the room, and Claire relaxed back into her pillows. "Now I know I'm in trouble."

Captain Ramos graced her with a big smile. "For once you're off the hook, young lady. I'm so relieved everyone is all right, but I must tell you Derek Ruger wants to file an assault and battery charge against you for the damage he sustained to his wrist. He's in surgery as we speak. Good job, Claire!"

"Are you serious?" she asked, sitting up straight a little too fast and making her head swim.

"Don't worry about it. With all the pending charges against him, I'm sure his attorney will advise him to forget about it."

"Can anyone fill me in on what happened? And how's Jillian Garcia?"

"She's okay and in the room next to yours. Jillian is singing your praises," Captain Ramos said. "She says you kept a cool head and found a way to free both of you. As a sidebar, it turns out her co-anchor, Scott Christie, hasn't left her bedside. He apparently has feelings for her. It wouldn't surprise me if she sports a new ring in the near future."

"Actually, Frankie's fingernail clippers let me cut the plastic straps off her wrists and ankles. Without it I don't know if we would have made it out unharmed."

"For now, I'll let Jack and your brother fill you in further. It seems I have a press conference awaiting me as a result of your heroic efforts. If you need anything, have Patrick let me know. I'll be going now." The captain started to leave.

Claire called out, "How about a few days off with pay for your favorite detectives?"

"Claire, you can't ask the Captain for that." Patrick looked embarrassed by her request.

The captain grinned. "Sure she can. Would four days with pay do the trick?"

She smiled back. "Thank you. That would be great."

"Okay, everyone's leave starts after the reports are written and on my desk." Captain Ramos waved as he left.

Patrick pulled a chair up alongside the bed. "I can't believe the captain went for your suggestion," he said.

"I can," Jack said, leaning against the wall. "I think the captain likes Claire as long as she behaves. This time, she stayed within the lines even though it took three strong men to keep her there. Of course, she basically saved Jillian Garcia single-handed, which I'm sure was a big relief."

"Jack, either find another chair or sit on my bed. I can't wait to hear how this all played out," Claire said.

"Hey, am I too late for this party?" Michael Keeley entered the room, carrying a vase filled with beautiful fall mums. "These are from the entire Keeley clan."

Claire was delighted. "Oh, Michael, please tell everyone thank you from me."

Michael set the vase on a side table. "I think we owe you, Patrick, and Jack a thank you for putting an end to our long nightmare."

"Will someone find Frankie and a couple of chairs? I don't know how much longer I can stay awake, and I want to hear the entire story," Claire said.

Within a few minutes everyone settled down as the various parts of the story came together. Patrick showed the pictures of the Keeley family tree from Derek Ruger's apartment and shared how he'd remembered the secret compartment in his grandmother's desk, which happened to be identical to Ruger's. He couldn't believe his luck when he discovered Ruger had left the funeral home business card behind in the secret compartment.

Claire was floored when she looked at the pictures of the Keeley family tree covering an entire wall. Even more creepy was seeing a picture of herself and Jack posted on it, too. "I wasn't comfortable when I met him at Chicago General. I felt like something was off. He seemed to be hiding something, but I sure wouldn't have guessed all of this."

Frankie jumped in, telling how he called security the minute Claire was late and how they found the empty surgical case cart in the morgue.

"Do you know what he hit me on the head with?" Claire asked.

"I think Ruger said he used a bladder retractor," Patrick answered.

"Those things are huge. I can't believe he didn't crack my skull."

"You've always been a little hard-headed," her brother responded. This brought on a round of laughs, which was just what she needed to relax.

"We had no idea what had happened to you," Jack said. "Then I reviewed the security tape that showed Ruger loading a gurney with a covered body on it at the back entrance of the hospital, and I realized I was watching you being kidnapped."

Claire shook her head. "I probably remember the least, since I was either knocked out or covered up. When I met Jillian, neither of us had any idea we'd been brought to the basement of a funeral home. Frankie, tell your dad his fingernail clippers saved Jillian and me in the end."

A knock at the door drew everyone's attention. It was a hospital volunteer, delivering a huge vase with three dozen red roses. Jack placed them on the table next to the mums and handed her the card.

"Who are those from?" Patrick asked.

"Scott Christie and the WTLV television station. This is overwhelming."

The next knock was the nurse. "Okay, everyone out of the pool per the doctor's orders. The patient needs some rest. You can visit again after four this afternoon, but only two at a time." The nurse stood guard as everyone made their goodbyes.

Patrick and Michael were the last to go. Her brother squeezed her hand. "You get some shut-eye. The rest of us could sure use it. Hopefully, after Ruger recovers, he'll confess and we'll finally understand his motive."

Michael patted her shoulder. "Claire, because of you and our fine police department, my family is going sleep a whole lot better tonight."

Claire smiled as she watched them leave. A feeling of satisfaction came over her. Then she closed her eyes and slipped into a sound sleep.

# Chapter 60

A week had passed since Claire's release from the hospital. She marveled over how great it felt to wake up in her own bed with her apartment all to herself. Well, almost to herself. Curled up, snug against her side, lay a year-old yellow tabby cat named Tucker. He was a gift from Jack the day she'd been discharged. Her new watch kitty's purring motor had come on full blast. She'd already fallen in love with this bundle of fur.

He'd told her he thought at first of giving her a dog. However, with her long days at the morgue, he knew it wouldn't be fair to the animal. Even he and Patrick couldn't be guaranteed regular hours to help with dog-walking duties. So they scouted out several cat shelters. At the last one Tucker kept tapping Jack's leg for attention, as if to say, "Take me!"

"Tucker, would you like some breakfast? I have your favorite, salmon and shrimp." Tucker jumped off the bed and raced to the kitchen. Claire quickly dressed in jeans and a sweatshirt and followed him. "I swear you understand every word I say, at least when it comes to food." She stirred warm water with half a can of wet food and placed it on his tray. Tucker scarfed it down while she filled the dry food bowl, washed out his water bowl and gave him fresh water.

She'd started to make a pot of coffee when the doorman rang. He told her she had a couple of visitors, namely Patrick and Jack. Several minutes later she opened her door to the most heavenly scent.

"Sylvia baked her pecan coffee cake for you," Patrick said as he handed her the warm foil-wrapped plate. "Is the coffee ready?"

Claire took the plate and sniffed the wonderful aroma. "Have a seat. The coffee will be done in a few minutes." She placed the gift on the table and finished putting the coffee on, then gathered cups, plates, silverware and napkins.

"Wow, look at Tucker clean his bowl. The vet said he'd have a growing appetite until he was almost two." Jack bent over and petted Tucker's head. Tucker raised his back in thanks and tapped Jack's leg for more attention. "Hi there, little guy."

"Besides Sylvia's wonderful coffee cake, to what do I owe the honor of having two of Chicago's finest detectives in my home this morning?" She put cream and sugar on the table and poured the coffee. Tucker jumped up on Jack's lap and fell asleep.

"First of all, I've been medically cleared to return to full duty," Patrick said.

"Are you sure you're not pushing yourself too fast?" Claire asked.

"No. But there is one restriction, and this morning doesn't count. I have to stay on my diet and do some moderate exercise. Jack offered to be my trainer. I figured you and Tucker could be his backup when needed. How's your head and when do you return to work?"

"Patrick, that's great news. The headaches are gone. The stitches come out this afternoon, so I should be back to work by tomorrow."

"We also have some new information on the case," Jack added. "Even though Derek Ruger's recovery is far from over, he keeps babbling about how unfair life has treated him. We learned earlier from Paul Keeley that Ruger's father, George Ryder, was fired for theft from Keeley Liquor Distributors. At the time, Ryder told his son that his job had been given to Michael. Here's where the plot thickens. Apparently, Ruger is Derek's mother's last name. She never married George Ryder. When Derek's father lost his job, his mom took off with another man and left her son behind. In the meantime, good old Dad turned to selling street drugs when he couldn't find work, which eventually cost him his life. Derek was in high school at the time of his father's death. He grew up believing Michael Keeley was the root of his problems. I guess the building manager took pity on him and let Derek live in a spare basement room, so he wouldn't end up on the streets."

"That's really sad. In a sense, Derek was a victim too. Look how many people have suffered as a result of his father's choices," Claire said.

"Anyway, he developed a plan to seek revenge against the Keeleys for the loss of his own family. Michael's youngest sister, Mary Ann, became his first victim. The evidence tech at Ruger's apartment found several folders containing newspaper clippings, articles from the Internet, and notes on the Keeley family dating back more than fifteen years, to before Mary Ann's accident." Patrick reached for a second slice of coffee cake. With an *oh no, you don't* look, Claire slipped the plate away from him and set it on the kitchen counter.

"What about Elizabeth's death?" she asked.

Jack raised his coffee cup. "It turns out one of the clients at Floyd's Funeral Home died from gas gangrene. Ruger collected a sample. A few days later Elizabeth's name appeared on the surgery schedule at Chicago General. Naturally, the staff knew her brother was the mayor. Ruger saw an opportunity to make Michael really pay. He infected the donor tissue prior to the surgery date."

"Did he admit to this?"

"Surprisingly, he did. He almost seemed proud of what he'd done. He'll go down for it," Jack added. Tucker woke up and tapped Jack's hand for attention. He stroked the top of the kitty's head.

"What about Fred Drake's murder, and why kidnap me and Jillian?"

"Sis, he can't deny the kidnappings, but he's not admitting to Fred's murder. Because of Jack's and my personal involvement in the case, Captain Ramos assigned other detectives to do the questioning. We want to make sure we get him for everything. I doubt he'll see the outside of the prison walls in his lifetime."

"Oh, and he kidnapped you because he felt you were too nosey and asked too many questions," Jack said.

Claire scowled. "Well, too bad. Elizabeth wasn't only my patient, but an old friend. I'd do it again. I'd do it for all my patients. More coffee, anyone?"

Patrick stood, then moved around the table and gave his sister a hug. "Thanks, but we have to get back to work. The bad guys didn't take a break while we were on leave."

Jack handed Claire her kitten. "How do you like him?"

"It was love at first sight," she said, cuddling the purring kitty close to her heart.

"I know how that goes," he answered. Claire felt herself blushing. She still didn't know what to say about Jack's hug and kiss outside the funeral home.

Patrick rubbed Tucker's head as they left. "Now make sure she behaves," he instructed the kitty.

From out in the hallway, Claire heard the elevator arrive. She couldn't quite suppress a shudder at the memory that came with the sound, but she'd get over it eventually. Frankie's voice carried as he greeted Patrick and Jack. She caught a few words, and got up to stand near the closed door so she could hear better. Something about Dr. Johnson, and Frankie having called and checked with his office . . .

"We left some of Sylvia's coffee cake in case you're hungry," Patrick said.

"Thanks," Frankie answered. "I thought I'd check out our new security officer. I hear he's purrfect."

Frankie's footsteps came closer, then stopped. Claire waited just long enough for him to raise his hand to knock, then opened the door. "Hi, Frankie." He was carrying a large, multi-colored floral arrangement. "Are those for me?" she asked innocently.

"Yes. They're from Dr. Johnson."

"Come on in. Sylvia made her special pecan coffee cake and the coffee is fresh." Claire took the flowers and placed them on the coffee table. "Thanks for carrying them up for me. What brings you here? By now you must be tired of coming over."

"I'm just doing a follow-up visit for my report."

"Frankie, you are so full of it! Come on in the kitchen."

"How's your new security guard working out?" Frankie followed Claire into the kitchen and put a pet store bag on the counter.

"He tends to sleep on the job, but if you rattle the treat bag, he's Tucker on the spot. Thanks for the kitty treats."

"I have a catnip mouse for him, too." Frankie removed the toy from the bag and placed it on the floor. Tucker leapt out of Claire's arms in a flash and started batting the toy around the kitchen floor.

"I have another reason for my visit, besides checking on you and Tucker," Frankie said.

Over coffee and Sylvia's cake they discussed plans for the memorial service for their friend Sarah Murray, who'd been found murdered several weeks ago. Claire had solved that case and almost gotten herself killed in the process. That was when Patrick suffered his heart attack. Elizabeth's death followed right on the heels of that one, and plans for Sarah's memorial service ended up on hold.

"Since next weekend is Thanksgiving, why don't we look at the following weekend?" Claire suggested.

Frankie dropped a treat on the floor for Tucker. "Sounds good. By the way, my dad is telling all his customers how his fingernail clippers saved you and Jillian Garcia from certain death!"

# Chapter 61

"Right there, Captain." Patrick pointed out Derek Ruger standing off to the left of Jillian Garcia's live coverage feed the night the transport van brought Elizabeth O'Connor's body to the morgue. "This proves he was present. This film clip may be the reason he kidnapped Jillian. It shows he was there and he didn't have a plausible alibi for his presence at the morgue. Why was he so interested in being there when the body of the mayor's sister arrived, unless he had something to do with her death?" Patrick said. He, the captain, and his partner were viewing the film on his desktop screen. It boggled his mind what was possible in the twenty-first century.

"I think he was proud of his work. In a sick way, it brought him personal satisfaction to see the pain he caused the mayor," Jack suggested.

"As a sidebar, Ruger denies being involved with the heart Claire received," Captain Ramos said. "I spoke with Mr. Floyd from the funeral home this morning regarding who might have owned the heart, and gave him the date Claire received the package. He promised to research his records for deaths he handled during that period. His funeral home isn't in the best of neighborhoods. I think he'll cooperate because he doesn't want any bad press affecting his business.

"Also, the lab sent over their preliminary report on the fluid in Fred Drake's IV bag. A potent medication had been added. Since no one witnessed the attack on Mr. Drake in the alley, and at the moment we can't prove Derek Ruger tampered with the IV bag, we can't charge him for that murder."

"In other words, Fred Drake was collateral damage," Jack said. The case reminded him of his friend Tad's murder. He knew who those killers were, but in Tad's case the evidence hadn't been collected properly, and the two guys walked. It still made him angry to think about it.

The captain pulled up a chair, sat down and drained his coffee mug. "But there is some good news. We might have other charges against Derek Ruger, theft of body parts and forgery of family signatures on documents allowing the harvesting. The forensic tech guys have finished with the funeral home's computer hard drive and we have some interesting developments. Apparently, Ruger sold bone and tissue, without any of the deceased's families' permission, to companies with a history of looking the other way on where the donor tissue came from. The scam is working its way across the country. Several years ago, a New York dentist lost his license because of his drug addiction, so he went into the body snatching business.

"By chance a New York detective had been sent to settle what he thought was a routine business dispute at a recently purchased funeral home. When he looked around, he found a sealed space on the floor above the embalming room, set up like a surgical suite. Shipping receipts showed cadaver bone and tissue sold to various companies. Upon exhumation of several of the deceased, the NYPD discovered that the bodies had been packed with disposable gowns, gloves and supplies in order to hide the evidence. They used plumbing pipes to replace arm and leg bones. One of the victims happened to be Alistair Cooke, who used to host *Masterpiece Theater*. These shoddy practices are a billion-dollar body parts industry."

Patrick let out a breath. "This case has more branches than the Keeley family tree. Wait until it hits the courts. The news media will have a field day. I can almost hear the conversations across Chicago bars and restaurants. This'll definitely sell newspapers. If there are any other funeral homes working the same angle, they may consider the cash benefits aren't worth jail time."

"What cases do you want us to work on now?" Jack asked the captain.

"As much as I know you want to work the Derek Ruger case, we have to play it safe. We don't want to give his defense attorney any leverage." Ramos picked up a stack of files and handed them to Patrick. "Here are a couple of cases that came in while you were on leave. See what you can do with them. When does Claire return to work?"

"This morning was her first day back," Patrick said. "I should give her a call and see how she's holding up. She might be going through withdrawal."

"What do you mean, withdrawal? Was she on strong pain meds?" Captain Ramos frowned. "I can't believe Claire would ever allow herself to have that problem."

Jack and Patrick broke out into laughter. "No," Patrick said. "She has a new kitty and this is the first day they've been separated." He continued to chuckle.

"I don't suppose the two of you are planning to stop by on your lunch hour to check on the kitty?" Captain Ramos asked.

Both men shook their heads.

"Right," the captain responded. "Let me know where you are on these cases by the end of the day."

"No problem," Jack answered as the captain headed for his office. "Patrick, you want to divide up the stack and then compare notes?"

Patrick grabbed several folders. "We can probably evaluate all of them before we take Tucker his lunch. Sylvia cooked him some chicken. Don't worry, she sent us chicken salad and homemade croissants."

# Chapter 62

Claire vowed she'd focus on her charts and never fall behind again. She might have an excuse for the past week, but if she'd worked a little harder before all this ruckus began, she'd have about half the work to do now. She missed having Frankie's thermos of hot, velvety cappuccino on her desk. The machine coffee was nowhere close to the real stuff. But something else seemed to be making her feel out of sorts.

Everyone welcomed her back. Dr. Johnson praised her efforts to save Jillian. Sam dropped off a card from the staff and told her the next round of pizzas was on him. Her apartment smelled like a wonderful flower shop and Tucker was home alone. *Oh my word*, she thought, *I'm having separation anxiety over a kitten. Claire, pull yourself together!* If she had an old-fashioned answering machine, she could call and talk with him during the day. She wouldn't be able to hear his meow, but at least he would hear her voice.

"Dr. O'Shaunessy, we're ready for you down in autopsy," Ian called out.

"I'll be right there." She checked the clock. No time to run home for lunch today. The sooner she finished, the sooner she'd be home with Tucker. Just as she stepped out of her office, her cell phone rang. "Dr. O'Shaunessy speaking," she answered. She heard a strange rumbling sound.

"Hi, Claire. That was Tucker telling you he enjoyed the chicken Sylvia cooked for his lunch. He's doing fine and he used the litter box."

"Patrick, you checked on Tucker! How sweet. Please thank Sylvia for me. Of course you better tell my kitty that today was a special treat and he shouldn't expect this on a regular basis. Thank you. I feel so much better. Is Jack spending his lunch hour with Tucker too?"

"Yes. Sylvia packed us chicken salad," Patrick said.

"I have to run. Ian is waiting for me downstairs. Love you, big brother!"

"Mission Tucker accomplished. Back to crime," Jack joked in the background.

* * *

"How does it feel to be back?" Ian asked as he finished stitching closed the 'Y' incision on their last patient for the day.

"Great. You can't believe how much I missed my normal routine. Work sure beats being kidnapped and tied to a cart in the creepy basement of an old funeral home," Claire answered. Several co-workers had asked about her experience. Now that she was on safe ground, she had to admit when she re-told the story there was a certain air of excitement tied in with the adventure. If the outcome had been anything but positive—she wasn't going there.

"I'll put our patient in the cooler and clean up before going home," Ian said.

"Thanks. I've almost completed my notes. I've recorded all the organ weights in the computer, so you can erase them from the board. Don't stay too late. I'll see you in the morning. Good night, Ian."

Claire returned to her office to find Jack lounging in a chair. "What are you doing here? Is Patrick with you?"

"The answer to your first question is, I'm waiting for you, and no, Patrick is at home with his family. We have twenty minutes before my order is ready, so hop to it."

"What order?"

"Try orange chicken from your favorite Chinese restaurant. Now get a move on."

"Yes, sir," she said. It only took a few minutes to close up shop. Then she and Jack picked up their food. Before Jack could ask her how her day went, she wanted to hear all about his and Patrick's lunch with Tucker. "Don't skip any details," she told him.

Minutes later they pulled into her building's garage, grabbed their dinner and caught the elevator. As Claire inserted her key into the lock, mewing sounds could be heard from the other side of the door. She opened it and bent down to scoop up her bundle of joy.

"I'll put dinner in the kitchen until you're ready," Jack said, with a broad grin.

Claire couldn't stop kissing Tucker. "I'm coming. We can eat as soon as I feed Tucker. Is that okay with you?" she asked her kitty. In response, he butted her chin and purred.

Moments later, Claire served up their food while Jack took over holding Tucker. "Thank you for ordering dinner."

"Figured you could use a little extra break on your first day back," he said, scratching Tucker behind the ears.

Once they'd eaten and everything was cleaned up, Claire turned to Jack. "Thank you again. I hadn't even given dinner a thought. Do you mind if I turn on the news? I feel like I'm behind the times." Claire cuddled a sleeping Tucker in her arms, wondering why Jack had shown her this extra attention. After all, she'd recovered from her head injury and the whole horrible stalker-kidnapping experience. There was that moment outside the funeral home . . . and what he'd said a couple of days ago, about love at first sight . . . but maybe it was her imagination, or just that she'd been hurt and vulnerable. Or maybe he'd bonded with Tucker and wished he'd kept the kitty for himself.

"I'll turn the television on, although I think you're preoccupied." Jack reached for the remote and clicked the "on" button. WTLV's nine o'clock news flashed onto the screen.

"Good evening and welcome to the nightly news for WTLV Chicago. I'm Scott Christie."

"And I'm Jillian Garcia."

"Jillian, it's been a week since you and Dr. Claire O'Shaunessy escaped from the funeral home where you were held captive by Derek Ruger. I'm sure you've been in touch with the police, especially since you're one of the victims. Can you bring us up to speed on the case?"

"Yes, I can, Scott. Derek Ruger confessed to killing Elizabeth O'Connor and has been charged with first degree murder. At this time, it's believed I was kidnapped because my cameraman caught Derek Ruger on film the day I reported from the morgue when Elizabeth O'Connor passed. Ruger's presence there will not help his case. Even if he'd learned about her death in the course of his work, why would he be at the county morgue? As for his reason for kidnapping Dr. O'Shaunessy, we believe he had a concern that she was getting too close for comfort in her effort to discover the reason for Mrs. O'Connor's death and to find who was responsible.

"The police are still collecting all the pieces to the puzzle, but it appears Derek Ruger is solely responsible for an enormous number of unexplainable accidents and attacks on the mayor's family. Also, there are reports of missing and dead family pets. This period spans over the last fifteen years. Some of our viewers may recall that Mayor Keeley's youngest sister sustained permanent brain damage as a result of a bicycle accident about fifteen years ago. From information the police are withholding at this time, it's believed Ruger may have caused the accident."

"Why was he targeting the Keeley family?" Scott asked.

"He was seeking revenge. His father, George Ryder, was fired from Keeley Liquor Distributors for theft but told Ruger the owner had given his job to his own son, Michael. Ruger blamed Mayor Keeley for his father's loss of employment and for the destruction of his family. Captain Ramos has stated more charges will be forthcoming as the case develops."

"Thank you, Jillian. And on a happier note, let's go live to the Chicago Stadium, where I hear the Bulls are leading in the third quarter."

While the two anchors talked, Claire felt Jack's arm slip around her shoulders. Instead of shying away, she took a chance and leaned into him. Between the warmth of his body and Tucker's soothing purr, Claire's eyelids grew heavy. The end of the broadcast faded out as she drifted into a wonderful, peaceful slumber.

# # #

# About the Author

Sue (Schreck) Myers was raised in Libertyville, Illinois and lives in the next town over with her husband Gene, their cats, and a backyard full of birds and squirrels. Her first encounter with a dead body was in third grade. Whenever a classmate lost a relative, the nuns would march the students up to the funeral home to say prayers over the deceased. Sue would stare at them, daring them to wink. Lucky for her, none did.

In her twenties, Sue worked as an ER Tech in a Chicago hospital between Rush Street and the projects. Because of the ER's interesting cliental, she was exposed to a whole array of situations involving the 18th District Police. Years later, Sue became a registered nurse, but her experiences in the ER never left her. She spent her nursing career in Labor and Delivery, Neonatal ICU, and Infertility. Her career in the medical field fueled stories that begged to be told. When Sue isn't writing, she can be found in her garden or quilting.

71816021R00132

Made in the USA
Columbia, SC
06 June 2017